Red Bird

Red Bird

Stephanie Grace Whitson

THOMAS NELSON PUBLISHERS
Nashville • Atlanta • London • Vancouver
Printed in the United States of America

Whi

Published in Nashville, Tennessee, by Thomas Nelson, Inc.

Unless otherwise noted, Scripture quotations are from The King James Version of the Holy Bible.

Scripture quotations marked NKJV are from THE NEW KING JAMES VERSION. Copyright ©1979, 1980, 1982, 1990 Thomas Nelson, Inc.

Library of Congress Cataloging-in-Publication Data

Whitson, Stephanie Grace.
  Red bird / Stephanie Grace Whitson.
    p. cm. – (Prairie winds : bk. 3)
  ISBN 0-7852-7484-7 (pbk.)
  1. Frontier and pioneer life–West (U.S.)–Fiction. 2. Indians of North America–West (U.S.)–Fiction. 3. Women pioneers–West (U.S.)–Fiction. 4. Dakota Indians–Fiction. I. Title. II. Series: Whitson, Stephanie Grace. Prairie winds : bk. 3.
PS3573.H555R43 1997
813'.54–dc21   97-14039
                                                                CIP

Printed in the United States of America

9 10 11 12   02 01 00

FOR BOB

My leader, my example,
my beloved, my friend

ACKNOWLEDGMENTS

I am truly humbled to think that with all the demands on your time you, dear reader, have chosen to read this book. In so doing, you have shared a precious part of your own life with me—moments that could have been spent in a million other ways. I do not take the time you have shared with me lightly. I pray that after you have "played" with me and my "imaginary friends" that you will return to "real life" refreshed and encouraged in your own walk of faith. God bless you.

This is a book about letting go—giving up one's own plans and dreams and allowing God to lead. In the last weeks of this book's preparation, I have been challenged to give up some of my own plans and dreams.

I have always loved the Browning poem that contains the lines, "Grow old along with me, the best is yet to be.' Recently, my husband was diagnosed with an incurable form of lymphoma.

Only a few women have become a real part of my inner soul. The day after my husband was diagnosed, I lost the dearest of my soul sisters to cancer.

I am being forced to learn the same lesson that I have created for my characters—to let go of my own idea of tomorrow and to walk by faith into a new plan, accepting that it was fashioned by a loving hand "before the foundation of the world" (Eph. 1:4 NKJV)—a hand that has only my best interests at heart.

My beloved friend Celest loved 2 Corinthians 4:17–18:

> *For our light affliction, which is but for a moment, is working for us a far more exceeding and eternal weight of glory, while we do not look at the things which are seen, but at the things which are not seen. For the things which are seen are temporary, but the things which are not seen are eternal.* (NKJV)

Celest has fully realized that verse. I am still struggling to apply it hour by hour, praying often, "Lord, I believe—help my unbelief."

If this seems a strange thing to write for this section of acknowledgment, let me just say that in light of the past few weeks of my life, I feel burdened to simply acknowledge *Him.*

I will extol You, My God, O King;
And I will bless Your name forever and ever.
Every day I will bless You,
And I will praise Your name forever and ever.
Great is the Lord, and greatly to be praised;
And His greatness is unsearchable. . . .
The LORD upholds all who fall,
And raises up all who are bowed down. . . .
The LORD is righteous in all His ways,
Gracious in all His works.
The LORD is near to all who call upon Him,
To all who call upon Him in truth.
Psalm 145:1–3, 14, 17–18 NKJV

CHAPTER 1

Foolishness is bound in the heart
of a child.

Proverbs 22:15

Everett Higgenbottom indeed! Perched on the edge of her chair on the lawn of Chouteau Preparatory School in St. Louis, Missouri, Carrie Brown made a tiny motion with her left hand to ward Everett off. He had leaned forward to whisper to her, but when she raised one tiny gloved hand, he sat back abruptly, resisting the urge to caress one of the deep red tendrils that had fallen out of her abundant hairdo.

Commencement day, and he has to whisper nonsense, Carrie thought. *"The sky is only a reflection of your eyes today, Carrie."* *Honestly*—Carrie tapped the earth nervously with one elegantly booted foot. As furtively as possible, she turned her head from side to side, searching the crowd. As the commencement speaker droned on, Carrie fidgeted, brushing her hair back into place. She picked up the nosegay that lay in her lap, inhaling the sweet scent of lily of the valley, unaware that Everett was adoringly watching her every move—and misinterpreting the cause of her nervousness.

The commencement speaker finally concluded his presentation. As Carrie's class rose to sing a hymn, Everett leaned towards her, drinking in the aroma of lemon verbena and lily of the valley that had followed Carrie like a cloud all morning. She felt his breath on the back of her neck as he whispered, "Relax, Carrie. You'll do fine. Your speech is perfect."

Carrie turned to glare at him, but movement in the crowd towards the back of the lawn caught her attention. She was too tiny to see who had just arrived, but someone had definitely come late to the commencement. Carrie stopped singing, her heart pounding. *LisBeth said she was coming and bringing a surprise—someone I would be glad to see.*

The hymn ended Everett nudged Carrie from behind and she turned towards him, furious. But Everett just smiled back and nodded towards the podium. Carrie blushed with embarrassment, realizing it was her turn to speak for the class. She hurried to the podium, but once she was facing the crowd she took time to look past the familiar faces to the edge of the lawn, ever hopeful that Lis-Beth and—but LisBeth wasn't there.

Carrie's eyes sought out her grandparents. They sat in the front row smiling encouragement. Surveying her class-mates, Carrie thought of how quickly the time at Chouteau had gone. There was Clara Delacroix, so proud of the fact that her parents were among the earliest French settlers of St. Louis. Philip Canard, who told jokes every day and never seemed to care that his own lineage was far more illustrious than Clara's. And Everett. Carrie's eyes glanced past Everett, but not before he had caught her eye and winked. Poor Everett. From his name that barely fit on his commencement certificate, to his arms that extended far beyond the limits of shirts and coats, everything about Everett Higgenbottom was long. Well liked, but teased mercilessly, Everett had even been nicknamed "Dan" because he shared the long face and protruding teeth of another Dan in town—a firehorse.

Carrie pondered Everett for only a brief moment before launching into the address she had agonized over for weeks. As she spoke, she continued to search the crowd, ever hopeful that LisBeth—and her surprise—would still appear.

Her speech concluded, Carrie took her seat among her classmates, heedless of the applause and the beaming faces of her grandparents in the front row.

Disappointment set in. Suddenly, it didn't matter that she had won the right to deliver the address. He hadn't come after all. She was so certain that he would be there. She had dreamed of it for weeks. As soon as LisBeth's letter had been read promising a surprise guest, Carrie had believed it, imagined it, become breathless at the thought of it. Now, as she sat primly on her chair and fumed, Everett leaned forward, shyly touching her shoulder, murmuring congratulations. Carrie flushed with emotion at Everett's attentions. *Everett Higgenbottom, indeed!*

For weeks she had been planning this moment . . . when *he* would come in, LisBeth on his arm. He would probably be dressed in a suit by now. But that wouldn't matter. He would watch only her through the entire commencement, and when it was over, he would be there, smiling, coming back into her life, instantly amazed at how grown up she was and how beautiful she had become.

She knew what she would do. She would deliver her commencement address smiling at him, showing him that she remembered everything. She would introduce him to Everett—and to snobbish Clara Delacroix. And then they would be amazed, a little afraid, and speechless, as their classmate, little Carrie Brown, took her rightful place beside the truly beautiful Lakota man named Soaring Eagle.

But the speech was over, and only Everett was present to admire her. Sighing again, Carrie resigned herself to the absence of Soaring Eagle. She mechanically walked forward to accept her diploma. As soon as the ceremony was over, she found her grandparents accepting congratulations and

Everett's request that she ride in his buggy back to her grandparents' house where the entire class had been invited for a reception.

Everett drove slowly up Chouteau Avenue, wondering about Carrie's unusual quiet. She was unresponsive when he poetically commented on the way spring had "assaulted" the river town of St. Louis. As the carriage made its way along the river, sunlight glanced off the spire of the riverside cathedral. A freshly painted steamboat bobbed at its moorings. Light danced on the surface of the river. Carrie was oblivious to the beauty around her.

Everett tried another topic of conversation. "You did a wonderful job, Carrie. With the commencement speech."

Carrie nodded noncommittally.

"You seemed—well, kind of distracted. I was worried you'd forget something." Everett kept the carriage horse at a walk.

"Oh, it's nothing—just some friends from Nebraska said they would come—I hoped—" Carrie blushed. "I was just disappointed, that's all." At last, Carrie pushed aside her dark mood. Forcing herself to smile brightly she patted Everett's arm and nodded towards the bay filly that pulled the carriage. "Did Mazie forget how to trot—or is there some reason we're supposed to arrive last at my commencement reception?" Ever hopeful that a "surprise" encounter still lay in her future, Carrie raised one eyebrow and eyed Everett.

Everett grinned back. "I'm just enjoying having you here—with me." They had rounded the last corner that led up the hill to a lovely home overlooking the river. Everett could see Carrie's grandparents waiting on the front porch, waving happily as the couple approached. Flicking the reins lightly, Everett urged Mazie into a trot. The carriage pulled up just as another buggy approached from the opposite direction.

Everett hopped down and reached up to help Carrie. But Carrie didn't see Everett. She stood, entranced, watching the other carriage's occupants. LisBeth called out from the buggy, "I'm so *sorry* we missed the ceremony, Mr. Jennings—Mrs. Jennings—the train was late." LisBeth looked past Mr. and Mrs. Jennings, noticed the other carriage, and saw Carrie. Laughing, she called out, "Carrie! I'm so sorry we're late—" LisBeth crossed the distance between them and smiled up at Carrie warmly. "But, I hope to make up for it. As you can see, I have brought you a surprise."

Carrie nodded, speechless.

Everett reached up and took her hand. "Carrie—"

At the sound of Everett's voice, Carrie started and looked down at him. Biting her lip, she hurried down from the carriage, waiting for her surprise to step forward.

Everett looked past LisBeth and frowned slightly as LisBeth turned to complete her introductions. "Mr. Jennings, Mrs. Jennings, allow me to introduce my brother, Jeremiah Soaring Eagle King. He's just finished his courses at John Knox in Illinois and he's been asked by the Society of Friends to speak to a few of the congregations in St. Louis. Jim couldn't come because of spring planting, so my brother will be my escort while we're here."

Jeremiah Soaring Eagle King stepped forward and bowed low.

Everett Higgenbottom moved to take Carrie's arm, but she stepped away from him towards the visitor.

Carrie couldn't trust her voice. Turning one gloved palm outward, she raised two fingers and moved them skyward. Soaring Eagle returned the sign and, finally, the corners of his mouth turned up slightly. "You remembered, Red Bird."

Carrie nodded, her heart full. Shaking her head in wonder she turned to LisBeth, who filled the silence. "Well, Carrie, thanks to a late train we missed your commencement speech, but we are here to share in your joy. I know your grandparents are very proud of you." LisBeth's voice softened. "And your mother, Carrie. I'm certain she's watching from heaven . . . and she's no doubt very pleased with how you've turned out."

The door to the house opened and Carrie's classmates tumbled out. Much to Carrie's delight, Clara Delacroix looked wide-eyed at Soaring Eagle and stood to one side. Carrie's grandmother and LisBeth started up the stairs, followed by Mr. Jennings and Soaring Eagle. Carrie took Everett's proffered arm and followed, barely resisting the urge to reach out and touch the long braid that trailed down Soaring Eagle's back.

He's here. He came . . . to me.

CHAPTER 2

The LORD is my strength and song, and he is become my salvation: he is my God, and I will prepare him an habitation; my father's God, and I will exalt him.

Exodus 15:2

He had charged into stampeding herds of buffalo astride a racing pony where one false step would have meant certain death. He had fought in battle against better-mounted and better-armed soldiers. But nothing he had ever faced had produced the quaking knees that carried Soaring Eagle to the podium of the Congregational Church in St. Louis, Missouri, one spring morning in 1883.

Reverend Hodge had reluctantly agreed to see if perhaps Soaring Eagle could make more of an impression for his people if he wore native dress. As Soaring Eagle stepped up onto the podium, the beads and thimbles that hung from his elkskin shirt jingled. The faint sound carried throughout the church as the parishioners sat, entranced by what was, for many of them, their first look at a "real, live Indian."

As Reverend Hodge stepped back and sat down facing the crowd, Soaring Eagle turned to the audience. Grasping the sides of the pulpit to hide his shaking hands, he bowed his head, waiting for the words to come, begging God to still his racing heart and help him say the right things.

When he looked up, his eyes sought out his sister's face. LisBeth smiled encouragement. Next to her, Carrie Brown sat, beaming. She was dressed in a new cadet blue gown that made her red hair flame and her blue eyes glimmer. With a tiny smile on her lips, she held up her right hand, signing "Friend." Carrie saw an almost imperceptible relaxing of the muscles around Soaring Eagle's mouth, and she knew that he was smiling inside.

With the sign of friendship, Soaring Eagle had been given the words to begin his speech. He looked over the congregation. "Friends." Signing the word he explained, "That is what this means. The Society of Friends has asked me to come here to speak to you in the hope that, by God's grace, we can become friends." Clutching the sides of the pulpit, Soaring Eagle paused. Glancing towards the cornflower blue eyes, he continued, "I have no complicated plan to solve the many problems that face my people. Instead, I come with a prayer that perhaps, if you and I can come to understand one another, we can learn to live together in peace."

Soaring Eagle paused before continuing. "There are some among your people who believe that the Indian is little more than an animal. I have read that one of your great warriors believes that 'the only good Indian is a dead Indian.' I hope that after hearing me, you will come to see another way."

Letting go his death grip on the podium, Soaring Eagle looked around the congregation. More than a few sat arms crossed, jaws clenched against his presence. Others seemed more receptive. Concentrating on the latter group, Soaring Eagle continued, his rich bass voice taking on a gentle tone as he spoke.

"Let me tell you of the first white I ever knew. She came to live among my people when I was only an infant. She came to love us, and she was known to me as *Ina*—which is *mother* in your language. This good woman read to me from your Holy Bible. She taught me about God. Knowing this good white and hearing the words she read from the Bible began the road which has brought me to you today."

Soaring Eagle looked over the crowd and sought out the most challenging male countenance as he added, "When I first realized that my way of living was dying—that the land would no longer be mine to hunt in and to live in, I was filled with bitterness and rage. I think that you, too, would feel anger if someone came into your homes and said that you must go elsewhere and learn a new way to live." Lowering his voice, he added, "That anger would become rage in any man if this person who came to say that you must leave also killed your family."

The belligerent listener blinked and looked away from Soaring Eagle. A few feminine eyes blinked back tears. Soaring Eagle continued matter-of-factly. "That is part of my past. But the apostle Paul reminds us to *'forget what lies behind.'* I speak of it only to help you understand the anger that lies in the hearts of my people. We feel loss and pain just as you do. We love our families. We grieve and mourn—just as you do.

"As I have said, when I realized that my old way of life was gone forever, I was filled with bitterness and rage. It was in this state that I arrived at the Santee Normal Training School. That was seven years ago. At the school, I met more whites. I observed their ways, and I waited for them to show their true feelings towards the Indian. I believed they were only pretending to be kind to us. But this was not the case. At the Santee Normal Training School, I saw children being taught how to live in the new world. I saw whites like my mother, who knew how to look beyond the skin and into the heart."

Soaring Eagle sought out Carrie's eyes. "Once a white girl at the school gave me a gift. It was a paper cross and on it she had written 'Jesus loves Soaring Eagle.' It took a long time, but I finally came to realize that truth. Through the kindness of those at Santee, I learned that Jesus loves me. I read the Bible and it told me of His love. Now I know that I belong to Jesus, and that although my people are weak in the face of this new world you have brought to us, Jesus is strong, and He will help us.

"It is difficult for older Lakota—like me—to change. But the message of Jesus' love can change the future of every man—even the Lakota. So I come to you today, saying that my people need your help to travel a new road—a road that will take them from hunting on the prairie and into a new life. I pray that we will be able to put aside the old hatreds and begin to walk a new road. We can do this if we remember that it is Jesus who loves us all and it is Jesus who can help us love our brothers, even when their skin is a different color from ours. Even when their ways are strange to us."

Soaring Eagle dropped his hands to his sides and stepped away from the podium. Quietly, he concluded, "I pray peace for my people, and I wish peace to you." He walked back to his place beside Reverend Hodge, who closed the service with announcements about a clothing and food collection for Santee and a brief prayer.

People moved forward to shake Soaring Eagle's hand— among them the man whose hardened gaze Soaring Eagle had first noticed. He was holding a boy by the hand. Impulsively the boy broke away from his father. Squinting up at Soaring Eagle from beneath his cap, the boy asked loudly, "You got any *scalps* I can see?"

A woman gasped. Everyone was immediately silent. The boy's father moved forward with an exclamation of dismay, but Soaring Eagle sat down quickly on the edge of the platform and beckoned to the child, asking, "What is your name, young man?"

"Benjamin Whipple."

With a glance at the boy's father, Soaring Eagle asked patiently, "Why have you asked about scalps, Benjamin Whipple, when I have said that I come in peace?"

The boy jutted out his lower jaw and retorted, "My uncle rode with Custer. I read all about it in the paper. Indians *scalp* people."

Emboldened by the attention he was receiving, the boy pointed to Soaring Eagle's shirt. "You got hair tied on that shirt. Must be scalps. My pa said so."

Thus singled out, the father offered another embarrassed protest, but Soaring Eagle remained calm, nodding soberly as he continued. "Well, I will tell you the truth. Benjamin. Do you think that you are ready to hear the truth?"

Benjamin thrust out his chin. "I'm ready." His father shifted his weight nervously, enduring the angry glares of several adults—among them his wife.

Soaring Eagle answered carefully, "The truth is, Benjamin Whipple, that the hair on this shirt is from the tails and manes of my favorite ponies. And some of the hair is from the people I have loved who have gone on to the next life." Soaring Eagle's voice dropped as he added, "When I learned to love Jesus, I gave up killing. I have no scalps. I have only these reminders of the old way of life and the people I loved."

Heartily disappointed, Benjamin made a face and turned to look at his father.

Soaring Eagle called out to a group of boys clustered by the podium. "Do you boys have questions, as well? If your parents say it is all right, you can ask me questions. I will tell you whatever I can."

Immediately, a question rang out as one boy fairly shouted, "Where'd you get that scar? Fightin' soldiers?"

Soaring Eagle reached up to point to the scar on his left cheek and began the story. "When I was only a boy—just about your age—my father and I went on our first great hunt. To be invited along at such a young age was a great honor, and I was filled with excitement." Soaring Eagle went on to describe the hunt, drawing his young audience into the story as he described the skill with which Rides the Wind tracked game.

"This hunt was not only for getting meat. It was for learning my place in my tribe and for learning to be a man." Soaring Eagle stopped briefly before going on to explain. "Our ponies were carrying much game when we returned home. We took a way along a ravine. We spotted two eagles, and then we stopped and watched as they flew down to their nest."

Reaching up to touch the feathers that adorned his gleaming black hair, Soaring Eagle said, "Every Lakota desires to show his bravery by capturing an eagle and taking its feathers. I was no different. My father helped lower me to the nest—but we were caught by a storm. Then the grown eagles began to attack. My father came down beside me to fight—but one of the eagles raked his neck here—" Soaring Eagle lifted his chin and pointed. "There was much blood, but my father managed to kill the two grown eagles before he lost consciousness. The storm blew over. And there I was, a Lakota boy perched high on a cliff with two young eagles watching me. And beside them my father lay, dying."

Soaring Eagle looked into the eyes of each young boy and side quietly. "And I had to find a way."

A boy whispered hoarsely, "What'd you do next?"

"I prayed. I prayed to what I knew as the Great Mystery I prayed to what my mother had called God. I asked for help. Among the Lakota there is a legend of a warrior who was carried from a cliff by two eagles."

The boys who were listening looked at one another unbelieving. But Soaring Eagle nodded "Yes—far below me in the canyon was water—it was deep, and I knew that I had only one chance to save my father—and myself. So, I grabbed each of the young eagles around the legs." Soaring Eagle made a fist with each hand and held it above him. "And I jumped."

After a dramatic pause, Soaring Eagle concluded. "The eagles stretched their wings and we fell together into the deep water. I swam upwards and climbed out of the water and ran for help." He reached up to touch the scar on his cheek. "My father was saved. My mother sewed the wound on my cheek closed."

". . . and you got your eagle feathers." Benjamin Whipple's voice croaked.

Soaring Eagle smiled. "I did not know the Great Mystery then. I did not believe that He loved me, that He had sent His own Son to die for me. But I knew that Someone helped those eagles get me down from that cliff. And that," Soaring Eagle concluded, "is why I have this scar on my face."

Pastor Hodge spoke up. "Perhaps we can arrange a more informal evening where Soaring Eagle can answer questions?"

Soaring Eagle nodded his agreement and Carrie Brown spoke up immediately. 'I'm certain my grandfather and grandmother would be more than happy to offer our home for a gathering."

Soaring Eagle stood up and offered LisBeth his arm. The assembly broke up adults murmuring as they departed.

Reverend Hodge enthusiastically declared the evening a success. "You made more friends for your people tonight than you may realize, Mr. King. Those boys' parents would never have had the courage to ask those questions—but you can bet they were *thinking* them. You did a wonderful job—wonderful."

As the small group left the church, Carrie tripped happily alongside LisBeth, discussing plans for a reception for Soaring Eagle. "I'll arrange everything."

Much to Carrie's frustration, Everett Higgenbottom interrupted, "And I'll see Carrie home."

CHAPTER 3

Hear counsel, and receive instruction, that thou mayest be wise in thy latter end

Proverbs 19:20

I was formerly alienated and hostile in mind, engaged in evil deeds. But God has reconciled me through the death of Christ. Now I am striving to continue in the faith, firmly established and steadfast—never moving away from the hope of the gospel I heard." Dressed in a dark suit, his long hair neatly braided down his back, Soaring Eagle sat in the parlor at the home of Lucy and Walter Jennings, concluding his description of his transition from wild plains Indian to educated university graduate What Soaring Eagle had intended to be a brief autobiography had taken up most of the evening as men broke in to ask question after question, not a few of which had been whispered in their ears by their fascinated wives.

At last, the crowd dwindled to only a few influential parishioners and the talk grew more intimate as those in a position to support him discussed Soaring Eagle's personal future. Soaring Eagle looked about the room and said quietly, "If you want to change the hostility of the Indian, give him Christ. Only Christ can change the heart and set a man on a new road." His gaze settled on Reverend Hodge as he concluded, "I hope to be one who takes the message of the gospel to my people."

A listener offered, "I think the missionaries are already

doing a fine job of that, Mr. King. It seems to me that you can do the most for your people by speaking to groups like us—who want to help, but don't know how. I don't need to tell you that seeing an educated Indian who carries himself as well as you does a lot to influence us. You talk about the spiritual side of things, and that's all well and good, but your people need a spokesperson to influence people of consequence to send money for the school—clothing for the children—textbooks—whatever else is needed. I think you are the man for that task."

Soaring Eagle shook his head slowly. "I respect your opinion, friend. But *what is a man profited, if he shall gain the whole world, and lose his own soul?* I agree that there are physical needs to be met—but making the outer man comply when there is no change of heart does nothing lasting to help the Indian." He paused before adding, "I could have been *forced* to cut my hair and dress like a white man. But what good is that? What good are clothing and log cabins and education if there is no hope in the soul? The need for missionaries to share the gospel—for pastors to teach the people—is just as desperate as the need for physical help."

"But you can't deny that the physical needs are real."

Remembering the thinness of the soles of his own boots, Soaring Eagle nodded in agreement. "The need is real. But there must be a balance. The Lakota believe that the earth is their mother—that there is a balance to all things. Just so, there is a balance in this matter. Of course the physical needs must be provided for—it's just that—"

LisBeth interrupted softly, "I think what Soaring Eagle is trying to say is that his *personal* burden is for the *souls* of the people."

Soaring Eagle smiled at his sister appreciatively and nodded.

Carrie Brown interrupted. "But surely, Soaring Eagle, you can see that you are needed here—speaking like you did. Why, I'm certain the collection for clothing and books will be a great success, just because *you* were here."

Reverend Hodge agreed. "Little Carrie, here, may be one of the youngest among us, but I must say I agree with her. The Friends of the Indian have been looking for a spokesperson—and I think we've found him."

Little Carrie Brown. From the doorway where she stood, Carrie listened and stamped her foot impatiently—right on top of Everett Higgenbottom's boot. She had been hounded by Everett all evening. Everett met her at the punch bowl, insisting on pouring them both "some refreshment." When she walked in the garden, hoping to meet up with Soaring Eagle, Everett was there, taking her arm, plucking a rose blossom for her. Now, as she stomped his foot and saw him blanche, she whispered, "Oh, for heaven's sake, Everett!" and pushed past him. Making her escape out into the garden she slipped along the back of the house, in the kitchen door and up the back stairs to her own room. She was trembling with anger and frustration.

Nothing's working out the way I want it. Nothing. Carrie paced around her room, furtively watching the front porch from her window until nearly every guest had left. She especially watched for Everett, who was the last to go.

"Are you all right, Carrie?" A knock at the door and Lis-Beth's concerned voice called her away from the window.

"Oh—LisBeth—don't *you* go too. Not yet. Please. Come in."

LisBeth complied, settling at Carrie's dressing table. Picking up a silver hand mirror, LisBeth commented, "You certainly received some lovely graduation gifts." She set the mirror back down before adding, "Your young man was disappointed that you weren't there to say good evening. He was quite concerned—afraid you were ill."

"*My* young man?" Carrie snorted. "Oh—you mean Everett." She settled on her bed. "He's not *my* young man."

LisBeth grinned. "Certainly not from lack of trying."

"He's such a *baby*.

"Just your age "

Carrie blushed. "You know what I mean Everett's nice—but he has school to finish—and a lot of growing up to do He just *fawns* over me, LisBeth. I hate it "

LisBeth was suddenly serious. Is there something you need to talk about, Carrie?"

Carrie drew her knees up and wrapped her arms around them, bowing her head

"You seem, well, unsettled. Unhappy. Is there something wrong? Your grandparents are concerned too. Mrs. Jennings mentioned it over tea yesterday."

Carrie looked up abruptly. "They needn't be worried. I've just—so far to go before I—" she sighed. "When Mama and I had to leave Santee I promised I'd go back. I haven't forgotten the promise. I want to go back, LisBeth. To Santee. To teach at the mission. To—" she bit her lip.

LisBeth smiled indulgently. "I think that's a fine plan, Carrie." She sat beside Carrie before adding, "But have you prayed about your plans, Carrie? Have you considered your grandparents? Everett?"

At the mention of Everett's name, Carrie snorted. "I don't *need* to pray about this, LisBeth. I know what I want to do. I know what I *have* to do. I have to go to the university so I can become a teacher. Then I can go back to Santee." Carrie moaned. "It's just that everything *takes* so long. I've been away years already. Things have changed. Soaring Eagle has changed. I'm supposed to call him Mr. King. And it'll be *years* before I can really *do* anything."

LisBeth tried to assimilate the reference to Soaring Eagle into Carrie's speech. When she failed, she responded carefully. "I understand your impatience, Carrie. Soaring Eagle has experienced the same feelings. Why, just tonight he was bemoaning the years away from Nebraska while he trains for a pastorate."

Carrie sat up alertly. "He s going away to school? Going away *again?*"

"Yes, isn't it wonderful?" LisBeth answered, ignoring the disappointment in Carrie's voice. "Reverend Hodge said just tonight, after you left, that he's been in touch with Dr. Riggs at Santee. Together they are certain they can secure a scholarship for further study. Theology. Pastoral training. All the things that Soaring Eagle will need to go ahead with his life. And while he's studying, he can do some traveling for the Friends and publicize the needs Isn't it wonderful?"

"How long? How long will he be gone?"

"Two years, I think—"

Two years, Carrie was thinking. *I've waited half my life and now I have to wait at least two more years. What if—*her heart began beating faster as she considered the horror of the thought. *What if he meets someone else. What if he—Oh, he couldn't. God wouldn't let it happen, not after all the time I've waited. God just wouldn't.*

With a start, Carrie realized that LisBeth had stopped talking and was looking at her curiously. "Is something else wrong, Carrie?"

"No, of course not Nothing's wrong. I'm glad for Soaring Eagle. It will be wonderful. It's just that—" Youth won out and Carrie lost the battle to hide her feelings. "Two years is so long. And what if—"

LisBeth's dark eyes suddenly glowed with understanding and no small amount of amazement. "Carrie Brown! You're worried that he'll meet someone, aren't you?"

Carrie blushed and LisBeth laughed, "Land sakes, child, I had no idea you had a crush—"

Carrie frowned and interrupted. "It's *not* a crush, and I'm *not* a child. I'm seventeen years old." She drew her tiny frame to its full height of slightly less than five feet and looked unflinchingly back at LisBeth who rushed to apologize.

"I m sorry, Carrie. I didn't mean to—"

Carrie interrupted her. "Oh, yes you did, LisBeth. You and everyone else. No one takes me seriously. I'm little and I'm spoiled and no one takes me seriously. Even Everett Higgenbottom treats me like a little doll to pour tea for and take to parties."

Carrie marched across the room angrily and stared out the window Calming her trembling voice she went on. "But I'm going to show them. I'm going to be a woman that Soaring Eagle can be proud of. I'll go to school while he goes to school. I'll be ready to teach the Indians when we go back. We'll make a home together and we'll—help them!"

Turning around to face LisBeth, her blue eyes snapping, Carrie repeated, "Everyone says I'm such a beautiful little china doll. It makes me sick! I'm *not* a china doll, LisBeth. I'm a woman " She paused for a moment and when she continued, Carrie had regained her composure. Her voice softened as she talked.

"LisBeth, I was only a little girl when I first saw Soaring Eagle. I thought he was the most beautiful thing I'd ever seen. Everyone else was afraid of him that day he rode into the mission on that old pony. He looked wild and fearsome. But, still, I couldn't imagine why they were afraid. I could see how tired he was, feel how much he was hurting. And when I asked him to see that locket of your mama's— I could see him smiling, inside, the way he does.

"I've prayed for him all these years, and God did something inside me as I prayed. I grew to love him. At first, I thought maybe it was only the memory I loved. But now I've seen him, talked to him, and I love him more than ever. And—" Carrie blushed and laughed a light, happy laugh. "And I still think he's the most beautiful thing I've ever seen." Her cheeks blazed crimson and she raised her tiny hands to hide them before whispering to LisBeth, "I want to be his wife, LisBeth."

LisBeth blinked in amazement. Carrie perched on the edge of her bed. "You won't tell anyone, will you, LisBeth? They'd only laugh." She sighed miserably. "Even Soaring Eagle would laugh if he knew. But when I'm a college graduate, and I'm teaching out west, then I just know he'll see me as a woman and forget the little girl."

LisBeth opened her mouth to say something, then deliberately clamped it shut. She shook her head before answering. "I won't tell anyone, Carrie. I promise."

Impulsively, Carrie placed a gloved hand over LisBeth's and squeezed. "What you said about praying about it. That's all right too. Will you pray for me. for us, LisBeth?"

LisBeth nodded. "Of course I will, Carrie. I've prayed for you for years. I'm certainly not going to stop now."

The two women descended the stairs to the parlor together Soaring Eagle looked up from his chair and said, "Is my little Red Bird all right?"

Carrie blushed furiously and retorted, "Your *little* Red Bird grew up and flew away, Mr. Jeremiah Soaring Eagle King In her place is Miss Carrie Brown—high school graduate—soon to be student at the University of Nebraska. If all goes according to plan."

At the sudden announcement, Carrie's grandfather raised his eyebrows and puffed furiously on his pipe. Her grandmother looked up from her needlework in amazement and Carrie bit her lip nervously waiting for their response.

LisBeth cleared her throat meaningfully and Soaring Eagle rose to leave. After Soaring Eagle helped his sister into the carriage and climbed up beside her, LisBeth saw him take a long look back up the stairs of the Jennings' house where Carrie Brown stood in the doorway, watching them until they were out of sight.

CHAPTER 4

The way of a fool is right in his own eyes, but he that hearkeneth unto counsel is wise.

Proverbs 12:15

Thank you for coming, Mrs. Callaway." Lucy Jennings ushered LisBeth into her home, leading the way across the parlor and out into the garden. "I hope it hasn't inconvenienced you too much." Mrs. Jennings lead LisBeth to a secluded arbor and settled onto a garden bench as she continued, "But this is the only day before you leave that I am certain Carrie won't be about. She's gone on an outing with some of her fellow graduates. Sort of a farewell picnic, I believe. Everett picked her up in his carriage just before you arrived and they won't be back for hours."

LisBeth sat quietly, listening while Lucy Jennings rambled. It was apparent that Lucy Jennings had something of great importance to discuss. Still, she steered conversation to every polite and meaningless topic available. Finally, she and LisBeth settled into uncomfortable silence.

After a few moments of dutifully admiring every variety of blossom in the garden, LisBeth asked, "Is everything all right, Mrs. Jennings? You mentioned that it was important for Carrie to be absent for our meeting. I hope there isn't some problem with Carrie. But, if there is, and I can be of help—"

"Problem?" Mrs. Jennings replied, strain in her voice,

"Problem? With Carrie? Why, no, there's no problem." She continued, choosing her words carefully. "Carrie has never been a problem, Mrs. Callaway. She's been a joy for her grandfather and I since the day she arrived." Mrs. Jennings chuckled, "Albeit a very *active* and *energetic* joy. There have been no dull moments in our lives." Mrs. Jennings sighed and stood up before she continued. She began to walk slowly back and forth beneath the arbor. As she walked, she reached up to pluck a rose, which she began twirling in one hand as she collected her thoughts.

"LisBeth—may I call you LisBeth?" Mrs. Jennings asked, continuing when LisBeth nodded. "As I have already said, Carrie has been the joy of our lives. However, she has never been an easy child Always active, energetic, asking thousands of questions, and not always accepting the answers she was given. She has, I think, had a happy life with us." Mrs. Jennings sat down beside LisBeth again and continued. "But she has always kept the dream alive of going back to Santee someday. At first, Walter and I thought it was just a childish wish for the only home she'd ever known—a very natural yearning for life to be the way it always had been— a desire to return to where her mother's memory would be more fresh. However, as Carrie has matured, she has reminded us regularly that she would one day be returning to Santee."

Mrs. Jennings dropped the rose on the brick path and turned to look at LisBeth. Her brown eyes squinted as she said earnestly, "Walter and I are both sincere Christians, LisBeth. The thought of one of our children—or grandchildren—giving her life to the Lord is a dear one. Normally, we would encourage Carrie along the way." Lucy paused before continuing, "However, in Carrie's case, we are concerned that her motive may not be quite so simple as a desire to serve the Lord wherever the Lord leads."

LisBeth nodded. "I think I know what you are going to

say, Mrs. Jennings Carrie hasn't sincerely given herself to serve the Lord wherever He would use her. She has already decided that the Lord will use her at Santee."

Lucy Jennings looked past LisBeth and took a deep breath before continuing. "She is *such* a strong-willed child, LisBeth I have urged her to pray for the Lord's guidance—"

LisBeth interrupted Mrs. Jennings. "And she says that she doesn't need to pray, she already knows what the Lord wants her to do."

Mrs. Jennings nodded. "I see that you've already spoken with Carrie. I should have guessed that she would share her plans with you." With difficulty, Mrs. Jennings went on, choosing her words carefully. "Did Carrie mention any *other* plans to you, LisBeth?"

LisBeth hesitated, not certain what to say.

"May I speak frankly, LisBeth?" Lucy Jennings lowered her voice and when LisBeth nodded encouragement, she continued softly. "I believe that Carrie wants to return to Santee because she believes that she will be able to make your brother fall in love with her." When LisBeth showed no surprise at the revelation, Lucy Jennings continued, "It's become such an obsession with her, LisBeth. She's taken her memories of your brother and written a fairy tale." Suddenly, Lucy frowned. Reaching out she squeezed LisBeth's hand. "Please, LisBeth, don't misunderstand me. There's no bigotry in my concern. From what I have observed and heard, Mr. King is a fine man. However—"

LisBeth interrupted, "However, Soaring Eagle has shown absolutely no interest in Carrie, and you're worried that she's rushing headlong to Nebraska to meet with great disappointment. To perhaps make a fool of herself and to do damage to her fragile relationship with God."

Lucy nodded her head sadly. "The latter concern is the greatest, LisBeth. Walter and I have spoiled Carrie. I admit

It. We couldn't help ourselves. She's a delightful child—beautiful, talented, sweet—everything grandparents desire. However, I fear that in spoiling her we have not prepared her for the realities of life. She believes in God, LisBeth, but hers is a God who—" Lucy sighed. "I think that God, for Carrie, is a lot like her grandfather—a kind old gentleman who delights in giving her just what she wants." Mrs. Jennings paused and looked at LisBeth soberly. "I fear what will become of Carrie when God does not make her fairy tale come true."

LisBeth nodded sympathetically. "It will be a shock, that's certain." Shifting the focus of their conversation slightly, LisBeth added, "I know that Soaring Eagle is very fond of Carrie, Mrs. Jennings. But sincere friendship is all I've observed." LisBeth paused briefly before continuing. "I know that you are right about Carrie's feelings, Mrs. Jennings, and I share your fear that she will be disappointed." Laying one hand on Mrs Jennings's arm, LisBeth asked, "What can I do to help?"

Mrs. Jennings reached down to retrieve the rose. A few petals fell to the ground, and as the faint aroma of roses filled the air, she continued. "You were here when Carrie so abruptly announced her plans to return to Nebraska this fall. She wants to attend the university there and then return to Santee as a matron or teacher. To her credit, she seems to realize that she *is* very young and inexperienced—that she has some growing up to do. But she wants to be in Nebraska, near Santee. She's already written to the university. She's even written to Augusta Hathaway for a job at her new hotel."

At LisBeth's look of surprise, Mrs. Jennings smiled. "I told you that Carrie has a way of getting what she wants. She had the entire thing so well planned before she even told Mr. Jennings and me, we didn't know what to say. She took our silence as permission."

LisBeth pondered the revelation before answering sincerely, "Aunt Augusta is the perfect person to watch over Carrie, Mrs. Jennings. She'll make Carrie work hard enough to keep her out of mischief. She'll see to it that Carrie attends church," LisBeth laughed, "and she's intimidating enough to ensure that no unwholesome company ever dares to approach Carrie."

Lucy Jennings smiled. "That's good to hear, LisBeth. Mr. Jennings and I had hoped Carrie would remain in St. Louis and attend a private school. We have the funds to make that possible. But Carrie becomes positively livid whenever the subject is broached. Still, it's asking a great deal of Mrs. Hathaway."

LisBeth laughed. "Aunt Augusta will love it, Mrs. Jennings. She's been a great supporter of the university since its inception, and she'll adore having responsibility for a female student. She'll also delight in having someone as adorable as Carrie back under her wing to mother. If anyone can handle Carrie, Mrs. Jennings, it's Augusta."

"I hope *you'll* be able to keep in touch with Carrie, LisBeth." Lucy paused doubtfully. "Does you brother visit often?"

LisBeth shook her head. "He's never been to our home. And he'll be away at school for at least two years. Dr. Riggs has already said he will arrange summer work to help with Soaring Eagle's finances. Jim and I usually visit Santee twice a year. Carrie will want to go along, but there won't be much chance for her to——." LisBeth hesitated before continuing. "We'll do our best to chaperone Carrie, Mrs. Jennings. Attending the university will open up new worlds for her. Our pastor in Lincoln is very interested in young people, and I know he'll have an impact on Carrie as well. She'll have plenty of opportunity to find a real—well, a real *heart* knowledge." LisBeth lowered her voice before continuing, "I remember what it was like to just believe in things because I'd been raised to believe them, Mrs. Jennings. That's probably what's going on with Carrie." LisBeth reached across to pat Mrs. Jennings's hand. "But Carrie has had a wonderful example in you and Mr. Jennings. The Lord will use that. And I have no doubt that, in time, He will bring Carrie to a fuller understanding of what it means to follow Him."

Lucy Jennings was surprised by the sudden tears that pressed against her eyelids. She managed a reply, "I hope you are right, LisBeth. I pray for it daily."

LisBeth reassured her. "You *are* doing the right thing for Carrie, Mrs. Jennings. The university in Lincoln is young, and the faculty is small, but comprised of excellent men. At least Aunt Augusta says so. Carrie will get a fine education there. She won't be unhappy like she would be if you forced her to stay in St. Louis. And there will be time for the Lord to work in her life. Time for her to grow into *His* plan for her; time for her to let go of her own plan."

"I hope you're right, LisBeth. Mr. Jennings and I have prayed for guidance. It seems that letting her go back to Nebraska is the only way to avoid bitter rebellion. We can keep in touch. From what you say, Mrs. Hathaway is definitely equal to carrying a young woman through a challenge, and," Mrs. Jennings sighed, "I fear that our little Carrie is in for some very great challenges before she truly becomes a woman. It is so very difficult to give up on childhood dreams and step toward adult responsibilities."

LisBeth answered sincerely, "We'll do everything we can to help, Mrs. Jennings. You can be sure of that."

The morning of their departure from St. Louis, LisBeth and Soaring Eagle were invited to breakfast at the home of Walter and Lucy Jennings. Carrie chattered happily about her plans to study in Nebraska and insisted that she and her grandparents escort LisBeth and Soaring Eagle to the train station.

Throughout breakfast Soaring Eagle was unusually quiet and distant. At the train station he absented himself from the small party as often as possible. Only at the very last moment before their trains departed did he reappear. He bowed formally to the Jenningses and Carrie before helping LisBeth aboard her train. Sprinting across the tracks to bound up on his own train, he turned to wave at the Jenningses. Carrie stood quietly by her grandparents, dressed in a blue suit that made her eyes sparkle. Just as the train pulled away and her grandparents turned to go, Carrie pressed her lips to the tips of her fingers and blew a kiss in his direction.

Soaring Eagle withdrew into the train coach. He didn't watch Union Station disappear into the distance. Instead, he hurried to an open seat, opened his New Testament, and began to read. Soon, the words dissolved and his mind wandered, finally settling on the image of a petite figure stylishly dressed in blue, blowing a kiss. Jeremiah Soaring Eagle King was disturbed to realize that pondering the image gave him great pleasure.

CHAPTER 5

Anger resteth in the bosom of fools.

Ecclesiastes 7:9

The train lurched. Soaring Eagle looked up from reading and knew he was in trouble. Opposite him sat a grizzled, overweight man with a wad of tobacco in his cheek and stains from various meals dribbling down the front of his shirt. The man belched loudly and stretched. As he lit a cigar he looked about him. His eyes narrowed as he inspected Soaring Eagle.

Quickly, Soaring Eagle thrust his New Testament into his shirt pocket. He had armed himself with an unread newspaper, but in this instance the newspaper did no good.

Gilbert Slater had already noticed what were, to his eyes, totally incompatible qualities in his fellow passenger. An impeccably groomed Indian was a square peg that did not fit into the round holes in Slater's brain.

As soon as Soaring Eagle opened his newspaper, Slater shoved it aside. Taking a puff on his cigar, he thrust his face across the aisle towards Soaring Eagle and blew a trail of smoke into his face. Soaring Eagle blinked back tears and managed not to cough.

"Well," Slater half shouted to no one in particular. "Lookee here, folks. Here's an Injun tryin' to be white." Slater took in the details of Soaring Eagle's garb, with special attention to the well-polished boots. "Didn't know I'd be sharin' my ride to Chicago with an escapee from the reservation," Slater drawled, scraping the bottom of his manure-caked boots across Soaring Eagle's feet.

When Soaring Eagle didn't move, Slater leaned back, took another puff on his cigar, and was quiet for a moment. He was slow-witted, and it took effort for him to find exactly the right words with which to hurl another insult. In that moment, Soaring Eagle looked about the train car, hoping to find sympathetic eyes—someone he could pretend to know—some excuse to get up and move. Unfortunately, the only sympathetic eyes on the train were feminine. He had long ago learned never to address a woman to whom he had not first been introduced. He steeled himself for what he knew was coming. Slater didn't disappoint him.

"You unnerstan' what I'm sayin'—boy?" Slater waggled a tobacco-stained finger in Soaring Eagle's face. "You talk-ee English—or do you jus' *look* white?"

"I speak English."

"He speaks English!" Slater shouted to the train car. "Dresses white. Talks white. Next stop maybe I'll see if he *fights* white too." Flicking ashes on Soaring Eagle's boots, Slater challenged, "What about it, Injun? You fight white? Or do ya sneak up *behind* a man and shoot him while he ain't lookin' like the rest o' your blood brothers?"

Soaring Eagle said quietly, "I have no quarrel with you."

The comment made Slater angrier. His face reddened and his eyes narrowed to two slits. "Well, I got a quarrel with *you*, Injun. 'Fore I was mustered out I had my fill of cleanin' up after battles with you and your kind."

Soaring Eagle swallowed. He had placed one hand on each of his knees and he was gripping them hard, praying for supernatural help to control his own anger. He was surprised and a little frightened by the rage that was growing inside him. He looked about, praying for some way of escape. Someone was standing in the aisle. A gravelly voice said, "Excuse me, sir, but I believe my sister and I heard you speak in St. Louis." While Gilbert Slater looked on, the stranger shook Soaring Eagle's hand. "Woodward. George Woodward." The stranger turned sideways. "And this is my sister Julia." After a brief pause, Woodward added, "Would you care to join us for coffee in the dining car?"

With a grateful nod, Soaring Eagle fairly leaped out of his seat and followed George Woodward and his sister Julia into the adjacent dining car. As soon as they were seated, Soaring Eagle shook George Woodward's hand again. "Jeremiah Soaring Eagle King. Thank you for rescuing me. I can usually avoid those situations. But today I had to see my sister to her train. I was much too late to choose a seat judiciously. I probably should have just stayed outside. Sometimes riding on the platform between cars is preferable to meeting men like that."

Julia Woodward's warm brown eyes were angry as she asked, "You mean this kind of thing happens often?"

"Often enough," came the reply.

Julia looked at her brother and blurted out, "See, George. That's just what I meant at last week's meeting. There are ignorant savages in every culture!" The minute the words were out, she wished them back. Blushing furiously she stammered, "Oh, dear. I'm so terribly sorry. I didn't mean—"

George interrupted. "Julia and I are members of the Friends of the Indian Committee in Boston, Mr. King. My sister participated in a particularly heated discussion at last week's meeting with a gentleman, although I hesitate to use that word, not unlike the one you just encountered." Woodward smiled warmly at his sister.

Soaring Eagle replied, "You'll forgive me if I don't remember you from my audiences in St. Louis. I was rather overwhelmed there—so many new people."

Julia laughed. "You mean you really *did* speak in St. Louis?" She winked at her brother. "George and I came up with that concoction to rescue you from a difficult situation."

"Then I'm doubly in your debt," Soaring Eagle offered. Coffee was ordered while he briefly explained his presence in St. Louis.

"You'll be speaking in Boston as well?" George wanted to know.

"In truth I am to spend the summer in Wisconsin working on a farm. The plan is for me to arrive in Boston barely in time to register for classes and begin my studies at Harvard. There probably won't be much time for speaking, although I'm willing if the Lord provides opportunities."

The trio ordered lunch, and while they waited George Woodward asked, "Would you indulge us, Mr. King, with the specifics of how you made the journey from the west to St. Louis?"

Julia laughed a low, warm laugh. "George Woodward, had I asked that question you would have lectured me all evening for my impertinence." Turning to Soaring Eagle she added meaningfully, "And I'm in my brother's debt for saving me the necessity of being so forward. Please, Mr. King, would you indulge us?"

Grateful for an excuse to postpone his return to Gilbert Slater's company, Soaring Eagle recounted his coming to Santee. "By the time I finished my studies at Santee, I was hungering for more—more knowledge of God, and more education to enable me to understand the new world that had been thrust upon me. Dr. Riggs was able to gain me admission to the preparatory department at Beloit College in Wisconsin. Thankfully, he also obtained government aid to help pay expenses. I spent three years at Beloit. I studied geography, history, mathematics, grammar, bookkeeping, and English. I watched how the other students dressed and talked. I studied people as much as I studied books."

George smiled broadly. "Well, I'd say the study of people was quite a success if you've already managed a lecture tour."

Soaring Eagle answered, "There was so much to learn. I was in an alien culture. I even wrote notes—what to say when being introduced, reminders to shake hands, phrases for taking one's leave."

Julia's voice was sympathetic. "You must have been miserable."

Soaring Eagle's dark eyes smiled warmly and he nodded. "Lonely, yes. But not miserable. God helped me to take refuge in His Word. It was a difficult time, but it was also a growing time. I grew closer to God—and perhaps, a bit closer to becoming the type of man that He can use in the world."

Lunch arrived. George ignored his food and asked, "What happened after Beloit?"

"Another school. Dr. Riggs guided me, making arrangements for me to go to John Knox College in Illinois."

"And what did you study at John Knox, Mr. King?" Julia wanted to know.

Soaring Eagle cleared his throat and hesitated. "There were many new things to learn at John Knox."

"I have no doubt of that." Julia grinned, turning to George with a comment about John Knox being coeducational.

It was nearly two hours before the Woodwards and Soaring Eagle finally folded their napkins and returned to the coach. With relief Soaring Eagle saw that Gilbert Slater was snoring loudly, his head leaning against the dirty train-car window. When the Woodwards insisted that Soaring Eagle move to an open seat across from them, he retrieved his newspaper and gladly made his way toward the opposite end of the train car where George Woodward had taken a seat opposite his sister, leaving Soaring Eagle no choice but to sit beside Julia Woodward.

When the train finally made its first stop, Soaring Eagle waited until every passenger had disembarked before rising to leave the car. He climbed down the ladder that led along the tracks opposite the platform, but his elaborate attempt to avoid an encounter with Gilbert Slater failed.

"Forgot to tell you I was a tracker for the army," Slater snarled, shoving Soaring Eagle against the side of the train car.

"I have no quarrel with you," Soaring Eagle said wearily.

"That's where you're wrong, Injun." Slater licked his lips.

"Why do you want to fight me? I've done nothing to hurt you."

"I got so many scores to settle with your kind it'd take all night just to list 'em," came the reply. "But this here stopover's only for twenty minutes. I got to be about my business. Those Injun lovin' friends aren't around to rescue you now, are they?"

Just as Soaring Eagle held up his hands to try to reason again, Slater grabbed him and threw him flat on his back. Wiping his nose, Slater loomed over Soaring Eagle, spitting a stream of tobacco juice into his face.

Slater gave a menacing kick to Soaring Eagle's ribs. "That's for my brother you savages killed." He leaned over and held up his hand in Soaring Eagle's face, kicking him again. "And *that's* for the two fingers you see missin' off that hand. Lost 'em when they froze. Winter of '68. Tracked a bunch of Crows through the mountains when it was forty below. Half my company had body parts lopped off. Couple of 'em died." Slater grabbed Soaring Eagle's shirt and pulled him up, slamming him hard against the train car. He doubled up his fist and slammed it hard into . . . the side of the train. Soaring Eagle had disappeared.

Slater howled with pain as two arms reached around him from behind, pinning his arms to his sides. Squeezing the air out of Slater's corpulent mid-section, Soaring Eagle whispered angrily, "I am *not* going to fight with you. You told me you have a list of people you want to avenge." Soaring Eagle squeezed tighter and Slater grunted. "Shall I give you *my* list? Shall I tell you of the day I was asleep in my tepee and soldiers rode into our village—past an American flag our chief had raised in honor of a treaty he had just signed—and began shooting? Shall I give you the names of my sisters, my mothers, my children—who all died that day?"

Soaring Eagle squeezed Slater tighter and tighter, realizing he was longing to break the man's back over his knee. With supreme effort, he forced himself to let Slater go, slamming him against the train and pinning him back with one forearm. He thrust his own face inches from Slater's. Still holding Slater against the train he said, "I could tell you more. There is a *better* way than revenge."

Slater spit in Soaring Eagle's face again, muttering foul epithets. In the wake of his hatred, Soaring Eagle released some of the rage he had held in check. Grabbing Slater by the throat, he whispered ominously, "I want you to know something. I am dressed like a white man. I am going east to a white man's school. I believe in the same God as the white man. But I'm still Lakota." He tightened his grip, shutting off some of Slater's air supply. "I remember very well how to kill a man." Soaring Eagle squeezed Slater's airway shut momentarily before releasing his hold. Slater slid to the ground, gasping for breath and rubbing his neck.

Soaring Eagle squatted beside Slater and said quietly, "I'm getting back on that train. I am going to Chicago. I will probably be having supper in the dining car with my friends. I do not expect to see *you* again."

Soaring Eagle stood up and brushed the dust off his jacket. He turned his back on Slater and climbed stiffly up the ladder at the back of the car. Crossing to the platform, he made his way toward the station where he tried to wipe away all vestiges of the encounter.

When the passengers climbed back aboard, Julia Woodward insisted that Soaring Eagle settle next to her again. The Woodwards noticed that Slater was absent from the train, commenting happily on the fact. Soaring Eagle was quiet on the subject. Only when the three got up to go to dinner did George Woodward guess that Soaring Eagle had had something to do with Slater's absence. Soaring Eagle moved carefully, wincing visibly when he pulled out Julia's chair to seat her in the dining car. He sat down slowly, trying to protect his bruised ribs from further trauma. Looking across the table at George Woodward, he saw understanding and respect shining from his new friend's eyes.

CHAPTER 6

Use hospitality one to another without grudging.

1 Peter 4:9

Carrie Brown boarded the Chicago, Burlington & Quincy train for Lincoln, Nebraska, on June 15, 1883. Walter and Lucy Jennings accompanied their granddaughter on the trip, unwilling to allow her to travel so far unescorted. When the train pulled into the new Gothic train station in Lincoln, Nebraska, Augusta Hathaway was waiting to greet them. She directed a young man to take their trunks to the hotel. Carrie paused just outside the train station to stare in disbelief at a three-story hotel directly across the street from the station. The building was brick, with ornamental cartouches over every window and an imposing covered entryway that welcomed guests to the Hathaway House.

Augusta reveled in Carrie's open-mouthed admiration. "My new hotel, Carrie. It's quite a change from what you remember, no doubt." Augusta made no attempt to hide her sense of accomplishment. "Three stories high. We can accommodate three hundred guests—and lately I've wished I had more rooms." Augusta turned to the Jenningses. "Lincoln has become quite a metropolis. Nearly twenty passenger trains arrive each day and we're adding more every few weeks. Telegraph's in and I'm on a waiting list to actually get a telephone soon. Steam heat, gas lights—everything modern has come to Lincoln since you left, Carrie. We're not a little prairie village anymore. Of course we're not St. Louis, either—but we're growing fast." The trio made its way across the street while Augusta expounded. "Some believe, and I'm among them, that we'll have one hundred thousand citizens in less than ten years. The schools are growing, and commerce is good."

Once across the wide street, Augusta pointed out improvements. "Used to be a sea of mud around the railway station when it rained. Paving the road stopped that. Sidewalks improved things even more." They entered the hotel, pausing briefly for Augusta to introduce them to Silas Kellum.

"Silas calls himself 'my lowly desk clerk,' but he's actually learning everything he can about running a hotel so he can buy me out in my old age."

Silas saluted energetically and clicked his heels. "Yes, ma'am, that's right." He lowered his salute and bowed smartly to the Jenningses. "Welcome to the Hathaway House. We promise satisfaction or your money will be cheerfully refunded."

Augusta nodded. "Good boy. Lesson number one in business, Silas. Always remember that the guests come first. The day I forget to make the welfare of my guests my paramount concern is the day Hathaway House is on its way to losing its—"

Silas broke in, "losing its place in the community to the Lindell."

"Bite your tongue, young man!" Augusta ordered with mock sternness. "We're the largest hotel in Nebraska, but we also offer the most home-like service. Kate Martin over at the Lindell has been wooing the politicians for years, but they still meet in *my* dining room."

Silas chimed in, "And they always will—as long as we can keep the Schlegelmilch sisters cooking."

Augusta finally gave up her boasting and led the Jennings and Carrie toward the back of the building and through a simple doorway marked "private."

"This is my apartment," Augusta explained. "I keep talking about getting a house in town, but I don't really want to move. I've lived in a hotel for so many years, now, I wouldn't know how to act if I couldn't hear my guests tromping in and out—and if I couldn't preside over the dining room personally."

The Jenningses entered Augusta's private domain and were welcomed by the faint aroma of frying potatoes and roast beef.

"Something smells wonderful," observed Walter Jennings.

"That's Cora's cooking, Mr. Jennings. We're at the back of the hotel now, and the kitchen isn't far away. God has blessed me with two sisters who are among the best cooks in Lincoln." Augusta explained, "I thought you'd want to see Carrie's room first. Then I'll show you upstairs and you'll have a chance to get settled before dinner."

Augusta directed the party to a small room that opened directly onto her parlor. On either side of the only window in the room were a walnut bed and its matching marble-topped dresser. As Carrie looked about the room, Augusta offered, "I was going to order a new feathertick and comfortables, Carrie, but I thought you might want to pick those out yourself. We can get different draperies, too, if these don't suit. It will all be part of my welcome gift to you." A round table had been added to the center of the room. "You can do your book work in here when you like—away from distractions. I didn't think the writing desk would be quite big enough by itself." Augusta backed out of the room to allow Carrie and the Jenningses to inspect, which they did briefly before emerging with appreciative comments.

Augusta continued, "We'll talk details later, Carrie, but you can entertain here at the hotel any time—just please give me a few days' notice if you're planning an affair for more than a few classmates. I thought about giving you a permanent room upstairs—it would be larger—but I'm selfish and I wanted you close by." Augusta smiled sincerely. "I've been lonely since LisBeth and Sarah left me, and I'm looking forward to having a young person to spoil again—and I hope you'll accumulate a great many young friends to entertain often. I love having young people about."

Lucy and Walter Jennings had been overwhelmed by Augusta, but now they relaxed visibly, each one thinking that the decision to allow Carrie to return to Nebraska was a wise one after all. After a few brief but sincere thankful comments to Augusta, they gratefully accepted her suggestion that they ascend to their own room to unpack and rest before dinner.

Carrie bounded back into her little room, enthusiastically unpacking and arranging things while Augusta answered the few messages that had been left for her while she waited at the train station. When Augusta returned to her apartment, she peeked into Carrie's room to see Carrie seated at the small Circassian walnut writing desk positioned underneath the window that overlooked the service entrance to the hotel.

When Augusta appeared at her door, Carrie looked up with a bright smile. "Mrs. Hathaway, I can't thank you enough for all you've already done to help me. I want you to know that I intend to work very hard, and to make certain that you don't regret agreeing to let me stay here."

Crossing the small distance between them, Augusta patted Carrie on the shoulder. "I know you'll do wonderfully, Carrie. I was quite impressed with the fact that you took the initiative to write to me and to look for employment before you committed to the university. It speaks well of you that you want to make your own way in the world."

"When do I start work, Mrs. Hathaway?"

"Well, I thought you would want to enjoy Lincoln for at least a few days, Carrie. I want to drive you and your grandparents all around our budding metropolis, show them everything I can before they leave, and then, young lady, you will be put to work. There's plenty to be done. Laundry, dusting, window-washing, serving in the dining room, kitchen work—the list goes on and on. At present, I desperately need someone to keep the lobby and dining room spotless. We'll talk about all the details later, Dear. For now, you just enjoy getting settled in. Your grandparents will be down in about an hour and I've arranged to have Joseph take us on a tour of the city."

Aged Joseph Freeman drove the carriage that introduced the Jenningses to Lincoln, Nebraska. They drove east on P Street, turning north on 10th for their first view of University Hall. Three stories high, it towered above the homes that had only recently begun to reach the edge of its grounds, which were, this day in 1883, providing breakfast for two milk cows.

Augusta laughed, "There's a moooove-ment abroad to fence the grounds to prevent this. But the university is like everything else out here. It sprung up from the will of a people who refuse to admit that Nebraska is a 'worthless desert.' And, just like everything else, the university will outlive the rural lawn ornamentation. Two rows of trees were planted years ago, but the grasshoppers destroyed them in one afternoon. For now, we're still mowing hay on the grounds and working to keep the cattle away.

"The building's fine, though. There's a large chapel

inside. You'll be happy to know, Mr. and Mrs. Jennings, that chapel attendance is required." Augusta counted on her fingers as she enumerated the features of University Hall. "Twenty recitation rooms, a reading room, rooms for literary societies, music, and painting, a laboratory, a ladies' reception room, a printing office—" Augusta took a deep breath. "And something they call a 'cabinet' where they house the botanical, geological, and biological specimens."

Walter Jennings said, "I'm impressed, Mrs. Hathaway. Not so much by the university, but by your apparent knowledge of the details regarding its founding and function."

"I'm a very involved citizen, Mr. Jennings. And the founding of the university has not been unclouded by controversy," Augusta explained. "In the seventies when the grasshoppers ruined everything in sight, there were many who insisted that the university was unnecessary. The state teacher's association even passed a resolution to try to get the resources appropriated for the university diverted to the lower levels of public education. I was part of all that battle—on the side of the university.

"Our first chancellor, Allen Benton, did a great work. He traveled the entire state raising support and recruiting students. In only ten years, the university has grown to employ seventeen professors and boasts nearly three hundred students. I'd say the battle was worth it."

Carrie nodded appreciatively at the building. "See, Grandmother and Grandfather, I *told* you I could get a good education here. And I like the idea of going to a campus where there's only *one* building and fewer students." Carrie paused to explain to Augusta, "In St. Louis, I'd be on a huge campus." Carrie raised her hand to her forehead in mock woe, "A tiny speck on the sea of humanity."

"Well, Carrie," Augusta laughed, "you *are* a tiny speck of a thing, but at this university, you'll get plenty of individual attention from the professors, and plenty of opportunities to teach. There are many rural schools near Lincoln truly begging for teachers. It's not at all unusual for university students to take a term or two away from their studies to teach and build up their bank account."

Carrie nodded. "I thought I might even take a *year* off to teach after my first year here—if you think a rural school would have me. I'd like to get experience as quickly as possible. Which reminds me, Mrs. Hathaway, I'll be happy to accept that class of scholars for Christian Endeavor meetings—if it's still available."

At the surprised looks on the Jenningses' faces, Augusta explained, "When Carrie wrote about her desire to teach as soon as possible, I mentioned that our Sunday meetings have been growing right along with the city, and I suggested she might want to take on a children's class."

Walter and Lucy Jennings nodded approvingly.

"I think you'll discover," Augusta offered, "that the students at this university are older and more serious than those at many of the institutions back east. A large number of our students are here because they really want higher education—not because they were sent here. Many of these students have to sacrifice in heartbreaking ways to pay for their education. Last year I heard about one young man who walked forty miles to enroll. It's been my experience that most have to work to stay in school. They work hard and have little time for extracurricular activities."

Carrie was paying close attention to Augusta's every word, enjoying a rather dramatic picture of herself as overworked and undernourished, yet triumphing over all to gain her teaching certificate and head north to teach the beloved Lakota languishing in ignorance. The carriage jolted as Joseph began to pull away from the university, and Augusta went on with her recitation about Lincoln buildings. They drove by a neat row of frame houses with yards outlined by picket fences which Augusta announced were faculty and student housing.

"There's another three-story dormitory building just three blocks from campus. It's coeducational, which means about seventy female students receive room and board, and about eighty young gentlemen receive day board. Carrie will be the only student at Hathaway House, of course. I've rarely a free room any more, what with emigrants pouring into Nebraska from all over. The railroad offers free accommodations up at the Emigrant House. Even so, Hathaway House stays full. Not all the emigrants are poor, you know. We're getting German Mennonites now who brought sizable fortunes with them. I hear talk that they might even begin their own newspaper here in Lincoln soon."

Augusta broke off and pointed to a building. "That's the Merchant's Cafe, Carrie, and you'll do well to turn down any invitations to that place. They sell a two-dollar meal ticket that's good for twenty-one meals. The students call them 'sample meals' because the portions are so small. Silas used to eat there before he came to work for me. Told me he survived by taking all the bread in sight and emptying the milk pitcher as fast as it could be filled."

The carriage had been moving slowly back south into the busier part of the city. When it approached the capitol, Augusta called out to Joseph. "Turn in at the Braddocks, Joseph. I haven't seen Abigail in over a week now, and Sarah said to be certain that we bring Carrie over right away so they can get reacquainted."

The Jenningses looked at one another with raised eyebrows as Joseph turned the carriage into a cobblestone-lined drive that led through a massive gate and onto impeccably groomed grounds hidden by a high brick wall. Augusta quickly explained Sarah and Tom Biddle's arrival in Lincoln as runaway orphans, their coming to live with her and Jesse King, and Sarah's subsequent opportunity to be trained as a housekeeper for Abigail Braddock and her son David. "Sarah's done so very well for herself," Augusta said as she climbed down from the carriage. "I'm so proud of her. And she'll be delighted to get reacquainted with you, Carrie."

CHAPTER 7

Look not every man on his own things, but every man also on the things of others.

Philippians 2:4

Sarah Biddle leaned away from the heat of the open oven and wiped her moist forehead on her apron. Grasping hold of the leg bone of the mammoth turkey that had been roasting for hours, she gave a twist. The bone gave way easily and Sarah nodded with satisfaction, sliding the turkey back into the oven, but leaving the door open as she crossed to the pantry to retrieve a platter. Just then she heard a carriage coming up the drive. Sarah didn't wait for her visitors to knock before opening the door. Augusta Hathaway nearly fell through the open door into the kitchen.

"Sarah! They're finally here!" Augusta fairly pulled Carrie and the Jenningses into the kitchen. "It's been five years, and little Carrie Brown has finally come back to Nebraska. Carrie, you remember Sarah. Walter and Lucy Jennings, meet Miss Sarah Biddle—the finest housekeeper to ever grace a home."

Sarah blushed with embarrassment, laughing nervously and shaking her guests' hands. Augusta started for the front of the house. "Where's Abigail, Sarah? I know I should have called at the proper hour this morning to arrange it, but I'd love for her to meet Carrie and her grandparents."

Sarah shook her head. "I'm sorry, Aunt Augusta, Carrie, Mr. and Mrs. Jennings. Mrs. Braddock hasn't felt up to coming down today." Sarah's face brightened, "But Mr. Braddock will return from his bank meeting soon, and Tom's due any moment from school. Perhaps you'd all like some lemonade."

There was something in Sarah's voice that Augusta didn't like. She looked towards the front of the house, then up towards Abigail's room. "We'd love some lemonade, Sarah, but you must let me help to prepare it so you can tend your dinner."

The Jenningses were shown through another door and onto a small porch at the back of the house where bittersweet vines grew up a trellis, offering a shady haven from which to observe a beautifully manicured rose garden.

"Now, how does she get such roses, I'd like to know," Lucy Jennings said admiringly. She settled comfortably on a wicker swing with Walter beside her. Carrie took the opportunity to walk through the garden.

In the kitchen, Augusta and Sarah were quiet while Augusta made lemonade and Sarah bustled about preparing supper. Just then twelve-year-old Tom Biddle arrived home from school. He came up the back stairs slowly, contemplating the evening ahead. Miss Griswall had assigned an essay just when he had planned a game of ball with the neighborhood boys. But at the sight of Augusta he brightened. "Aunt Augusta!" he boomed, giving Augusta a hug.

"Well, Tom. How's Hortense Griswall treating you these days?"

Tom began a recitation of carefully practiced complaints against Miss Griswall and her demands on Tom Biddle, but Sarah stopped him. "Tom, you know that Miss Griswall pushes you because she knows you can do the work. She wants you to do well and to get into the university. If you want to read law, you've got to do well."

Sarah's speech was well-rehearsed, and Tom crossed the kitchen, helping himself to an apple fritter without so much as acknowledging Sarah's comments.

Sarah ordered, "Take those fritters out to the porch to our guests, Tom. Aunt Augusta has the lemonade all ready." She looked doubtfully at Augusta. "I need to do a few more things. Do you think they'd mind? I'll be out in just a minute."

"Of course not, Sarah. You go on about your duties. We're the ones who are being rude by turning up at this awkward hour. But I just couldn't drive by without stopping in."

Sarah turned to slide a mound of thinly sliced potatoes onto a griddle before turning back to Augusta and smiling warmly. "I'm so happy you did, Aunt Augusta. We've been a little lonely these past few weeks." Sarah turned away abruptly and Augusta frowned slightly as she took lemonade out onto the porch. She was back inside momentarily, and without a word from Sarah began to snap beans into a great blue crock.

"How is Mrs. Braddock doing, Sarah? Dr. Gilbert was in for dinner the other evening. I said something about Abigail, rather innocently, I thought. Well, he didn't say much, but I could tell that he is really concerned."

Sarah's blue eyes turned cool and she looked away before answering. "Not well. Not well at all, I'm afraid." Sarah stopped, carefully choosing her next words. "She hasn't been well enough to come downstairs in a few days. But we're still hopeful. David—Mr. Braddock is very attentive."

Augusta's voice was warm with affection. "I'm so pleased that you've made such a home for yourself here, Sarah. I admit, though, to having been a bit worried you'll make yourself sick caring so much for Abigail."

Sarah looked up quickly. "That's nonsense. Mrs. Braddock

has done so very much for me, Aunt Augusta. Both of you have. I'll do whatever it takes to care for her, to see that her house is run just the way she wants it, and to see that she is as comfortable as I can make her for as long as it takes until, until she gets better."

Abruptly Sarah changed the subject. "Thank you for bringing Carrie over so soon, Aunt Augusta. It's amazing how much she's grown up. I knew she grew up, of course. But seeing her is quite a surprise." Sarah turned the potatoes and lowered the fire. "I think I can get away for a few minutes now, to actually visit." Just as the two women headed for the porch, a bell rang in the pantry.

"That's Mrs. Braddock, Aunt Augusta. You'll have to excuse me." Pulling her apron off she opened a cupboard near the butler's pantry door and grabbed a bottle. As she left the kitchen she called back, "Tell the Jenningses I'm terribly sorry—I hope they understand—" Her voice melted away as she ran up the back stairs to Abigail's room.

In her haste to answer the bell, Sarah had left the cupboard door open. Augusta went to close it. One shelf was lined with bottles, next to which was a copy of a book. Feeling only a little guilty, Augusta reached for the leather-bound book. *Ladies Guide in Health and Disease, J. H. Kellogg, M.D.* There was a torn piece of paper marking a page. Augusta opened the book and caught her breath. The page had been studied carefully. It was stained and several lines were marked under the heading that read *Lotions for Use in Cancer of the Breast . . . Ex. Bella., dr. 1., Ex., Stramon., dr. 1. Vaseline, oz. 1. . . . to be used as an ointment . . . excellent to relieve pain arising from the rapid growth . . .* Augusta looked up at the shelf. Two bottles bore the labels *Ex. Bella., Ex. Stramon.*

Reaching up to take down another bottle, Augusta jumped as Sarah said, "The first recipe is still giving some relief. Dr. Gilbert has already shown me how to mix . . ."

her voice faltered and she took a deep breath. "Dr. Gilbert has already shown me how to mix what we'll need next."

"Oh, Sarah, I had no idea. Abigail never mentioned, I never guessed."

Sarah's eyes filled with tears, but she willed them away and took a deep breath. "No one knows, so far, Aunt Augusta. Not even Mr. Braddock. Mrs. Braddock won't have it. She doesn't want to cause any trouble—any worry."

Augusta closed the book that lay open on the counter and put it away along with the bottles. Closing the cupboard door, she wrapped her arms around Sarah, feeling the slim body tremble with emotion. "*You* know. You've had this burden—alone—for how long?"

Sarah shrugged and pulled away. "Not so long. It's only in the first stages. The medication helps, and Mrs. Braddock still has good days. She may even come down for supper tonight." Sarah looked boldly at Augusta. "She needs me now. I'm glad I'm here for her."

"But, Sarah, you shouldn't have to bear it alone."

"I'm not bearing it alone, Aunt Augusta. Dr. Gilbert is very good about checking in. Every evening Tom reads to her." Sarah lowered her voice as if sharing a great secret. "We've taken to calling her 'Mother Braddock.' She seems to like it. Tom reads and I quilt. Some evenings it's almost like I'm back at the hotel with you and Aunt Jesse."

Augusta was apologetic. "I didn't mean to snoop, Sarah. You left the cupboard door open. I was just closing it, but I saw the book—I was curious. I should have just closed the door and let well enough alone. I'm sorry."

"It's kind of a relief to have someone else know, Aunt Augusta—someone who can pray with me." Tears welled up in Sarah's eyes. "I guess it *has* been kind of a lonely burden."

Augusta reached for Sarah's hands and squeezed them,

whispering, "I'll pray every day, Sarah—more than once. If I can help—"

Sarah shook her head and pushed herself away. "No, there's nothing you can do. Just don't tell anyone, yet, and pray." Tears threatened again as Sarah looked away, adding, "I don't know what this will do to Mr. Braddock when he finds out. He's already suspicious that there's something seriously wrong. He's always been so close to his mother."

Reaching for her apron, Sarah returned to the stove where she began looking under lids and stirring things. "He'll be home soon. I hope you'll come back for another visit, Aunt Augusta. Can you explain to the Jenningses? They must think me very rude."

"Do you think you can get away to join us for dinner at the hotel tomorrow evening, Sarah?"

Sarah opened the oven and hefted the turkey onto the counter. "Yes, I promised Tom. Mr. Braddock will be home with Mother Braddock. She knows about it and she'd be very angry with me if we didn't come."

Augusta nodded with satisfaction. "Good. Now, we'll be off. I'll send Tom in with the lemonade pitcher and glasses, Dear. You don't even need to say good-bye. We'll just slip away and look forward to seeing you tomorrow evening."

Tom came back into the kitchen with the lemonade pitcher and glasses. Sarah heard her guests' footsteps go down the porch steps and around the back of the house towards where Joseph waited in the carriage. Just as Tom was rinsing the glasses, Augusta opened the kitchen door and called softly, "Good-bye, Dears. God bless. I'm praying." She closed the door softly behind her, joined the others in the carriage, and was gone.

Tom quizzed his sister. "What's she prayin' about?"

"About us. Mother Braddock."

"Good. She needs it."

"We all need it, Tom. Now help me set the dining table for supper. David should be home any minute."

"How come you call him David when you're with me and Mr. Braddock the rest of the time?"

"Because he's my employer, and that shows respect."

"You don't respect him to his face," Tom argued. "You call him David then too."

Sarah blushed. "That's because he asked me to. Just like Mrs. Braddock asked us to call her Mother Braddock. Mr. Braddock asked me to call him David."

"Well, I like it. Makes it more like we got a real family."

They had walked through the butler's pantry and begun to set the table, four places of fine china, with only two forks and two goblets, simple fare for the evening.

"Will Mother Braddock be down for supper?"

"I think so. The medicine is definitely helping."

"I hope she gets well soon."

"Me, too, Tom." The sound of carriage wheels on the cobblestone drive brought a smile to Sarah's thin lips. "There, David's home. Now you finish this, and I'll check on Mother Braddock."

David Braddock ascended the side stairs of his mansion slowly, stopping outside the leaded glass door to remove his hat. He passed one hand over the thick dark curls the hat had crushed down and then opened the door and went in. Tossing the hat onto a small settee he turned left and went straight into the kitchen where he pulled out one of the two chairs at the small white table in the corner and sat, waiting.

Sarah and Tom entered the kitchen at the same moment. When David looked up at her, Sarah said to Tom, "Tom, see if Mother Braddock needs help coming down, will you? I'll begin to dish up our supper." She stood motionless, watching David carefully.

Tom left the room. When David finally spoke, his mellow voice was strained. "I saw Dr. Gilbert today." Anguish filled his eyes and he bowed his head and covered his face with his hands.

Sarah crossed the spotless white kitchen floor and laid a hand on the broad shoulders. At her touch, David took in a deep breath. Then he wrapped both his arms around her. He was holding her so tightly that she could barely breathe. She stroked the dark curls.

When David finally let go he looked up at her, his eyes shining with unspilled tears. "You knew."

"Yes."

"Why didn't you tell me?"

"I promised I wouldn't. Not yet."

David stood up. He was not a tall man, and his eyes were nearly level with Sarah's. "I have to go back to Philadelphia sometime this year—"

Sarah didn't let him finish. "You should go as soon as possible. Get it done and come back home, so that you'll be here when—"

He raised two fingers and touched them to her lips. "I'll go in two weeks. It will take that long to arrange things here. I'll wire my cousin Ira to get things going in Philadelphia. It shouldn't take long." Reaching down to take one of Sarah's hands, David said quietly, "When I come back we'll be married. Mother will be able to attend." He looked up at her doubtfully. "Do you think?"

Sarah bit her lip, didn't reply.

David sat down abruptly, running his hand through his hair again. Sarah started to move away, but he grabbed her hand. "That wasn't a proper proposal, Sarah. In fact, it was miserable. I'm sorry."

"It's all right, David. I understand."

He looked up at her hopefully. "Do you love me, Sarah Biddle?"

"I don't think Lincoln will approve of your selection of a wife, David."

"I don't give a rip what Lincoln thinks."

Sarah smiled down at him. "That's one of the things I love about you."

Tom called from upstairs that Mother Braddock was coming down for supper.

"Shall we tell Mother tonight?"

"Oh, I think not, David."

"Why not?"

"Because you should be sure before you tell Mother Braddock."

"Sarah Biddle." David's voice was angry and Sarah faced him, surprised at the emotion. "You are the sweetest, most humble, most capable girl I've ever known. I'm too old for some wild romance, but I want to marry you just as surely as snow flies in December. Now, will you or won't you?"

Sarah looked about the kitchen doubtfully. "I think I belong in the kitchen, not in the parlor."

David turned her face towards him. "Don't look at the *house*, Sarah. Look at *me*." His voice took on a reassuring tone. "Every man I know has commented at one time or another that they wish their own daughters could be as genteel as you."

"I don't have the right background for—"

"You don't need a *background* to be my wife."

"That's not what your friends will say."

"Then they aren't my friends."

"Don't be immature, David."

"I'll be immature if I want to!"

Sarah picked up the platter of turkey and headed for the dining room, her eyes blazing. "Then you'll be immature alone, because Tom and Mother Braddock and I are eating supper now!"

David wandered sheepishly into the dining room just as Sarah and Tom settled at their places. He kissed his mother on the cheek and took his place at the head of the table, snapping his napkin angrily and shoving it into his lap.

Abigail Braddock's eyes sparkled with mischief as she said innocently, "Did I hear a bit of an argument coming from the kitchen?"

Sarah's cheeks reddened and David's eyes blazed as he stabbed a piece of turkey and shoved it into his mouth, preventing him from answering.

Abigail chuckled. "My, my, children, such a lot of fuss over a simple engagement."

Sarah laid down her fork and looked up.

Tom plunked down his water glass and let out a loud "*What?*"

David emptied his glass of wine and speared more turkey.

Abigail's mellow voice continued, "We'll have the ceremony in the parlor. I'll have Elsie Thornburn in yet this week and we'll discuss the gown. Sarah will want a simple ceremony . . . not much fanfare." Abigail turned to David, "But I insist that you announce it in the Philadelphia papers—and move me into the room across the hall so that my room can be redecorated for the two of you."

Sarah began to protest, but Abigail held up a thin hand. "My beloved child, of all the things that could have happened to me today, *this* is the very happiest." She smiled warmly at Sarah and asked, "It *has* happened, hasn't it?" Looking sternly at David she scolded, "And shame on *you*, David Braddock. Proposing in the *kitchen!*" Clucking her tongue she asked, "Don't you have any romance in you at all, Boy?" Abigail turned back to Sarah. "Just like his father. All business. Closes in on a wife like he closes in on a banker to finalize some financial plan." Abigail chuckled. "Think you can put up with him, Sarah?"

For once, Tom Biddle remained so amazed he had nothing to say. It gave Sarah a rare occasion to formulate a heartfelt response. Casting a sidelong glance at David Braddock, she reached out to pat the back of his hand as she answered Abigail. "A woman can put up with a lot when she loves a man, Mother Braddock."

Unromantic as he was, David Braddock was given wisdom at that moment. He took Sarah's hand in his own and squeezed it. And he didn't let go.

CHAPTER 8

The LORD is with you. . . . and if ye
seek him, he will be found of you.
2 Chronicles 15:2

Great thunderclouds were rolling in from the west on the day that Carrie Brown stood on the platform of Lincoln's train station to bid good-bye to her grandparents. A multitude of passengers had gathered that morning to compete for seats on the train, and Carrie tried to hurry her grandparents, admonishing, "Now don't worry. You've met Mrs. Hathaway, and you both like her immensely. You've seen that she has a good job and a nice room for me. I'll have weeks to work before registering for the fall term. I should easily be able to save up enough to get me started through the first year."

Walter Jennings looked towards the darkening sky before answering gruffly, "I don't understand what all this figuring is about, Carrie. We've already told you we support your decision. Seeing Lincoln and the university and meeting Mrs. Hathaway for ourselves has put any doubts we had about your coming here to rest. We're going home to St. Louis with few worries about you. But Carrie," he pleaded, "you know we can pay the tuition and your expenses. I don't understand why you have to work."

"Grandfather," Carrie said shortly. "We've been through this and through it. I want to do this on my own. I've got to grow up, Grandfather. Make my own way."

A great clap of thunder resounded, and with a harrumph and a grunt, Jennings bent to kiss his only grandchild, angrily brushing an errant tear off his cheek.

Lucy Jennings gave in to her emotions, crying quietly as she smiled encouragement to Carrie. "We're both so very proud of you, Dear. We know you'll do well. Be sure you write. Be sure you let us know if you need anything. Be sure to come home for Christma—" her voice wavered and she put a lace-edged handkerchief to her face.

Another clap of thunder reminded the Jenningses of the need to hurry. Lucy Jennings regained her composure. Straightening her shoulders she gave a little toss of her head and said, "Goodness, what's gotten into us. As if we didn't raise you for this very moment." She sighed deeply. "It came too soon, that's all, Carrie. Here. Let me look at you." Laying a gloved hand on each of Carrie's shoulders, Lucy Jennings gazed down at her granddaughter with love and said, "We've done our best, Carrie. I know we've spoiled you, but you'll outgrow it. I hate to go, but in the end, I know it's for the best. Now—" Emotions threatened again, and Lucy hugged Carrie as she whispered, "May the Lord bless thee and keep thee, dear child."

When Carrie was released from her grandmother's embrace, she stood back and looked up at Lucy with serious eyes. "I'll work hard, Grandmother. I'll write, just like you asked, and everything will turn out."

Walter Jennings interrupted gruffly. "Promise us you'll go through with teaching the Christian Endeavor Society meetings, Carrie. There is no greater training ground than that of serving the Lord. You know, Grandchild, that our greatest concern is that you walk with God, that you transfer your dependence upon your grandmother and me to dependence upon God. If you learn to do that here in Lincoln, Nebraska, whatever else happens will be fine with us."

The train whistle blew just as it began to rain. Walter

Jennings grabbed Carrie up and swung her about, hugging her tightly and whispering, "God be with you, Granddaughter."

Lucy began to cry again as she and Walter boarded the train. Carrie backed under the overhang of the station and watched through the car windows as her grandparents pushed their way past a few passengers and settled by a window. Lucy struggled in vain to open the window, but it began to pour rain and the two were carried out of sight, waving furiously.

The moment she lost sight of them, Carrie felt a pang of loneliness—a flash of panic-stricken fear. *I'm on my own now,* she thought. *It's up to me to make something of myself.* The enormity of her first steps of independence washed over her as she darted through the rain back to the hotel, grateful that Augusta Hathaway was occupied elsewhere and could not observe her young charge's feeble attempts to fight back tears.

The summer of 1883 proved to be one of the most difficult periods in Carrie Brown's life. She had asked Augusta Hathaway for work without realizing just what she was requesting. As a child in her grandparent's home she had amused herself by "helping" servants clean windows and dust furniture. When Augusta's head housekeeper introduced Carrie to cleaning, Carrie was amazed.

Norah Murphy stood at the door to the dining room and recited, "Three times a day, Dearie. Hoist the chairs onto the tables. Sweep the floor first. Then mop. You *do* know how to mop?"

Carrie assured Norah that she knew how to mop.

Norah smiled. "Good. Now, when your university classes begin, you'll have only the morning and evening mop. I'll have another girl take care of noon. That way you'll have the day free for your classes."

When Norah first witnessed Carrie's attempt to mop, she stepped in immediately. "I don't know what they do in St. Louis, Dearie, but here in Lincoln we do things differently." Taking the mop from Carrie's hands, Norah demonstrated. "Out and back, over and back—ugh!" Norah held up the mop. "You didn't sweep first, did you, Miss Brown?"

Carrie blushed with embarrassment, but after the next meal, the floor was thoroughly swept before she mopped. Norah inspected and approved.

"Now, then, Miss Brown, we'll add the windows to your schedule. Twice weekly Mrs. Hathaway wants the dining room windows washed. You can do that after the evening mop. Do not use soapsuds. Use a clean cloth and clear water." Norah hauled a clear pail of water from the kitchen and wrung out her cloth. "Wet but not dripping, Miss Brown. Wash clean. Here, you try it." Carrie took the cloth and began to wipe. "Good. Now wring the rag dry and go over them again. Then polish with a dry cloth. Rinse the cloth and change the water as often as necessary." Norah Murphy grinned. "You'll make several trips to the kitchen and back."

Norah added, "Once a month polish the windows. Mix a little dry starch with water to the consistency of cream. Wash the windows with it, then let it dry on. When its dry, rub it off with a damp newspaper. Gives a high polish—no streaks."

The morning after her first window polishing, Carrie's arms ached so much she found it difficult to put up her hair. She dragged herself through the "morning mop," grateful when lunch arrived. That afternoon cleaning the hotel lobby was added to her list of duties.

"Silas Kellum will help you hang the rugs out back, Miss Brown. They're to be beaten clean on Saturday. Each

Wednesday evening, after the guests have retired, you'll sprinkle table salt over the rug and then sweep it clean. Do this to both sides.

"Be certain you wipe down the stairs, polish the woodwork, and dust all the lamps daily. No feather dusters, Miss Brown." Norah looked at her suspiciously. "Do they use feather dusters in St. Louis?"

Carrie nodded meekly. "Yes, I think we did use feather dusters."

Norah shook her head. "Well, Miss Brown, the object of dusting here at Hathaway House is to *remove* the dust from the room—not to simply move it to another location. Use these." Norah handed Carrie a neatly hemmed cotton cloth. "Begin in one corner of the foyer and dust thoroughly as you go. Don't overlook the stairs and the woodwork. The turnings on the railing are particularly challenging. Commence with the highest articles. *Wipe* with the cloth, Miss Brown, don't simply brush off dust. Remember: The object is to cause all the dust to lodge *on the cloth*. You will need to shake the dust out frequently. Do this out the *back* door, please. We do not want our guests having dust shaken in their faces, now do we? Once you have finished the dusting, wash out the cloth and hang it to dry on the lines in back."

Norah Murphy walked away, clucking to herself doubtfully about Miss Brown's lack of training and Mrs. Hathaway's "eternal patience with the present generation."

In spite of the hard work, Carrie Brown enjoyed her summer. She frequently sent Silas Kellum into gales of laughter with her flawless imitation of Norah Murphy, but she eventually learned to clean so well that even Norah Murphy was pleased.

"Look at that, won't you. An original hayseed, for sure."

"Straight off the farm. Look at that dress!"

Cruel comments and jabs continued until Carrie, who stood in line waiting to register for her university classes, couldn't resist glancing at the object of her classmates' attention. The girl was in the line next to Carrie. She was dressed in outmoded clothes. A few pieces of hay clung to the back of her hair. More hay was stuck on the back of her dress. She was thin and blond, and she stood with her eyes on the ground and a worn carpetbag clutched in her hands. Carrie knew the girl had heard the cruel remarks, but although she seemed to be fighting back tears, she kept her place in line.

When another cruel jab was whispered, Carrie stepped out of her own place in line and crossed to where the new-comer stood. "You've got something—" Carrie smiled and reached back to pull the strands of hay out of the girl's hair.

"Oh!" the girl's hand shot up to her hair. She blinked and said softly, "Thank you."

Carrie put a hand on her shoulder. "Here, just turn a minute." Quickly, she brushed the hay off the girl's clothes.

"Thank you," the girl repeated before thrusting out one hand and introducing herself. "Myrtle Greer."

"Carrie Brown," Carrie answered. "Are you from Lincoln?"

Myrtle smiled shyly. "Oh, no, not me. I'm from forty miles west."

The line moved forward and Carrie stayed next to Myrtle, who said, "You'll lose your place in line. You were way ahead of me."

"Oh, I don't mind," Carrie answered. "I'm from far away, too. St. Louis. I've been working here this summer, saving money for tuition."

Myrtle nodded. "I've been saving for years to get to

come here. I finally got the money for the first term, though." She reached up to touch her hair and grinned. "Didn't have train fare, though. I hitched a ride with a neighbor to get here. He was bringing a load of hay to market. Thought I had it all brushed off."

"You rode forty miles in a wagon just to get here?"

Myrtle nodded.

"You've been saving for years?"

Myrtle nodded. The line moved again. Myrtle asked, "You said you'd been working here this summer. You don't know where I could get a job, do you?"

"We can ask Mrs. Hathaway. She owns the big hotel here in town. That's where I work. If she isn't hiring right now, she'll know who is. You can walk back with me after we get registered."

Carrie introduced Myrtle to Augusta Hathaway. "John Cadman needs kitchen help, Miss Greer," Augusta offered. Surveying Myrtle's worn clothing, Augusta added, "And if he's already hired someone, you come back to me. We'll find something." Turning to Carrie, Augusta said, "Now you two scoot into the kitchen and ask Cora for two big pieces of lemon cake. And some hot cocoa."

Over lemon cake and cocoa, Myrtle and Carrie discovered that although they had nearly identical university schedules, they had very little else in common. Carrie had been an only child. Myrtle had grown up on a farm, the eldest in a family of twelve children. While Carrie grew up in a house where she had few responsibilities, Myrtle had only recently escaped the duties of running a house. Two sisters had grown old enough to help, and Myrtle's parents had finally given in to their eldest's incessant begging to attend the university. Myrtle had studied by lamplight long into the night to get her primary certificate. She had sewed for neighbors and even helped one season with harvesting, just to add to the small cash savings she had designated for her first term. When she had finally reached what her parent's thought to be an impossible goal, they had reluctantly watched her pack her two dresses and hop onto the neighbor's hay wagon for the ride to Lincoln.

Myrtle told about herself in a matter-of-fact way, but when she finished, she said firmly, "And I don't plan to go back until I have my certificate and a teaching position. I'm not staying on the farm to be worked to death like my moth . . ." Myrtle looked up sheepishly and changed the subject.

The first few weeks of school, Myrtle and Carrie were too busy working or studying to have much chance to build their friendship. Carrie complained to Augusta one evening. "I can't believe they expect us to virtually *memorize* every word they say."

"Is that so impossible, Dear?" Augusta wanted to know.

"Not for Roscoe Pound, it isn't. Have you met him?"

Augusta nodded. "I know the family. Amazing. Mrs. Pound educates the children herself. She has always been suspicious of the abilities of the local schools. I was their guest one Sunday afternoon. The family read the Scriptures aloud. In Greek."

Carrie nodded. "Just what I heard. Young Mr. Pound is only twelve, Mrs. Hathaway—yet he'll graduate in '87 with a degree in biology. He speaks fluent German, and Miss Smith's Latin class holds no horrors for *him!*" Carrie added, "We applaud for our professors, you know. I don't mind when it's Professor Collier. But applauding for a cross old hen like Miss Smith is almost more than I can take."

"Carrie!" Augusta scolded. "Miss Smith is an excellent teacher. I remember when she was hired. She's created a fine Latin department."

"Maybe so, Mrs. Hathaway," Carrie said doubtfully. "But every time I try to recite I see her frowning at me and I just can't remember anything. Silas Kellum has been tutoring me, but I think I'm a lost cause. And there is no sure salvation except in being thoroughly prepared for Miss Smith every day."

Carrie's "sure salvation" failed her one morning in Miss Smith's class. Carrie had prepared carefully, but Myrtle Greer was late to class, and when she finally arrived she looked unusually thin and quite ill. Carrie whispered her concern to Myrtle, and Miss Smith called out loudly, "In Nebraska, Miss Brown, young ladies do not talk while their professors are lecturing." Carrie blushed profusely and sank back in her chair. Her embarrassment eased significantly when Miss Smith approached another student, sniffed loudly and said, "Young man, you need a bath. You may return to this class when such has been accomplished." The student slunk out the door.

At the end of class, Carrie caught up with Myrtle. "Myrtle, what's wrong?" Myrtle looked blankly at Carrie. "Wrong? What do you mean? Nothing's wrong."

"You don't look well, Myrtle."

"I'm all right, Carrie. I've been working hard and studying 'til all hours, that's all."

"You look thin. Haven't you been eating *anywhere* but that Merchant's Cafe? I told you how bad it was."

Myrtle looked back at Carrie. "You told me, Carrie, but it's all I can afford and it'll have to do."

"But, Myrtle—"

Myrtle waved at Carrie and hurried away. When she didn't attend class the rest of the day, Carrie expressed concern to Augusta, who took immediate action. "I'll send Dr. Gilbert over to that boarding house right away, Carrie. Myrtle will have to talk to Dr. Gilbert."

Myrtle *did* talk to Dr. Gilbert. Dr. Gilbert talked to Augusta. And Augusta talked to Miss Smith, the heartless Latin teacher. To Carrie's amazement, Myrtle returned to classes a week later, with color in her cheeks and a new home. "Would you believe it, Carrie? Miss Smith came to see me at the boarding house and simply begged me to come keep house for her. Said her own housekeeper had left on short notice and she simply couldn't keep up with teaching and all. Gave me a nice room and said I'm to keep up with my studies *first* and—"

Carrie stared in amazement. "Myrtle, are you talking about Miss Smith. *The* Miss Smith. Latin?"

Myrtle nodded. "Yes. Carrie, she's really very nice. She lives all alone in a neat little house just a few blocks from campus. Compared to helping raise eleven brothers and sisters and cooking for farm crews, cooking and cleaning for Miss Smith will be so easy. I can't believe it, Carrie. I just can't believe it."

Carrie couldn't believe it, either. For several days after Myrtle's announcement, Carrie watched Miss Smith carefully. It took great effort on her part, but Carrie finally saw evidence of Miss Smith's closely guarded secret. At times she demanded things that were nearly impossible. But then a student would accomplish that nearly impossible thing, and when the student smiled triumphantly, a light glimmered in Miss Smith's eyes, and a smile graced her lips, and Carrie discovered the secret. Underneath her stern exterior, Miss Elvira Smith harbored true love for her students.

CHAPTER 9

Be strong and of a good courage, fear not, nor be afraid of them: for the LORD thy God, he it is that doth go with thee: he will not fail thee, nor forsake thee.

Deuteronomy 31:6

The summer that Carrie Brown was working as a maid at the Hathaway House in Lincoln, Soaring Eagle was working on a dairy farm in Wisconsin. Owned by friends of the Riggs family who were also Friends of the Indian, the farm had often been host to various students from the Santee Normal Training School. Soaring Eagle was heartily welcomed and kept physically fit by every form of manual labor available on the farm. He spent the summer mowing hay and driving dairy cattle to and from the fields, using spare moments to study language—English, Latin, and New Testament Greek. He missed the open spaces of his homeland, but outdoor work offered some compensation so that when the fall came and he boarded the train for Boston, he felt ready to meet the demands of academic life in a big city.

No unpleasant encounters were endured on the long train ride from Chicago to Boston. Soaring Eagle kept his books nearby and used the time to study. He scarcely looked at fellow passengers until a man settled opposite him after a stopover in Pennsylvania.

"Jeremiah King, I believe?"

Surprised, Soaring Eagle looked up at the stranger who stretched out his hand. "R. J. Painter. St. Louis *Post Dispatch*." Painter took a vacant seat opposite Soaring Eagle and continued, "I believe I heard you speak in St. Louis this past spring."

"Entirely possible," Soaring Eagle replied. "I was there with my sister for a few meetings."

"Would you be willing to give me an interview, sir? I've been trying to follow the news from the west closely—just a personal interest. I'd like to do a piece on the Santee Normal Training School—something on this issue of the value of teaching Indians in the vernacular—or requiring only English instruction. I'd be interested in your views."

Soaring Eagle took a deep breath and reluctantly lay aside the anonymity he had enjoyed for one entire summer in northern Wisconsin. Once again he took up the mantle of being the token Sioux Indian for the Santee Normal Training School and the Friends of the Indian. It was a heavy mantle that he would soon weary of wearing.

In Boston, Soaring Eagle climbed down from the train into a mass of humanity that nearly overwhelmed him. Men and women shoved and pushed against one another, hurrying in different directions. Baggage handlers shouted and cursed, newsboys and vendors hawked sandwiches and newspapers, and each one seemed to pause momentarily in his activity to stare at Soaring Eagle. He tried to remain calm. Still, as he was carried along with the crowd, his heart began to pound. He could feel the tightness of his collar and reached up to loosen it, finally managing to make his way out of the throng. Waiting with his back against a column, he tried in vain to remember the names Alfred Riggs had given him. What if they didn't come? If he couldn't remember the names, he would be alone in Boston.

"Jeremiah King, welcome to Boston!" A short, balding man with a ridiculously tall hat was pushing through the crowd. He pumped Soaring Eagle's hand enthusiastically, turning to pull a tall, thin woman toward him. "Robert Davis. My wife, Nancy." Without further ceremony, Davis apologized. "I'm sorry we weren't here the moment you disembarked, Mr. King. There's so much traffic in the street today, we just couldn't—"

"You don't need to be gallant, Mr. Davis," a familiar voice sounded. "You were late because I couldn't get my bonnet tied on to suit me."

Soaring Eagle looked over the top of Nancy Davis's head and saw Julia Woodward. The bonnet in question was enormous, lined with just the right shade of emerald to accent her dark eyes. Her gown of emerald silk was trimmed with black lace. Soaring Eagle didn't really listen to what she said. Julia was shaking his hand, taking his arm, welcoming him to Boston, guiding him through the crowd. Robert and Nancy Davis looked meaningfully at one another and followed.

Julia explained, "George waited with the carriage so we could make a quick getaway. We'll send someone for your trunks. You'll be staying with Mr. and Mrs. Davis. It's just a short walk across the river to Harvard from their home."

Once the four were seated in the Woodward's carriage, Julia was quiet, content to watch Soaring Eagle. He was on edge. His eyes continually moved from the street to the shops, to the tops of the buildings they were passing. At the Davises' home, things were no better. Everyone was seated in the formal dining room around a huge table. A meal of elegantly prepared foods with elaborate table service was spread before them. Soaring Eagle sat on the edge of his chair, answering questions with meaningless monosyllables, trying to remember the lessons he had been given in etiquette.

As a hostess, Nancy Davis had always tried to anticipate her guests' needs. She was well aware that Soaring Eagle was uncomfortable. Finally, she manufactured a reason to check on someone in the kitchen. As she passed her husband's place at the table, she stooped and whispered something. Robert Davis immediately stopped pressing Soaring Eagle to participate in the conversation. Turning instead to George and Julia Woodward, he skillfully guided the conversation away from Soaring Eagle and towards planning the details of one of his speaking engagements at a meeting of the Society of Friends.

No longer the center of attention, Soaring Eagle took a few more bites of food and then excused himself from the table. He rose and went to a window, peering down at the traffic on the street below, contemplating his surprising reaction to the Boston train station. Nothing anyone had told him had prepared him for Boston. He had gone through St. Louis and Chicago, but apparently at "off" times. He was somewhat perplexed at the feeling of absolute panic he had experienced when confronted with such a crowd of strangers. He tried to sort through the feelings, but could not reason his way to an explanation. *How do they live like this . . . so cut off from the land?* He smiled ruefully, took a deep breath and prayed, *Help me, God, to endure it. The months of school . . . the tall buildings that block out the sky . . . I want to do the right thing, Father. But, please, take me back to the prairie before too many moons.*

Soaring Eagle turned around and put his back to the window. An oil painting over the fireplace in the parlor across the hall drew his attention, and as the Davises and the Woodwards continued in deep conversation, he walked across the narrow entryway and into the parlor to inspect the painting.

"Shhhhhhhhhhhh," a child's voice whispered. "Be quiet, Sam."

"But he's in *here*, Sterling. He wasn't supposed to come in *here*. Mama said we could watch as long as we were quiet. So *shhhhhhhhh*."

The conversation was taking place in stage whispers emanating from behind a pair of heavy draperies at a window to the right of the portrait. Soaring Eagle approached the painting on the right side and studied the scene of an Indian village arranged at the foot of a mountain. He took in every detail and decided the artist must have actually visited the spot—it was a perfect recreation of *He Sapa*, the favorite wintering spot of his childhood.

The voices had ceased, but there was still a tiny bit of movement behind the drapes. Soaring Eagle sat down in the chair near the drapes and waited. Waited. Waited.

"Ah-choo!"

In mock terror, Soaring Eagle yelped softly. In a low voice he directed an order to the curtains. "Come out from behind those curtains!" Two boys emerged, white-faced, wide-eyed, terrified.

Soaring Eagle sat back down and folded his arms, staring at the two boys. He demanded, "Who are you and why do you spy on me?"

"Samuel Davis, sir," said one boy. He was stoutly built, with a round face and ruddy cheeks almost as red as his flaming hair.

"St-St-Sterling D-D-avis, sir," said the other boy. He was only slightly smaller than his brother, with the same round face and the same flaming red hair.

The boys stood side by side, facing Soaring Eagle. They trembled, and Sterling nudged his older brother. It was a signal, and the two boys turned to flee. But Soaring Eagle was too quick for them. In a flash he had jumped up and grabbed the two boys around their waists. Too terrified to struggle, they hung like limp sacks, staring sideways at one another, awaiting their fate.

"Mama's gonna be real mad at us, Mister. She said we had to be good. Not bother anyone. She's gonna be real mad."

"Shut up, Sterling. She's gonna be more than mad. We're probably gonna get *killed*."

Soaring Eagle set the boys down on the floor. They scooted away from him, their backs against a ridge of cushions that hung over an ornate couch, not daring to move as he asked with mock seriousness, "Is this a custom among the whites of Boston? Do they often kill their children because of disobedience?"

Sterling, the smaller one, spoke up. "Naw. She won't *really* kill us. But she'll be *really mad*. We bothered a guest. That's against the rules in this house."

Soaring Eagle let a very slight smile soften his features as he said, "What if the truth is that you didn't *bother* a guest. What if the truth is you *rescued* a guest?" He looked from Samuel to Sterling, then sat down with them on the floor, crossing his legs and leaning forward to rest his elbows on his knees "I was just wishing that I was at home, around my campfire, telling stories to the boys in the village." He pointed up to the painting. "When we moved to our winter campground, my village looked just like that." Samuel and Sterling relaxed a little, even crossing their legs and sitting like their guest. Soaring Eagle continued. "Now, I know you are not Lakota, but I think that perhaps boys everywhere like to hear stories. Would you let me tell you a story?"

Samuel and Sterling Davis nodded their heads.

"So," Soaring Eagle said. "I will tell you of a time I disobeyed my mother—and of what happened to *me* because *I* was spying on a stranger who came to visit."

Half an hour later, Samuel and Sterling Davis had not

moved from their places on the carpet with Soaring Eagle. They had, however, howled with laughter to the extent that Nancy Davis had stormed across the hall and to the doorway of the parlor, ready to pounce on them both. When she saw the scene before the fireplace, she motioned to her guests, who followed her to the door.

Sitting on the floor with Samuel and Sterling, Soaring Eagle was totally relaxed. His face was animated and his eyes sparkled as he described scenery and characters in the story from his youth. He motioned and gestured, lacing his anecdotes with Lakota legend and Bible truths.

Sterling and Samuel Davis suddenly looked past Soaring Eagle and at the look on their faces, he stopped talking and turned around. Sterling and Samuel stood up abruptly. Soaring Eagle stood behind them, putting a hand on each boy's shoulder. "Your sons have made me feel welcome to Boston, Mrs. Davis."

Nancy Davis answered with mock sternness, "Then they've just gotten out of a tight spot, I'd say. Well, Samuel, Sterling, you've heard us talk about Mr. Jeremiah King, who's to be staying with us this next year while he attends classes at Harvard. Now you have met him, and it is time for you both to retire."

Robert Davis interjected. "Boys, Mr. King has been very kind to entertain you when he has just arrived and is no doubt weary of meeting new people. You two get right upstairs, and remember the rules."

"Yes, sir" the boys echoed, making their way for the stairs. "Never go in his room, never interrupt when he talks, and don't ask rude questions."

Following the boys up the stairs, Nancy Davis swatted them and whispered intensely, "Your father didn't request a *recitation*, boys . . ."

Robert Davis turned to Soaring Eagle. "I hope they didn't make too much of a nuisance of themselves."

Soaring Eagle shook his head. "No. Never. Samuel and Sterling will never be a nuisance. They let me talk of home, and I like to tell stories."

Robert nodded as he guided George and Julia Woodward to be seated in the parlor. As he took a seat, he laughed. "Well, one thing is for certain, Mr. King. You have just made Samuel and Sterling Davis the two most popular boys in school tomorrow. When they tell their friends that they spent tonight sitting on the floor hearing *real* Indian stories from a *real* Indian!" Robert chuckled. "Why, the notoriety might even make them *like* school—for an hour or so."

CHAPTER 10

Restore unto me the joy of thy salvation; and uphold me with thy free spirit.

Psalm 51:12

His full schedule of studies and speaking engagements prevented Soaring Eagle from spending much time with Samuel and Sterling Davis. He did, however, manage one visit to their school. When he arrived in native costume, Samuel and Sterling Davis were thrilled. They each took a hand of their friend and led him to the front of their class, delivering an elaborate introduction and nearly bursting with pride.

Soaring Eagle told the class of his life before his ride to Santee and his conversion to Christianity. He made the speech a brief one, because he wanted to give the young students plenty of time to ask questions. He was not disappointed. The young scholars delighted him with their openness and their honest curiosity.

At the close of the session, Samuel and Sterling once again led their friend out of the classroom and to a waiting carriage. "When we get home, would you show us that game you talked about?" Samuel wanted to know. "The one where you throw the ball?"

As soon as they arrived home, the trio made its way to a little patch of green behind the Davis home. "The game is called *Tapa wankayeyapi*," Soaring Eagle explained. "On the prairie, we would cut out a piece of sod to be a symbol for the center of the universe. But your parents would not want us cutting the grass. So," Soaring Eagle took Sterling by the shoulders. "You stand here, in the center." Sterling complied, and Soaring Eagle went on to explain, "We would have four others, one at the north, one at the south, one at the east, one at the west. But we have only Samuel and me. So, Samuel," Soaring Eagle motioned to the boy to stand opposite him, on either side of Sterling, "when Sterling throws the ball, we will see who can catch it." Sterling threw the ball skyward and Soaring Eagle pretended to scramble for it, making certain that Samuel caught the ball.

"Now," Soaring Eagle explained, "among my people, this is a sacred game. It was taught by the White Buffalo Calf Woman, who told us that the ball represents God moving away from the people—and then coming back to join them." Soaring Eagle looked at the boys soberly. "As Christians we know that God never moves away from us. But sometimes, we move away from Him. That is something we must never do."

He tossed the ball up and caught it. "When the ball returns to the earth, it means that we have reunited with God, we have received knowledge. Everyone who is in the game must do his very best. Then he shows how much he wants to be near God and to have knowledge."

Soaring Eagle was more interested in the spiritual application of the game than the game itself, but he quickly realized that Sterling and Samuel were waiting impatiently for him to stop philosophizing and play. He stopped talking abruptly and tossed the ball to Sterling, beginning a rollicking game that ended with the three lying on their backs, looking up at the sky, panting for breath.

Late in the evening, long after the boys had retired and Soaring Eagle sat in his room poring over a philosophy text for a recitation the next day, a knock sounded at the door.

Robert Davis was standing in the hall. "Jeremiah," he offered, "I just wanted to thank you for spending so much time with the boys."

"It is I who should be thanking you, Robert, for allowing me into your home. You have two fine sons."

Robert nodded. "Yes, God has blessed us. But sometimes they can be demanding and rambunctious. I know they've interrupted your studies often, and I appreciate your patience."

Soaring Eagle indicated the stack of books on his table. He laid his book down thoughtfully and said, "It takes no patience for me to talk with Sterling and Samuel, Robert. If everyone I have met were as kind and as honest as those two boys, I believe the 'Indian question' would have been answered long ago. Then all these philosophy books could be set aside. I could go home, and perhaps have sons of my own."

Robert Davis cleared his throat. "Well, just the same, I wanted you to know that Nancy and I appreciate your putting up with them." He closed the door behind him and Soaring Eagle returned to his studies.

The following evening found Soaring Eagle on his way to yet another meeting of potential "Friends of the Indian." Julia and George Woodward and Robert and Nancy Davis sat near the front of the auditorium. As soon as Soaring Eagle was introduced and stepped through a small side door onto the platform, the auditorium grew quiet, with participants inspecting the native dress of what they had been told was a cultured Sioux Indian, and wondering what he would have to say.

"Honored guests," he began, his voice projecting throughout the hall. "Thank you for coming to hear me. I come to you to talk of the Santee Normal Training School in Nebraska. This school was established by the American Board of Commissioners for Foreign Missions for the purpose of raising up preachers, teachers, interpreters, businessmen, and model mothers for the Dakota Nation. You will have some idea of whether or not they are successful as you hear me this evening.

"This year, between the Dakota Home for Girls and the Young Men's Boarding Hall, the school at Santee will reach into the lives of over seventy young people with the gospel of Jesus Christ and the instruction they will need to make a new life for themselves and their families."

Soaring Eagle stepped to the edge of the podium so that his costume could be readily investigated by his audience. "When I came to Santee, I was dressed as you see me now. I was mounted on a pony, and I carried a few belongings with me, including deep anger in my heart against what was happening to my way of life. At Santee, I learned that there were people like yourselves who looked upon the Indian with compassion."

Soaring Eagle went on to share his own conversion to Christ before outlining the advantages of the Santee school in training children. "Santee is situated at the very gateway to the wild lands now inhabited by the Sioux. The staff at Santee understand the Indian character. There, the work of Indian education can be carried on more cheaply, more thoroughly, and with better results than by institutions farther removed from the Indian country.

"Only you can decide if Santee has been successful. You must hear what I have to say and judge for yourselves. I have told you of my former life, and you see me now. Santee is successful because at Santee the Indians hear the gospel of Christ. No influence is so effective in civilizing Indians as the gospel of Christ.

"The government wants to take over the education of the Indian. The government wants to say that the Indian cannot be taught in his own language. But a good knowledge of the English language does not change a bad

Indian into a good white man. An Indian needs a new heart just as much as a white man. And nothing can give that but the Holy Spirit, through the gospel of Jesus Christ. The only effective way to civilize Indians is to lead them to Jesus.

"There are churches that have been founded as a result of the work at Santee. They cover only a little corner in the eastern part of the state you call Nebraska. But their light is spreading. The Christian Sioux are trying to do their duty. Hope for taking the gospel to the entire Sioux nation was never so bright. Hearts are open to the truth. Now is the time to work.

"A great many tribes, under Red Cloud, Spotted Tail, and Sitting Bull, have not as yet had any religious teachers. Until they have native religious teachers they are not likely to receive the gospel in such a way as to be benefited by it. We are anxious to engage your interest to help us carry the gospel to the wild part of the Sioux Nation."

Soaring Eagle concluded with a ringing plea. "Men, brothers, sisters, fellow Christians—for the sake of our risen Lord who bids you, come! Come to the Indian, not with bullets, but with Bibles. Replace the 'theory of extermination' with the gospel of Christ."

Soaring Eagle left the podium, listening to the singing of hymns while he changed into his "Boston clothes" and returned for the discussion that was to follow his speech.

He was joined on the podium by George Woodward and Robert Davis. As soon as the session concluded, Soaring Eagle left to escort Nancy Davis and Julia Woodward home.

"It was a fine lecture this evening, Jeremiah," offered Nancy Davis. When Soaring Eagle didn't seem to hear her, Julia Woodward echoed Nancy. The two women soon gave up trying to engage their friend in conversation.

Hope was never so bright. . . . Hearts are turning. . . . Now is the time for work. Soaring Eagle felt his own words rising up to condemn him. Suddenly, his restlessness of the past few weeks, and his unhappiness came to mind. *Are you leading me to do something else with my life, God?*

The answer came as Soaring Eagle imagined God challenging him. *Who is better to take the gospel to the wild Sioux than another wild Sioux? Tonight you begged for help. You spoke of native Christians taking the gospel to the people of Sitting Bull. I called you out of the village of Sitting Bull. I called you to Santee where you learned of Me. Now, I ask you, who is better suited to take the gospel into Sitting Bull's village than Soaring Eagle?*

When the carriage arrived at the Davises, Soaring Eagle automatically bid Julia Woodward good night. Ignoring her proffered hand, he followed Nancy Davis into the house and mounted the stairs to his room where he spent a sleepless night, wrestling against his responsibility to represent Santee Normal Training School to the Easterners.

If any man lacks wisdom, let him ask of God. The verse called him to prayer and to study. Soaring Eagle began to do both. Over the next few weeks his desire to return home to the west grew, and the burden for his own people grew. It became a weight so heavy he felt its presence physically.

Dear Father, he finally prayed. *I want to return home, but I am a new child. How can I be certain that this is what You want? I ask, dear Father, that You show me this is from You. I tell no one of it but You. Please, Father, You tell Alfred Riggs what I am to do. It seems good to me, Father, to trust his advice.*

Soaring Eagle continued to speak, continued to study. His longing for the prairie grew until he daily had to fight the battle against melancholy. Those around him noticed, and grew concerned.

"I don't know, Julia," George Woodward said one day. "Perhaps we've expected too much. The studies are certainly demanding. Perhaps he just needs a break. Whatever it is, I'm concerned."

"He's lonely, George," Julia said.

"Lonely? He has more friends than he knows what to do with. They practically fight over who's going to entertain him next."

"He's not lonely for *entertainment*, George. He's lonely for *companionship*."

George looked suspiciously at his sister. "I suppose you mean female companionship?"

Julia Woodward didn't answer her brother.

"Be careful, Julia. Be very careful."

CHAPTER 11

He that refraineth his lips is wise.
Proverbs 10:19

*E*verett *Higgenbottom, indeed!* Standing in the foyer of the Hathaway House Hotel, Carrie Brown stared in amazement at the note in her hand. Looking up at Silas Kellum she stammered, "But, but, this can't be. It just can't."

Silas Kellum turned the guest register towards Carrie and pointed to Everett's name. "There it is, Miss Brown. He checked in about an hour ago and left this note for you. Said he'd be in the dining room." Grinning, Silas teased, "What's up, Kid? Long lost lover from St. Louis? He must have some crush, following you all the way to Nebraska."

"Silas Kellum," Carrie retorted. "*Just* because you are tutoring me in Latin, and *just* because you have saved me from certain death at the hands of Miss Smith, does *not*, I repeat, does *not* give you the right to be impertinent." Carrie slapped the card back onto the desk and headed for the dining room where the card had promised she would find Everett Higgenbottom.

He was there, having folded his long legs under the smallest table available in a corner by the windows that faced P Street. At sight of Carrie, he jumped up, hitting the edge of the table so hard it overturned his water glass.

"Here, Everett, let me help you." Carrie grabbed a towel

from a nearby bussing tray and mopped up the spill. Everett blushed and gushed his joy at seeing Carrie until she finally ordered him to sit down. She poured them each a glass of water and asked bluntly, "What on earth are you doing in Lincoln, Nebraska, Everett? What about Washington University?"

Everett shook his head. "Hated it. I'm transferring. Mr. Kellum said Mrs. Hathaway doesn't board college students. But she boards *you*, Carrie. Maybe you could get her to give me a room, too?"

He's coming here. To this university. He wants a room here. At the Hathaway House. Carrie leaned her forehead on her hand and contemplated a year of Everett Higgenbottom. Then she shook her head. "No, Everett, I can't. Mrs. Hathaway doesn't board college students for a good reason. She's too expensive. She boards me because I work here and because she's a family friend." Carrie looked at Everett convincingly. "But I know you wouldn't expect her to take less than her full rate for a room. I couldn't ask her to do that."

"She doesn't need to lower the rate, Carrie. I can pay my way. Mother fought it like—well, like you know she would—but when she finally realized I was headed here and she couldn't do anything about it, she finally gave in." Everett grinned. "I think she was almost glad about it when she realized how much less expensive the tuition is."

"But, Everett, the university doesn't even *have* a music department."

"I guess I know that, Carrie," Everett said with a winning smile. He grew suddenly serious. "I never wanted to be a pianist, Carrie. That was all Mother's idea."

"But why come here, Everett—when there are so many other institutions—older and probably better? Why not go back east?"

"There are good schools back east, all right," Everett

agreed. "But there's one thing none of those other schools have."

"What's that, Everett?"

"A student named Miss Carrie Brown."

"Oh, Everett." Carrie moaned.

"I know, I know. Carrie. You're going to grow up and go teach the Indians and marry Jeremiah King."

Carrie looked about the dining room. "Sshhhhh. Everett. You have no business talking like that where someone might hear."

Everett grinned. 'Yeah, all right, Carrie. All right. Look." His watery gray eyes were serious. "You've got this dream. I know it. I know I'm only your friend, Carrie. But I am your friend. That's something. Who knows?" Everett shrugged his bony shoulders. "Maybe you'll get to like me. Maybe something will happen, something that makes you change plans." Everett looked hopeful.

"Everett Higgenbottom. You followed me through high school like a—well," Carrie hesitated before continuing. "Everett. This is for your own good. You followed me through high school like a puppy. I don't want to be hounded all over Lincoln."

Everett Higgenbottom beamed at Carrie. His devotion to her was so complete that be knew no shame. "I won't hound you, Carrie. But you'll need an escort from time to time. That Indian fellow isn't exactly living in Lincoln, is he?"

"Soaring Eagle is living in Boston while he attends Harvard. I don't expect to see him for a long time."

"Good."

Carrie agreed. "Yes, Everett, it *is* good. I have some serious learning to do. Some serious growing up to do. Some serious teaching to do before Soaring Eagle will ever take me seriously. But he *will* take me seriously, Everett. Someday he will."

Everett snatched Carrie's hand and pressed it. "Listen, Carrie. I worry about you. What happens if this thing doesn't work out for you? What then?"

Carrie pulled her hand away. "It *will* work, Everett. I'm not considering failure."

"Carrie, I'm going to say something that's going to make you mad. I'll only say it this once, but somebody needs to make you face facts. You're building a future hope on a past memory. You haven't been back to Santee since you were a little girl. How do you know you'll like it? How do you know you even want to live there? Things change, Carrie. People change. You remember the way things were when you were a little girl. You played and had a great time. But your mother, God rest her, basically worked herself to death. Have you thought about that, Carrie. Have you thought about how much *work* it is to be a missionary? Or," Everett bit his lip. "Or do you think about that at all? Do you just have this romantic picture of the tiny redhead with the handsome Indian husband who lectures and travels? It's a pretty romantic picture, Carrie. I admit it. But what if it doesn't work out?

"Sometimes, Carrie, things just don't work out. What will you do if they don't work out? What if you hate things at a mission school? You're not exactly used to 'doing without,' you know. What if you don't even *like* teaching? What if this Soaring Eagle guy meets someone else in Boston?" Everett waved a hand at her. "All right, Miss Brown, all right. There's no need to explode. I can see you're really angry with me now. But *think* about it, Carrie. Think about it and remember." He smiled brightly. "If things don't work out, you can always call on me to, well, to do whatever. I care that much, Carrie. I really do."

"Everett, why did you really come all the way to Nebraska?"

"I really did come to be near you, Carrie." Everett

laughed suddenly. "Although, in the meantime, I plan to get a degree in something. That should be useful for the future, don't you think?"

"A degree in what, Everett?"

"Don't know yet. Guess it doesn't really matter much. I'm not much to look at, Carrie, but I'm pretty smart. I figure I'll try a few things until I land on something I like. One thing I know for sure. It *won't* be *music*."

Everett Higgenbottom checked into the Hathaway House Hotel, a fact which made him instantly well-known on campus as the one student rich enough to afford a real hotel and tuition without taking a job. He proved useful to Carrie Brown as an escort to every evening lecture she wished to attend. He also proved popular with his classmates. He was genuinely kind, lending a hand wherever he could and participating in enough pranks to almost get expelled. (It was Everett Higgenbottom who masterminded the entire affair over Thanksgiving when the cadets moved a cannon into Haymarket Square and set it off to protest the university policy that required military drills of every male student.)

Everett was on the staff of the student newspaper, the *Hesperian*. He played in the orchestra and was a favorite on the debate team. Everett Higgenbottom was a success in every undertaking except one. He could not get Carrie Brown to fall in love with him.

Although Carrie had been furious with Everett when he attacked her plans for her future, she finally admitted to herself that he had made some valid points. She hadn't been back to Santee since her childhood, and she didn't really know if she liked teaching. She set about planning to overcome those obstacles.

An opportunity to visit Santee in the spring presented itself when Jim and LisBeth Callaway came to Lincoln for Thanksgiving. As soon as LisBeth had settled on the couch in Augusta's parlor, Augusta launched into plans for the spring clothing collection for Santee. "We'll have several barrels of clothing, LisBeth. You'll have lots of sorting to do up at the mission," Augusta said.

LisBeth cleared her throat and said, "Well, Aunt Augusta, I don't think I'll be able to go this spring."

Augusta looked at her sharply. "Not go? You always go to Santee in the spring, LisBeth."

LisBeth blushed and said softly. "Yes, I know. But this spring I'll likely be, indisposed."

"LisBeth Callaway! You mean?" LisBeth nodded and Augusta engulfed her in a hug. "Praise be. I'm going to be a great-aunt!"

LisBeth beamed. "We've waited so many years, Aunt Augusta. I'd almost given up hope. But we just came from Dr. Gilbert's, and he assures me it's true." LisBeth looked thoughtful. "I'll miss going to Santee, of course, but—"

"*I'll* go to Santee to help, LisBeth." Carrie Brown had been in her room. Now, she stood in the doorway. She was apologetic. "I didn't mean to be eavesdropping, but Mrs. Hathaway's voice does carry and I couldn't help hearing."

Carrie stepped into Augusta's parlor to explain further. "I haven't been back to Santee since I was a child, Mrs. Hathaway. I'd love to go back and see things. See if things are the way I remember. Get reacquainted." She turned to LisBeth. "I want to go back there to teach, LisBeth. But friends have said I don't have a realistic view of what it's like. Maybe they're right. Going back with Mr. Callaway would take care of that. And I could be of help. I know I could."

LisBeth nodded. "Yes, Carrie. You could. And I agree, if

you think you want to work with the Indians, the sooner you visit the better."

"Just tell Jim to give me a few days notice, if he can, so I can get packed up and so that Mrs. Hathaway can plan for my absence." Carrie hesitated. "It is all right, isn't it Mrs. Hathaway?"

Augusta gave hearty consent. Carrie congratulated Lis-Beth and returned to her room, her heart pounding with excitement.

The winter quarter of school flew by as Carrie anticipated her return to Santee. She could think of little else. Everett wearied of her preoccupation and found himself avoiding her in order to avoid talking about the trip.

When the morning came that Carrie was to depart with Jim Callaway, Everett bade Carrie good-bye with a forlorn look.

Carrie was cheerful. "You're headed home for a wonderful summer, Everett. I'm only taking your advice. I'll be finding out what I think of Santee, and what working among the Indians is really like. I'll be dispelling all those romantic notions you've teased me about."

As the wagon trundled north, Carrie Brown settled back to read, unaware that the object of her "romantic notions" was at that moment boarding a train in Boston to escape romance.

CHAPTER 12

The LORD seeth not as man seeth;
for man looketh on the outward
appearance, but the LORD looketh
on the heart.

1 Samuel 16:7

December, 1883

Friends,

I have witnessed Thanksgiving among the white people at the home of Mr. George Woodward. They served much more food than we at Santee would see in many feasts. While the people in Boston have been kind to me, as I sat at the table with them I wished that I could see my friends at Santee again and wade through the snow to your Thanksgiving.

I have received a letter from Pastor Thundercloud. He has asked for prayers for the Dakota churches, but I think that these prayers need also to be made for the churches here in Boston where I speak. I copy it for you. Pray that they may be more consecrated to the work of saving souls. Pray that a deep and genuine revival of religion may be experienced in the Boston churches. Pray that Christ may be so formed in all the Christians, and the Holy Ghost come upon them with such power from on High, that they will have it in their hearts to go everywhere and tell the story of the cross to all the wild Dakotas on the plains and, thus, bring them to Christ.

The Friends here say that when I lecture, that sends help to you, because then more is donated to the barrels. I wish you would write to me and tell me—are you receiving more barrels from Boston?

I am your friend,
J. Soaring Eagle King

Throughout the fall and winter months, Soaring Eagle prayed and studied and lectured. When Dr. Riggs's letters continued to encourage him in his course of study, he tried to be content. Still, his longing to return to Nebraska grew. He spent many hours in the parlor of the Davis home, staring at the portrait of Indian tepees long after the Davis family had retired.

One evening late in December, Soaring Eagle was at dinner with George and Julia Woodward when George presented him with a document. "Read it over, old man. I think you'll be pleased. The Committee has finally accomplished something concrete."

With a flourish, George handed Soaring Eagle a carefully worded document titled *Platform of Principles on Which to Represent Our Indian Policy.* Soaring Eagle read the document. When he had finished, he set it down on the edge of the table and took a long drink of water.

"No comment, Jeremiah?" George was obviously disappointed.

Soaring Eagle shook his head.

Julia chimed in. "Jeremiah, we thought you'd be pleased."

"Pleased." Soaring Eagle was barely able to contain his anger. "I have been lecturing and speaking for months. Everyone has said that my speaking will result in help for the Indian. Do more barrels of clothing reach Santee? No. Is more food sent? No. Have any of these young men in Boston who sit and listen to me with smirks on their faces been converted to Christ? Has even one person come forward to say he will take the gospel to the plains? No. You hand me this document and expect me to be pleased. *More words on paper* is not progress. We Lakota know all about words on paper. They make the whites feel better about themselves. They accomplish nothing for the Indian."

Soaring Eagle's voice shook with rage as he snatched up

the document and began to read aloud. "*1. Indians are men, not much differing from others, with the same wants and governed by like impulses as other men.*" Sarcasm dripped from his voice as Soaring Eagle commented. "I am so pleased to know that it has only taken you five months to learn this from me."

He read on. "*2. In their native state, Indians are lawless, and often need to be restrained by force. 3. It is more economical to feed Indians than to fight them, as well as more humane and Christian.* I would have hoped," Soaring Eagle remarked, "that the Christian motive would have preempted the economic one. Forgive me for expecting so much from the churches of Boston."

Soaring Eagle tossed the document at George. "The final paragraph should have been the content of the entire document, George. Read it. Aloud. I want to hear you read it."

George Woodward complied. "*To successfully accomplish the objects herein enumerated—to civilize, to enlighten, to educate and bring up to the highest style of manhood—we regard the teachings of the gospel of our Lord and Savior Jesus Christ are indispensable, and therefore we urge that the prosecution of the missionary work among the Indians be imperative.*"

Soaring Eagle nodded. Leaning towards George he said, "I think, George, that your committee needs to be spending their time on the missionary *work*—not the *wording* of documents." Standing up abruptly, Soaring Eagle bowed to Julia and to George. "Excuse me, but I find that I can no longer continue this conversation and still honor my Lord God. Good evening." Throwing his napkin down angrily, Soaring Eagle strode out of the dining room.

It was nearly midnight before Soaring Eagle walked up the Davises' street and let himself in. The house was quiet, and as he started up the stairs, he stopped abruptly. Instead, he went into the parlor and sat, once again, before the portrait of the Indian village camped in the Black Hills. Leaning his head back against his chair, Soaring Eagle half closed his eyes, remembering. He could almost hear the drums beating, smell meat roasting over campfires, feel the softness of a buffalo robe wrapped about his shoulders.

He sat for a long time, remembering, longing for—Soaring Eagle sat up abruptly, looking more carefully at the painting. All at once he realized that his longing had crystallized into specific desires that he was able to name and pray for. The reading of the document that George Woodward had so proudly displayed had played a part in focusing his disappointment—the dissatisfaction that he had been feeling for weeks.

Lord God, Soaring Eagle prayed, *I want to return to my people. I want to tell them the gospel. I have been praying of this for weeks now, and still there is no answer.*

Dr. Riggs encourages me to stay here. I have asked You to show me Your will through him, and if that is to stay here, then I will try to be patient. But, God, I am so lonely.

Another specific need crystallized. *There are other things, Father. You have made me a man, my Father. Here among the whites they accept me as 'the educated Indian.' But to them, I am an object of interest. Not a man. Lord God, I want a wife.*

As he stared at the portrait of the village, Soaring Eagle thought of Winona. She had loved him, but his heart had been so full of rage and hatred that he had had no room for love. He began to think of other women he had met. *Lord God, I want someone to wrap in my buffalo robe. Someone who will enter into my life, become part of my soul, understand the things I cannot say. You have made me, Lord God. Have you not made a woman for me?*

In his memory, Soaring Eagle saw children skittering around the village, chasing dogs, shouting joyously. *Lord God, I want children. Before I knew You, I thought I would never want to bring a child into this world. Now, I want children. I want a son to take hunting, as my father did me. I want a daughter to tell stories to, to make toys for.* Soaring Eagle remembered the corncob doll that still lay in his parfleche back in Nebraska. He remembered a little girl wrapping it carefully and cradling it as tenderly as if it were an expensive china doll, the kind he had seen in store windows here in Boston.

Soaring Eagle sat before the painting in the Davises' parlor praying as tears of loneliness and despair spilled down his cheeks. *Why, God, why? Why do You let me have these desires when there is no one to fulfill them? Dr. Riggs says that I should stay here. Must I stay here, heavenly Father, where my spirit is dying?*

Finally, Soaring Eagle rose and went up to his room, falling into an exhausted sleep.

The New Year passed, and Soaring Eagle took advantage of poor weather to study more. He was booked for fewer lectures, but this created more opportunities to visit informally in the homes of various influential people. He plodded wearily through these evenings, doing his best to be patient with the often foolish questions he was asked, returning to his room after each encounter with a melancholy that would not lift.

Samuel and Sterling Davis went on holiday with their mother. The boys became seriously ill during their absence, and while letters assured their father and Soaring Eagle that they would be fine, their convalescence was expected to prevent their returning home until spring brought warmer, healthier air to Boston.

The one light in Soaring Eagle's life was his friendship with Julia and George Woodward. Julia, who took his arm and led him through uncertain situations in such a way that he appeared to be the leader. Julia, so beautiful that he was sometimes speechless when they first met after a few days apart. Julia, who gazed at him with something in her dark eyes that stirred him so deeply it frightened him.

Following their initial amazement at Soaring Eagle's reaction to the Platform, George and Julia Woodward had gone to their friend with an apology. "We want to understand, Jeremiah. We've missed something. Can't you help us poor ignorant Bostonians understand?" George said it with such pathetic sincerity that Soaring Eagle broke into laughter.

He smiled at his two friends and nodded. "I will try, my friends. But first, you must do something very difficult."

"Anything," Julia Woodward assured him.

"Try to see past what you call 'the Indian problem' to the men and the women and children who are hurt by this problem. God can help you do it." Soaring Eagle added sugar to his coffee and stirred it as he spoke. "You mean to do well, and I understand that, but you cannot solve 'the Indian problem.' That is what I have been trying to say for all these months."

He took a sip of coffee and continued. "Let the government wrestle with the laws and the proposals. While they are struggling to write documents and policies, you and your friends can be sending real help to real people. Collect more clothing. Send more money. Challenge your young people to consider becoming missionaries. Spend your time doing this—not writing documents and proposals."

Soaring Eagle leaned forward in his chair and looked from George to Julia intently. "If you could once see Santee, see the children learning, you would understand why I am impatient. Lives can be changed for the better, for God's glory, now. You do not have to wait for some document to give you permission to help. You can make a difference in all that, George and Julia." Soaring Eagle paused and sighed. "But these papers you write, they make no positive difference for my people. I said something in anger before, but I repeat it to you now. We Sioux have seen many well-written papers that promise great things. We have learned to ignore them."

Pausing again, Soaring Eagle collected his thoughts before continuing. "It is really not so difficult, my friends. Begin with me. Think for a moment. What am I to you? After all these months, am I still 'the Indian?' Or am I a man you know who happens to be Indian?" He sighed. "You must see beyond the problems and the issues, my friends. See the man. See the people I represent. When you see us as people, not as part of a problem, then you will begin to give real help."

Soaring Eagle lowered his voice and looked from George to Julia. His eyes rested on Julia as he concluded. Julia had listened carefully. Now, however, her eyes drifted away from his face, to his broad shoulders, his hands. She lowered her eyes and her cheeks took on a rosy glow.

George Woodward cleared his throat and pulled a piece of paper from his coat. "At the risk of having you storm off again, Soaring Eagle, I'd like to read you something. You mentioned that if we could see Santee for ourselves it would accomplish a great deal. Just last evening the committee wrote another resolution. I think you'll like this one." George handed the paper to Soaring Eagle, who read:

Arrangements have been completed for a visiting committee to go into Dakota and visit the mission stations. The Committee of Reverend Dr. A.C. Johnson, Robert Davis, Esq., and George Woodward will be accompanied by Mrs. Davis and Miss Julia Woodward. We expect to leave Boston by April 18. We are to be joined by Rev. John Thundercloud of Santee, who has consented to accompany the committee to the other stations. From Santee we shall go to Fort Sully, to Sisseton, and last of all to Berthold.

Julia Woodward spoke first. "You see, Jeremiah, some of us *have* been listening to what you say. But it took a while to convince the Committee to fund the trip." Julia smiled with excitement. "Once they've seen the work firsthand, there should be more response. More understanding."

George Woodward nodded. "That's right, old man. The committee has even engaged a journalist to go along. He'll join us in St. Louis. Remember R. J. Painter? Well, you made an impression, Jeremiah. He heard from the committee in St. Louis about our plans and offered to pay his own way if he could accompany us on the trip."

Dinner was concluded while Soaring Eagle tried to prepare George and Julia Woodward of Boston for their first view of the plains. As they listened to Soaring Eagle that evening, George and Julia Woodward realized that something was happening between themselves and their Lakota friend. He described the west, and they saw it for the first time, not as a foreboding wasteland, but rather as the homeland of a people. Soaring Eagle laughed and gestured, describing villages and people, transforming people who the Woodwards had thought of as helpless savages in need of a champion into men and women in need of many things, but nothing so much as the need for a Savior.

"You see, my friends, our bodies may be poorly fed and clothed, but if we can make progress in living truer lives, in being better men and women, that will make us happier and bring us nearer to God. This can only be accomplished through the gospel. Someday the things around us all will drop away. We will all stand face-to-face with the Real and the Eternal. We can afford to lose some of the poor pleasures of this life. When we pass over the unreturning way, we will need to hear 'well done' usher us into the gates of the other life."

Julia Woodward saw the west through Soaring Eagle's eyes, and she was surprised to feel herself blinking back tears as she contemplated the spiritual plight of an entire nation of people without the gospel of Christ.

George Woodward left the dinner table a few minutes early to reclaim coats for the frigid carriage ride home. While they waited, Soaring Eagle and Julia Woodward basked in one another's presence, saying nothing, but smiling with a new understanding. Soaring Eagle looked at Julia and wondered if this woman might, after all, be God's answer to his prayer for a wife. For her part, Julia Woodward realized that for the first time she was no longer seeking the attentions of Jeremiah King, the Indian. Julia rose from the dinner table and smiled warmly as she took the arm of Jeremiah King, a very attractive man, who just happened to be a Lakota Indian. *There is a difference,* Julia thought as they walked across the dining room together. She looked up at Jeremiah King with new eyes. Soaring Eagle looked down at Julia and smiled, covering her hand with his own.

CHAPTER 13

Flee also youthful lusts: but follow righteousness, faith, charity, peace, with them that call on the Lord out of a pure heart.

2 Timothy 2:22

George, I'm sure I don't know what you're talking about." Julia Woodward smoothed her damask napkin and took a dainty bite of breakfast.

George's voice sounded weary. "Julia, you have previously had very little interest in our nominal membership in the Society of Friends. Your position as recording secretary is purely ornamental—or at least it was, until the arrival of Jeremiah King." George took a gulp of hot coffee before continuing. "Suddenly you go to every meeting, every lecture. You don't flirt nearly as much. You're reading different books. *You're* different, Julia. Why, I believe you actually *listened* to Reverend Johnson's sermon last Sunday morning!"

Julia folded her napkin thoughtfully before responding. "And wouldn't you say it's about time, George? A few weeks ago I overheard Nancy Davis talking about me. She said, 'That woman is all ruffle and no garment.'" George sputtered with amusement at the analogy, but Julia went on. "I was furious. But she was right. I've always taken on whatever cause suited my fancy, just like adding a ruffle to a dress. Then I've sought out the best escort for the occasion and made myself the perfect adornment for him. Whatever was required, I said it, with no thought as to the real issue, the garment you might say. I don't really know why, but somehow that sort of thing doesn't seem right anymore."

Julia took a deep breath and chuckled softly. "I'm amazed to find that I am really interested in the issues we discuss at the Friends meetings. It's rather heady stuff for a girl like me to suddenly be seriously interested in national issues like the Indian problem." Julia looked at George soberly. "But you know, I've learned something about myself, George. I have a fairly good mind, and when I use it in the right way, people do take me seriously. They listen to what I have to say. Sometimes they even change their attitudes. And then sometimes they even *act* on those changed attitudes." Julia added thoughtfully, "I like that, George."

Julia returned to her flip self. "Of course, I still don't like it quite as much as I like being escorted by a handsome man, but I do like it." She laughed softly. "I guess you could say I'm 'less ruffle' and 'more garment' than in the past."

"But you haven't had to give up the handsome escort." George frowned. "Julia, you might be interested to know that there has been some concern about you and Jeremiah. The Committee has discussed it."

Julia bristled, "How dare they?"

"They dare, my dear sister, because they know of your past, uh, interests. They dare because it is their duty to protect Jeremiah and to make certain that he finishes his studies and accomplishes the purpose for which God sent him here. They dare because they are very well aware of the mutual attraction between you two. And they want to ensure that you both maintain a level of conduct that is above reproach."

Julia waved her hand in the air. "Oh, all right, George, there's no need to bring that up. Surely you must know I would never—"

"Absolutely." George sighed. "Let us make certain that our conduct remains impeccable. Social customs in Boston are completely new territory for Jeremiah. He's had no opportunity to learn about these relationships and he's no fool. He knows he should be very careful. And, I might add, so should you, for his sake."

"But what if he cares for me, truly cares for me, and just doesn't know how to, well, how we go about things here." Suddenly, Julia urged her brother. "Isn't there some way you can let him know that I wouldn't be averse to his attentions?"

George sighed. "You really do think men are idiots, don't you, Julia? If Jeremiah King thinks you'd be 'averse to his attentions,' as you so blandly put it, then he's blind. Once again, Julia, I have to ask you, what is it you want?"

Julia lifted her fine chin. "Anything, George. Anything *he* wants."

"Blast it, Julia!" George was nearly angry with her. "Do you really intend to pursue this attraction when you know he fully intends to return to Nebraska? I'm sorry, Julia, dear. But somehow I can't picture you making coffee over a fire in a cabin, or whatever they call those shacks they make from the earth." George began to laugh louder, oblivious to Julia's distress.

"George, stop. Stop laughing." The hurt tone in Julia's voice brought George's laughter to an abrupt halt. Julia concluded their conversation. "All right, George. I get the point. You see no future for me with Jeremiah King, so you won't intervene. Fine."

April, 1884

Dear Friends,
    It has been raining and snowing for weeks, it seems. When I walked in the rain, I caught cold. The Davises have been kind to call a doctor and I am well again now.

That is, my body is strong again. My spirit still feels weak, and I think it is because it longs to see the hills around Santee. I think of my little room at James and Martha Red Wing's. I wonder about the black mare that James said he would keep for me. I would like to be where I could catch that black mare and ride her over the hills to watch the prairie come to life again after this long winter. Here in Boston the buildings hide the sky, and there is little grass.

Do not think that I am too lonely here. Robert and Nancy Davis are very good to me. Their sons were very sick but are better now, and once again they want me to wrestle with them. It makes me think of the boys at Santee and how they made a game of trying to sneak up on me to tackle me from behind. I think I have grown slower now and, perhaps, they would be able to do it. I am forgetting my Indian ways.

George Woodward and his sister Julia will be coming with Robert and Nancy Davis and Reverend Johnson to visit Santee soon. You will like them, I think. They do care very much for the Indian and they have tried to understand what the real needs are. When they come, you must be certain to show them everything. If you lay the needs before them, I know that they can furnish great relief. Share the difficulties and trials fully.

I will be finishing my classes soon. Thank you for arranging for me to go to Wisconsin. I know you do this for my good. I am trying not to disappoint you.

Your friend,
J. Soaring Eagle King

Alfred Riggs read Soaring Eagle's letter with grave concern. He read anguish in every line, and his heart ached for the young man trying so very hard to please his mentor when he was obviously depressed and homesick. The moment he received the letter, he took up pen to write Soaring Eagle and order him back to Santee. The letter was unnecessary. The evening after Soaring Eagle wrote the letter, something happened that sent him back to the Davises to pack his belongings and leave Boston on the first train headed west.

At the sound of Soaring Eagle's footsteps in the hall, Julia Woodward rose from her seat by the fireplace. The maid who had shown him in took Soaring Eagle's hat and retreated. Julia called out a greeting, beckoning, "Please, Jeremiah, come in." Soaring Eagle was seated opposite her before she explained, "I'm sorry that George won't be joining us this evening, Jeremiah. He forgot that he had an engagement elsewhere." She had poured tea for them both before she gave the rest of her news. With just the appropriate tinge of regret in her voice, she said, "The Johnsons had to send regrets, as well—something about Mrs. Johnson being indisposed."

Soaring Eagle rose immediately to go. He didn't try to hide the disappointment in his voice as he said, "George has been very helpful in teaching me some of the rules of your culture. I know that I am never to speak to a woman to whom I have not been introduced, and I know never to be alone with a woman. Are those not true rules in your culture?"

Julia avoided answering the questions directly. "Don't be ridiculous," she said. "Two friends can certainly enjoy a cup of tea by the fire without doing damage to anyone's reputation. We've had this meeting planned for days. I see no reason why you and I can't visit about the Committee's trip—even though George and the Johnsons aren't able to be here. I can certainly relay your suggestions to them."

When Soaring Eagle looked doubtful, Julia added reassuringly, "And we're not alone. The servants are in the house. In fact, Molly will be in soon to collect the tea service. If you're that concerned, I'll go fetch her and ask her to stay in the room." Julia raised one eyebrow and Soaring Eagle realized he was being teased.

"Please stay," she begged. "You've been ill, and we haven't had the pleasure of your company—it seems like it's been weeks. George will be home later, and I know he'll be disappointed if he finds you were here and didn't wait." Julia took up her cup of tea. "I have at least two hours worth of impertinent questions that I've never been able to ask. After our dinner the other evening, I feel, well," she lowered her eyes momentarily and then looked back at Soaring Eagle. "I feel closer to you now."

Soaring Eagle shifted in his chair. A voice inside him was screaming for him to get up and leave, but he ignored it. Instead of obeying the voice, he took up a cup of tea.

"Don't worry," Julia laughed. "They aren't improper questions, just ones that would be considered impertinent by proper Boston society. I want to know more about the life you lead before things changed so drastically. More than what you tell everyone else." Julia settled comfortably in her chair, leaning her head against the high back. Soaring Eagle noticed her elegant, long neck.

"I've gathered from your comments that most of the things being written today about the Indian aren't accurate. I saw how angry you were at the Johnson's last Sunday evening when the subject of the Wild West shows came up. You don't think much of their portrayal of the Indian, do you?"

Soaring Eagle had not been alone in the company of a beautiful woman before. He was trying his best to pay close attention to what Julia was saying but finding it very difficult to do so.

Aware of his inner struggle, Julia offered, "You've had a stressful day of classes. Perhaps a glass of wine would help you relax." As she spoke, she crossed the room to the wine cabinet.

Soaring Eagle shook his head. "No. When I was a boy, my father made me promise never to drink what he called 'that evil stuff from the traders.'"

Julia repented immediately, closing the wine cabinet, crossing back towards the fireplace. Soaring Eagle fought the temptation to linger over how gracefully she moved. Julia draped an arm over the back of her chair and remained standing. Twilight shone through the window behind her, accenting her fine shoulders.

Soaring Eagle gulped some tea and stood up and moved to where his own chair formed a physical barrier between himself and Julia. Gripping the back of the chair he said again, "I should go."

Julia smiled. "Your father made you promise never to drink wine. Did he also make you promise never to be alone with an unattached woman?"

Shaking his head, Soaring Eagle studied the fire.

"Tell me about him. Tell me about your father, Jeremiah."

"He taught me everything I needed to know to live well in our world. He didn't prepare me for the changes that were to come, but he tried to give me his faith in God. I suppose he knew that that was, after all, the best way to prepare his son for the future." He concluded with regret, "He didn't live long enough to see me accept his God."

Julia sat down again by the fire, asking, "If it isn't too painful, I really would like to know what life was like for you before, before everything became such a, such a mess."

Soaring Eagle looked about the room, wondering how to begin to explain life on the plains to a product of Boston society. His eyes returned to Julia Woodward. She met his gaze directly. There was no hint of flirtation in her eyes or her voice, only a genuine interest in his life, his past. Loneliness swept over him, and Soaring Eagle realized that he wanted to share more of himself with Julia Woodward.

He was groping for where to begin his saga, when the answer appeared at his very feet in the form of a bearskin rug spread across the hearth. Seating himself on the rug, Soaring Eagle crossed his legs and settled comfortably by the fire.

"I killed one of these once." He ran one hand along the back of the bear's head. "I think the one I killed might have been a little larger. It took me three arrows."

"Only three?" Julia sounded surprised.

At the hint of admiration in her voice, Soaring Eagle shook his head. "Three arrows are two arrows too many. I should have done it with the first. By the third arrow I was shooting down at the bear from the top of a very tall tree. My heart was racing, and I was convinced there would be an empty space at my campfire that evening. Mine."

Julia perched her feet on a needlepoint footstool and took up some handwork. "Please, Jeremiah. Tell me more. I want to know everything, everything about you."

Something sounded a warning in Soaring Eagle's mind, but he brushed it aside. "You've heard many of the most exciting stories already."

"I don't want those stories, Jeremiah. I want the ones you don't share when you speak to groups." Julia laid her needlework in her lap and scooted to the edge of her chair. "Tell me about a normal day. What was a normal day like in your village? What did you eat? What did you wear? Just the everyday things, Jeremiah." Julia took a deep breath before concluding. "I want to know what makes Jeremiah King who he is. What's in your *soul*, Jeremiah?"

Seated on the bearskin rug in Julia Woodward's parlor, Soaring Eagle began to talk. He described a typical day in his village, a day when buffalo were plentiful and there were no soldiers to worry about. He talked about breaking his father's horses, and worrying his mother when he was gone too long on a hunt. He described his mother with special tenderness. When he spoke of his father it was with such pride that Julia felt his anguish when he related trotting across the prairie to find his mother kneeling by the crushed body that had been pulled from beneath a massive buffalo bull.

At some point during his lengthy recitation, Julia laid down her needlework, slipped out of her chair, and came to sit beside him on the bearskin rug. When he concluded his monologue, she had pulled her knees up under her chin and was staring into the fire. He reached out to trace her hairline with the back of his hand. Suddenly the picture of her dressed as she was tonight, sitting by a fire in his tepee, made him laugh.

Before he could pull away his hand, she had caught it in her own. "Tell me what I've done to make you laugh," Julia said, "so I can make you laugh often, when we're alone." She lifted his hand to her cheek and murmured, "I like the sound of your laughter."

"I was thinking," he answered softly, "of you, dressed as you are tonight, trying to tend the fire in a tepee." He pulled his hand away and leaned back on one arm. "The picture reminds me of how my mother must have looked when Rides the Wind brought her to our village. I was only a baby, but I heard the story many times. His favorite part was always describing her trying to start a fire." Soaring Eagle chuckled. "For a while they called her 'Makes No Fire.' She would work and work." He crouched before the fire, showing Julia the antics just as Rides the Wind had re-created them.

Julia laughed with him. Watching him smile, she suddenly asked, "Did you have someone?"

Soaring Eagle sat back down next to her. "No," he answered quietly. "There's never been anyone." When she turned to look up at him he corrected himself. "Once, long ago, there was a very young woman who cared for me." He paused before continuing. "The last winter her family moved north, into Canada."

"The last winter?"

"The last winter of that way of life."

Julia grasped her forearms tightly, hugging her knees to her chest. "You never saw her again?"

"Never."

"And there was never anyone else?"

"Things changed. Too quickly." Soaring Eagle smiled at her. "There were too many other things to concern myself with. Too much study. Never enough time to learn the rules about men and women in your world." He shrugged his shoulders. "As long as I am only Jeremiah King, the Indian, there is no need."

"Isn't there anyone you know who looks at you in another way?" Julia gripped her knees tighter, aware that she was trembling.

The moment the words escaped her lips, Soaring Eagle saw the image of a blue suit and red hair, the St. Louis train station, and a blown kiss. He answered Julia honestly. "There is one." He began to tell Julia about Carrie Brown, but she didn't let him finish.

"No, Jeremiah. There are two. I don't know about the girl in Nebraska, but I am here. Now."

Soaring Eagle had never kissed a woman before. The scent of her hair, the softness of her silk gown, everything about her was so compelling, the emotion that washed over him the moment they kissed terrified him. Instantly, the thing that had been trying to push its way to the forefront all evening succeeded in making Jeremiah listen. *Get out of here. Get out now or you will make everything you have ever said about God and faith and living a true life into a lie.*

It took more effort for Soaring Eagle to push Julia Woodward out of his arms than he had ever expended in his life.

He almost ran to the door. He heard her call his name, but he didn't look back. *Don't look back. You're not strong enough to look back and not stay. Don't look back. Just go to the door. Go to the door, Soaring Eagle.*

Soaring Eagle followed the voice of his conscience out the door, through the streets of Boston, and back to the Davises. He listened when it said, *You cannot remain in Boston. You're too lonely, and she is too beautiful. Go home to Santee, Soaring Eagle. Sort out your feelings. Ask God for guidance. Talk to Dr. Riggs. Don't let this happen without thinking things through. If it is to be, it will be. In God's time. Not this way. Write a letter to the Davises and to the Woodwards. Explain that you are too homesick. They will understand. They know you've been depressed. They'll be disappointed you left so abruptly, but they will understand.*

Dawn broke the next morning with the first sunshine Boston had seen in weeks. Sunshine broke into the parlor at the home of George and Julia Woodward where Julia still sat, staring at the ashes in her fireplace.

Light streamed into the breakfast room of the Davis home where Sterling and Samuel were eating alone, having just received the news that their favorite houseguest was gone.

Sunshine spilled into the train car where Soaring Eagle sat. But he was too immersed in thought to take notice.

CHAPTER 14

Precious in the sight of the LORD
is the death of his saints.

Psalm 116:15

Dr. Gilbert spoke in the voice he had learned to use when telling the thing he hated most to people he admired. He spoke slowly and distinctly, in his gentlest tone, trying to comfort even as he told Sarah what she was facing.

"Toward the end it could get," the doctor paused, "difficult for her. I'll do what I can. I'll teach you to administer morphine. We must pray that God takes her before she suffers unduly."

Over the doctor's shoulder, Sarah could see the door to Mrs. Braddock's room, the door that had always been open to her, welcoming her in, giving her endless gifts, gifts for a daughter, not a housemaid. Sarah stared at the door for only a moment before she fixed her eyes on Dr. Gilbert's and said calmly, "I'll be fine, Dr. Gilbert. Just see that she's cared for properly. Don't worry about me. I'll do whatever you say. And I'll be fine." Sarah hoped that she sounded more confident than she felt.

"You'll likely need help at the end," he said kindly, patting Sarah on the shoulder.

Sarah shook her head. "I'll get someone to help with the house if necessary, but I'll take care of Mother Braddock myself." She looked up at Dr. Gilbert. "I owe her so much,

Doctor. The least I can do is to be the one—" She bit her lip and stopped. The door loomed in the background.

Dr. Gilbert nodded and pressed her hand. "Abigail Braddock is a fine woman, Miss Biddle. And you are a fine friend. I'm only a short distance away. You send Tom for me whenever you need me. I'll come right away." He reached inside his medical bag and handed Sarah a new bottle. "Continue with the application we've discussed. Soon, you'll need to add this." He withdrew a note from his bag and handed it to Sarah. *Chloral hydrate, gr. 5, Vaseline, oz. 1. to correct fetor and allay pain.* "If you have any questions, don't hesitate to ask." He had only gone down three or four steps before he turned and looked back up at Sarah and added, "You don't have to do this alone, Miss Biddle. We'll do it together."

With a trembling hand, Sarah set the new bottle and the script on a hall table. She stood for a few moments, staring at the closed door that separated her from Abigail Braddock and the unavoidable. Then, with God's help, she put on a bright smile and went through the door to Mother Braddock.

In only a few days, she was forced to send Tom for Dr. Gilbert. "I know it's only been a few days, Dr. Gilbert, but I've tried everything you told me about, tamarind tea and rice milk. She can't tolerate anything on her stomach. I've given several injections of pancreas and cream. She's still losing weight and," Sarah's voice trembled, "she's still in so much pain. I can sense it, even when I'm out of the room."

"When is Mr. Braddock expected?" the doctor wanted to know.

"He wired yesterday. He should be home tomorrow."

Dr. Gilbert's face was somber. "Good." He picked up his bag. When Sarah started up the stairs, he stopped her. "I'm certain you've done everything just right, Miss Biddle. This is to be expected. You are nearly exhausted, and I want you to go into the parlor and lie down while I am with Mrs. Braddock. I'm going to give her an injection to make her sleep all afternoon. While she is sleeping I want you to stay on that sofa or, even better, retire to your own quarters." He looked at Sarah sternly. "You are going to need every ounce of strength in you during the next few days or hours. We must still pray for a miracle, but we must also prepare for the usual course of action. Now, go into the parlor and I will come for you when she is resting."

Leaving Sarah, Dr. Gilbert proceeded up the stairs. Gratefully, Sarah went into the parlor and collapsed into a chair. The blinds had been drawn. Sarah welcomed the dark, giving way to the tears she had held in for weeks.

"David!" Abigail moaned. "When are you coming, David? I've waited so *long*. I'm tired David." Abigail turned her face away from Sarah and began to thrash about.

Sarah lay a cool hand on Abigail's forehead. At the touch, Abigail grew still. "David's coming, Mother Braddock. He sent a telegram only yesterday. Remember? He said he was taking the next train out of Philadelphia. He'll be here soon. I'm sorry you have to wait and suffer so."

Abigail opened her eyes. The fog of pain cleared momentarily and she smiled weakly. With effort she whispered, "Yes, Dear. I remember. David is coming." She closed her eyes again and muttered, "I'll wait for David before—" She flinched again and gripped Sarah's hand. "I'll wait for David, then I'm going."

Sarah raised Abigail's head gently, coaxing her to sip some tea. It contained a mild sedative, but combined with an injection it took effect quickly, and Abigail sank into a deep sleep. Even though she slept, she moaned and tossed her head. Sarah sat by her bedside, replacing cool compresses on the beloved head and trying to fluff pillows to cushion the thin joints. When it was time to change Abigail's dressing, Sarah's hands shook and she prayed her way through it, prayed she would forget what she saw and be able to continue her labor of love.

When it was done, Sarah sat motionless in a chair, her clothing drenched with her own sweat, her face pale. She watched Abigail struggling to live until David arrived, and wondered at the spirit that could survive so long when the body was so near death.

Halfway through the night it became apparent to Sarah that Abigail was going to lose her battle to live to see David one last time. Tom ran for Dr. Gilbert, and he came momentarily, his shirttails not quite tucked into his waist, his dark hair rumpled. Abigail's moaning had increased until she let out a shriek that sent a chill down Sarah's spine. Dr. Gilbert pulled out a blue-tinted bottle. Turning to Sarah he said, "I didn't want to have to do this, Sarah, but we musn't let her suffer any longer. This will take the pain but it will also keep her unconscious. She may not know when David comes."

From the bed, a remarkably lucid voice said, "No. I won't have it. I must be awake when David comes."

Sarah and Dr. Gilbert turned to look at the frail body that was Abigail Braddock. Sarah looked beyond the shrunken, ashen face and into sparkling eyes that were bright and smiling.

At the look of amazement on Sarah's face, Abigail said, "I'm about to die, Sarah, dear. I know that. But I really do want to be awake for David. When do you think he will come?"

"I'm sure he'll be here by morning, Mother Braddock," Sarah lied.

"Then I shall wait until morning. This thing in my body and I have done battle for a long time, and it is about to win. But I will win one more battle." Without turning her head, Abigail said softly, "Dr. Gilbert, I'd like it if you'd stay in case I can't bear it. But, please, I feel better now. Don't do anything unless, unless—"

Dr. Gilbert interrupted his patient. "I'll stay as long as you like, Mrs. Braddock. And yes, I'll wait until David comes before administering more sedatives."

Abigail sighed, and seemed to relax. "Sarah," she called, and her hand patted the bed beside her. "Come here, Dear, where I can see you."

Sarah obeyed, and Abigail began to talk. "I have been so pleased with you, Sarah. You've been such a dear daughter. Dare I say that? There's only Dr. Gilbert here, and he won't tell a soul. Sarah, I'm so happy that David will have you when I am gone, to care for him. He's very fond of you, Sarah. As am I." Abigail changed subjects abruptly. "And Tom. See that Tom finishes school. Where is Tom?"

Sarah fetched her brother, who crept into the room with the reluctance of any child who fears the changes illness brings to beloved elders. But when Tom stood by the bed and looked into the blue eyes, he saw Mrs. Braddock, and the illness and the odd smells in the room melted away.

Mrs. Braddock smiled lovingly. "Tom, dear," she said, reaching feebly for his hand. "I've great plans for you. Now you study hard, and make me proud. I shall be watching you, young man. I expect great things. I'm leaving you enough money to finish school and go on to the university. Someday, when you're a great lawyer, you remember me, Tom. Do something good with your success and share it with others. Remember, Tom, when God blesses us, He expects us to pass that blessing on to others."

Tom mumbled 'Yes, ma'am," before impulsively leaning down to kiss the hollow cheek.

"There's a good boy," Abigail murmured. "Now run along. Youth doesn't need to watch an old woman die."

When Tom had gone, Abigail sighed again and began to

talk to Sarah. "I resent it highly, Dear, that I'll not be around to be a proper doting grandmother. You tell Augusta Hathaway that I expect her to dote enough for two of us."

"Yes, Mother Braddock. I will." Sarah forced herself to answer in a calm voice, denying the reality of the moment so that she could get through it calmly.

"And don't let David brood. I've had a good life. I'm looking forward to seeing William. Remind him of that. All my life I've looked forward to seeing William again."

"Yes, Mother Braddock."

"There are some in the family who aren't too kind, Sarah. They may be a bit rude to you. You just remember that Abigail Braddock loved you, Dear. And you're just as worthy of the Braddock name as anyone. Remember that."

"Yes, Mother Braddock."

Abigail drew in a sharp breath and added between clenched teeth. "Now, I think I'll have to take another rest, Dear. Is it morning yet?"

Sarah looked through the window at the black sky and lied again. "Yes, Mother Braddock. I think, I think dawn will be here soon."

"Dawn and David." Abigail sighed, sinking away from consciousness.

Sarah held her hand tightly and sank onto the floor, resting her head on the edge of the mattress until Dr. Gilbert came in and insisted she rest.

"I'll call you, Sarah, the moment anything happens."

Sarah shook her head. "No, Dr. Gilbert. I'm not leaving." Sarah dragged a rocking chair to the side of the bed and took Abigail's thin hand in her own strong one. "I'm not leaving until David comes, or—"

Night wore on and Abigail's enemy raised its wicked head and began to pound at her body again. Pain seared through her and the sound of it escaped from her pale lips.

At last, Dr. Gilbert was forced to administer morphine. Abigail sank into unconsciousness where her mind no longer knew the agonies of the body.

When dawn really arrived, someone pounded at the front door. Sarah dragged herself from her rocker wearily and started down the hallway. At the top of the stairs, she stopped and looked down at Tom, who was closing the door, a telegram in his hand.

"It's from Iowa, Sarah," He huffed as he hurried up the stairs. Sarah opened the telegram and read it and sank down onto the stairs. In disbelief she read it again and again. Her head sank onto her knees and she began to cry. Then, from behind her, came the sound of Abigail's voice screeching her son's name and calling for Sarah.

Sarah ran back into the room. Kneeling by the bed Sarah lied to Abigail. "Mother Braddock, Mother Braddock, it's David. He's coming. Please wait, Mother Braddock, David will be here any minute."

But Mother Braddock couldn't wait for David. Her body had fought against the pain as long as it could. Mother Braddock was being called across the pain and into eternity She opened her eyes and a smile lit her face. "David!" she called out in wonder. And she died.

Sarah fell into the rocker at the bedside, trembling, clutching the telegram. Dr. Gilbert sat very still beside his patient for a few moments before looking at Sarah. Tears streaming down her cheeks, Sarah rocked back and forth in the rocker while she patted Abigail's cold hand.

"Mother Braddock, Mother Braddock, please wait. David—" She stopped talking abruptly. The lie was no longer needed. And it was a lie. For David wasn't coming. The telegram clutched in Sarah's hand said that Mr. David Braddock had been killed in a train accident in Iowa the day before. Sarah rocked, patting Abigail's hand with her own left hand, while her right hand clutched the telegram.

Dr. Gilbert took the telegram from Sarah and read it. "Oh, my dear. My poor, poor, dear." He reached for his medical bag and produced smelling salts.

Sarah looked at him numbly. Tom was at the door and when he saw Sarah's face he came to her and held her. Sarah leaned on her little brother's shoulder and wept.

"It's David, Tom. David is, gone. Killed. Train derailed. In Iowa."

Tom said hopefully, "Maybe they mistook him for someone else, Sarah."

Sarah shook her head wearily. "No, Tom. I can feel it. He's gone."

Then she remembered and her face brightened. "Dr. Gilbert," she said hopefully, "do you think Mother Braddock saw David? Do you think he came for her after all? Is that why she called out his name?"

Now Dr. Miles Gilbert was a man of science. And as such, he was not given to nonsensical presuppositions about the afterlife. But Dr. Miles Gilbert was also a man of God, and as such he was given to kindness and a humble belief that in matters concerning the afterlife there were many things that only God knew. Thus, Dr. Gilbert put a caring hand on Sarah Biddle's trembling shoulder and said warmly, "I think that must have been it, Sarah. The good Lord let David come for his mother. They're together. God rest their souls."

Sarah pondered the thought, and it comforted her. She felt aged. Grief was beginning to grip her heart. Still, at the center of the grief was the still small voice that she had come to know so well since being welcomed into Augusta Hathaway's adopted family. It was the voice of hope. And while grief lay fresh over the lives of Sarah and Tom Biddle, hope covered it all.

CHAPTER 15

Let none of you suffer . . . as a
busybody in other men's matters.

1 Peter 4:15

God smiled on the farmers in Nebraska in the
spring of 1884, sending abundant rain that
would result in near-record harvests. But for Carrie Brown,
the fine, steady drizzle that made the farmers rejoice was
an unwelcome obstacle preventing her from exploring her
old haunts at Santee. During the first two days of her visit
it rained almost constantly, turning the school grounds
into an impassable mess. Mud sucked wagon wheels and
horses' hooves down into themselves, making travel a
nightmare. School children scraped their shoes along the
edges of every porch, forming tiny walls of mud that dried
and had to be knocked off with a shovel.

Carrie had to postpone her plans to explore, instead
joining Matron Charity Bond in a war against the mud.
The mud tried to break through the doorway of the Birds'
Nest, caking so thickly on shoes it was impossible to scrape
off. Charity demanded that the children remove their
shoes at the door. Mud clung to the girls' skirts, covering
every hem with several inches of filth. Charity met the
girls at the door with the admonition, "Pick up your skirts,
girls, and hurry up the stairs. Don't sling mud. Slip out of
that skirt and, here, give it to me. I'll just wash the hem.
Now change, and don't go out again." Charity stopped,

embarrassed, and wished for the indoor plumbing her mother in far-off Lincoln had just boasted of in a letter. "Oh, well, I guess you may have to. But stay on the path and hold your skirts out of the mud!" Turning to Carrie, she lamented, "If only we had enough money to get them more changes of clothing!"

Charity had the boys haul in a washtub and set it up permanently in the kitchen. A different team of girls met nightly after supper to heat water and attack the mud that left stains in their already threadbare clothing. Charity warned the girls not to scrub too hard. "You brought those donation barrels just in time, Carrie. These poor rags won't withstand too many more washings."

The school children grew restless, looking up from their work and out across the prairie towards home where soon they would be helping their parents tend meager crops in poor soil.

Her third day at Santee, Carrie awoke, excited that this was to be her day off. Moaning with dismay, she slammed her pillow over her head, trying to shut out the incessant drumming of more rain. When another half hour of sleep failed to change the weather, Carrie crept downstairs in the pre-dawn light. Lighting a lamp, she hastily read through a passage of Scripture, chuckling in spite of herself when her eyes lighted on the phrase *a continual dripping of rain.*

Reluctantly giving up on her plans to explore her old haunts at the mission, Carrie attacked the mending pile. She managed to sew on an entire row of buttons before becoming restless and heading for the kitchen.

Lighting a fire in the stove she began to heat water for coffee, setting the back door ajar and inhaling the promise of spring. The air was warm, and the rain had changed from an intense pounding to a slight drizzle. Still, the damage had been done. The mud holes had once again filled with water and the wagon tracks were a slippery mess.

Carrie sighed, thinking of the unhappy result she would have to deal with if she attempted to drag her ten yards of calico skirt and three petticoats across the prairie. *I'll be soaked to my waist before I get halfway to the creek.*

She finished half a cup of coffee, disconsolate at the prospect of another day of rain, another day of mud, another day of laundry. Jim Callaway would be heading back to Lincoln in only a few days. He was anxious to get home, concerned about leaving LisBeth alone with a baby on the way. Resting her hand on her chin, Carrie traced the pattern of a knothole in the table. Then her eyes fell on the answer to her dilemma.

They hung right inside the door, five pairs of them all clean and mended and ready for the boys to pick up. Carrie snatched down a pair of pants and a shirt and retreated to her room. She emerged cautiously, happy that no sound emanated from Charity's closed door. She didn't want to have to explain her sudden preference for men's dress.

Gone to explore. Thanks for the day off. She scratched a note and hastily finished her coffee, weighting the small piece of paper with the rinsed-out cup. Picking her way across the compound, Carrie ducked into the storehouse and dug through a pile of rejected clothes, coming up at last with a mouse-chewed bowler hat and a reasonably good pair of high-top boots that had been too small for any of the boys at the school. The boys had howled with laughter when the hat was pulled out of the donation barrel, snatching it from one another's heads, strutting around the wagon, and then tossing it aside. Carrie had flushed with anger at the thoughtless gift and promised herself to personally sort the boys' clothing before future donation barrels were delivered to the mission. *I wonder what banker back in Philadelphia is patting himself on the back for his generosity to the poor savages,* she had thought bitterly, kicking at the hat.

This morning, though, Carrie was grateful for the

outdated hat and undersized boots. She knew she looked ridiculous, but she had no plans to be seen, and the hat would keep the rain off the back of her neck and hide her piled-up hair from sight.

Peeking out the door of the supply shed, Carrie saw that smoke was coming from the chimneys of the Riggs' cabin and the Birds' Nest. Jamming her hands into her pockets she hurried from behind the shed and up the rise to the north, almost running in her haste to get away for the morning's adventure.

In spite of the drizzle, the morning proved to be a satisfying diversion from the endless work at the Birds' Nest. Carrie sat by the creek and remembered Sunday afternoons with her mother, her little girls' feet sinking into the white sand that covered the creek-bottom. She relived growing up at Santee, the natural beauty of this spot by the creek receding in the wonder of the presence of a Lakota Sioux who had, miraculously, allowed her to be his friend.

Chewing on the crust of bread she had stuck in one pocket early that morning, Carrie walked the familiar territory towards another favorite spot. Long before she got there, she could see that the gigantic cottonwood tree had been struck by lightning. One massive bough from high up in the tree had split, tearing at the tree trunk as it fell. Carrie shivered slightly, looking up at the blackened bark, picturing the ancient tree burning in the storm. Walking up to the tree, she leaned against it with outstretched arms, realizing at once that it was not quite so massive as it had seemed when she was a child. Still, her outstretched arms reached barely halfway around the trunk.

Turning around to lean against the tree, Carrie looked up to see a small patch of blue sky peering through the clouds. She settled down on the earth and took off the wet hat, shaking down her hair and leaning her head on her knees and speaking aloud.

"I wish you could talk, tree. You could tell me what it was like. Before. Before we came and messed everything up. Before there was killing and hate." She let drowsiness overtake her, and her mind wandered, imagining a circle of tepees in the shadow of the great tree. Imagining.

Thunder interrupted her imaginings and she barely had time to stuff her hair into the hat before rain began to fall in torrents. The small speck of blue sky was no longer visible, and a strong wind was carrying great, dark thunderheads across the sky.

Carrie moaned. *I should run for it, back to the mission.* But the true destination of her wanderings had not yet been reached, and she was determined to go there, whether she received a soaking or not.

I can build a fire and dry out. She struck out through the storm, grateful for the hat brim that made it possible to see, grateful that she didn't have far to run before the barn and lean-to loomed in sight.

The Red Wings had left a week ago to visit the small group of believers on the Yankton Reservation to the west. Carrie knew they would be gone, and this afforded her the opportunity to be near Soaring Eagle in a new way.

I shouldn't be doing this, she thought as she opened the door to the Red Wings' cabin. It was gloomy inside. Carrie shivered and started a small fire in the fireplace. A warm glow flooded the room and she sat down to pull off her boots and jacket. Arranging them by the fire to dry, she turned to face the door to the room she had wanted most to see. James Red Wing and Soaring Eagle had built a room onto their cabin for Soaring Eagle.

Her hands were shaking as Carrie opened the door to the room. It faced south, and a break in the storm provided enough light to view its contents. A low cot along one wall was covered with the yellowed quilt that LisBeth had returned to Soaring Eagle shortly after they had finally met face-to-face. Carrie knew the story of the quilt, and she ran her hand across its surface, trying to imagine the road it had traveled, from Jesse King's emigrant wagon to an Indian village, and a Lakota woman who would become Jesse's friend. Then to Jesse's adopted son, Soaring Eagle, who had given it to his half sister as a peace offering when they finally found each other as adults.

Carrie sat on the cot and looked around the room. Beside the cot was a crude desk fashioned from some crates and a plank. On it were a few books. Carrie read the titles, smiling softly as she pictured Soaring Eagle sitting at the desk, studying. She turned her attention to the framed diplomas that hung above the desk. One declared that Jeremiah Soaring Eagle King had performed all requirements in pursuit of full graduating honors from the Santee Normal Training School, Santee, Nebraska. A similar document marked the conclusion of his education at Beloit College in Wisconsin.

What she had come to find was not in view. Other than the cot and the desk, the room was spartan. Perhaps under the cot? She knelt down beside it and her hands touched the stiff rawhide of an old parfleche at exactly the moment a gruff voice rumbled from the doorway, "Just what do you think you are doing?"

With a start Carrie turned around and looked up stammering guiltily, "I—I—"

"Red Bird?" the voice softened and Carrie recognized him. Sitting on the floor she leaned over and put her hands to her flaming cheeks.

Before she could try to formulate an excuse for her snooping, Soaring Eagle held out his hand to her. "Your things are nearly dry. But *you*, I see, are not. Come."

Carrie obediently took his hand and stood up, following him into the cabin's main room. Sitting on the floor again, she pulled on her stockings and boots. When Soaring

Eagle was silent, Carrie stammered, "I, I came to Santee with Jim Callaway for the clothing distribution. Today was supposed to be my day to explore. But the rain—"

Soaring Eagle indicated her costume. "It appears that you have found a way to explore in spite of the rain."

Carrie looked down at herself and blushed. "I knew I couldn't drag petticoats and skirts over a wet prairie. I must look ridiculous." She looked up and smiled triumphantly, "But it worked. I got to do what I wanted."

Soaring Eagle's eyes looked toward his room. "I don't think you got quite everything, Red Bird." After a momentary pause he looked at Carrie. "I still have her." He got up and went into his room. Kneeling, he pulled his old parfleche from under his cot. He opened it and drew out something wrapped in skins. Leaving the parfleche on the floor, Soaring Eagle came back into the room, seated himself by the fire and handed the small bundle to Carrie.

"I told you I would keep her until you came back."

While he talked, Carrie untied the leather strips. Nervously, she unwrapped the little bundle and there, lying in her lap, exactly as she had remembered her, was Ida Mae, the corncob doll.

"It seems so long ago that Mother and I had to leave here." Carrie touched the little scarf she had tied over the doll's "head." "This calico was from a dress Mama made me." She lowered her voice. "I still have it back in St. Louis." Carrie cleared her throat and looked up at Soaring Eagle. "I'm sorry I snooped in your things, Soaring Eagle." Her blue eyes were shining with sincerity.

Suddenly, he laughed aloud. It began deep in his throat as a chuckle, but he couldn't contain it and it boomed out, filling the cabin and amazing Carrie who had seldom seen him smile, and never heard him laugh.

"I thought you were some good-for-nothing. If you hadn't been so small, I would have tackled you without asking questions." At the thought he laughed again, and Carrie joined him, although not quite as heartily.

He stood up. "I'll make you coffee. You need to dry off. Then you need to go. If you like, we can ride back together. I'll tell them I rescued you from the storm. I need to talk with Dr. Riggs." He went outside to fetch water from the well. When he came back in, he hung the pail on a hook and swung it over the fire.

Carrie asked, "I didn't think you were coming back to Santee this spring, Soaring Eagle. LisBeth said you would be going directly to Beloit as soon as your classes were finished." Carrie stopped abruptly. "I'm sorry, Soaring Eagle. It's really none of my business."

Soaring Eagle moved across the room to a crate where Martha Red Wing kept her supplies. He returned with the two mugs and finished preparing the coffee. He had handed Carrie a steaming mug and settled opposite her before he answered. "I had only one class to finish. It requires a paper. I can do that here." He took a gulp of coffee and looked down at Carrie as he said, "I needed to come home to Santee. It had been too long since I saw the sky without buildings in the way." He smiled sadly. "I guess I was homesick."

"Was it very lonely for you there?"

Soaring Eagle shook his head. "Not so lonely. I stayed with Robert and Nancy Davis. They have two boys. Sterling and Samuel. Wonderful boys."

"Did you make *friends* while you were there?"

Soaring Eagle looked into the fire and answered carefully. "I met many people."

Carrie shook her head. "Meeting lots of people isn't the same as having friends, is it? I know a lot of people in Lincoln, but I think I have only two real friends there—LisBeth and Everett."

"Everett?"

"Everett Higgenbottom. You met him in St. Louis."

Soaring Eagle laughed softly. "So, Everett Higgenbottom has followed my little Red Bird all the way to Nebraska." He looked at Carrie and nodded. "He is a good friend, Carrie. He cares for you."

"You didn't answer me, Soaring Eagle. Did you have friends in Boston?"

"I had, acquaintances. People who were interested in helping the Indians." He thought for a moment before adding, "And, yes, Red Bird, I had begun to have friends. George Woodward was trying to be my friend. George and his sister, Julia."

"Children always like you, Soaring Eagle."

Soaring Eagle laughed again. He set his coffee mug down deliberately and said nothing more. He stood up abruptly, scooting his chair back. "You should be getting back to the school, Red Bird. They will be worried."

Carrie stood up reluctantly. She pulled her borrowed hat down until it covered her ears. "Thank you for not being angry, Soaring Eagle. I shouldn't have come here. I know it. But I didn't think I'd see you again for a while, and well, I just had to know if—"

"I told you I would keep Ida Mae, Red Bird. When I say I will do a thing, I generally do it." Retrieving the doll from the table, Soaring Eagle wrapped it again and held it out to Carrie.

Carrie shook her head. "No, I want you to keep her."

Soaring Eagle opened the door for Carrie. "Are you certain you don't want to ride back?"

"I'm certain. I like walking. The storm's let up."

She stepped outside the cabin door, turning back when Soaring Eagle called her name. "Red Bird. No one knows I have come back to Santee. I think perhaps it would be best if *you*, too, are surprised to see me when I arrive at the mission tomorrow."

Carrie tilted her head back and peered at him from beneath the brim of the oversized hat. She nodded in agreement. He had nearly closed the door when she called out, "Soaring Eagle, thank you. For not being angry. I think you should have been. I'm glad you weren't. I really had no right. And, and, is it all right if I still call you Soaring Eagle? Jeremiah King seems so strange, somehow."

Soaring Eagle leaned against the doorway of the cabin, considering. "Soaring Eagle is my name, Red Bird. I like to hear it." He stood in the doorway watching until Carrie's form disappeared over a rise.

The rain continued. The mud grew deeper. As she walked, Carrie's sodden boots grew heavy. Her clothes were soaked through and she was shivering by the time she sneaked up the stairs to her room.

It had been a wonderful day off. *He still has Ida Mae. He kept her all these years. He said I could still call him Soaring Eagle.*

CHAPTER 16

Now set your heart and your soul
to seek the LORD your God.

1 Chronicles 22:19

Soaring Eagle paced back and forth in front of Alfred Riggs's desk, spilling out months of confusion and heartache. "I want to go west, Dr. Riggs. I want to see the open spaces and go hunting and, if God wills, maybe help a few of my people find their way to Him. I'm tired of getting up in front of crowds and being a 'fine example of my race' for everyone. I'm tired of starched collars and shoes that pinch. I'm tired of answering questions about scalps for impertinent little boys and running away from fights with their ignorant fathers."

Dr. Riggs leaned back in his chair and waited for Soaring Eagle to gather his thoughts. Soaring Eagle sat down next to Jim Callaway. He looked up at Dr. Riggs and continued with an almost desperate tone in his voice. "I want to take some other Lakota with me to heaven, Dr. Riggs. I don't want to make any more speeches. My speeches have not helped one Lakota soul find his way to heaven. Dr. Riggs, I *can't* go back to Boston. My people are dying while I sit in hotels drinking tea with white people whose only real interest is to see 'Jeremiah King, educated Indian.'" He looked away, concluding miserably, "I know I'm disappointing you, but I just can't go back to Boston."

Alfred Riggs's eyes shone with compassion. "Jeremiah,

you are *not* disappointing me." Reaching into his desk, he drew out a letter and handed it to Soaring Eagle. "This is from my brother Thomas, Jeremiah. Please, take a moment and read it."

Christmas, 1883

Reverend Thundercloud and I went to the new Dakota settlement up the Cheyenne River today. We reached an old trader's cabin in the evening. While we were rejoicing and talking together, there came an invitation to us from the Dakota tents. These Dakota live all together in a village by the river. The country around is hilly like the Missouri country. The water is clear and good. When we arrived, we went to the tent of a man named Reaching-to-the-Clouds. He made a speech. "My friends, we are a people of benevolent hearts. We have left off our roving habits, and we want you to come and give us knowledge. When one comes to us to teach us and stays only one winter and then leaves us, we don't like that. If a man does that, although he teaches us some good things, we forget them all when he is gone. We want a man to stay with us always. This is a good country to plant in. The soil is good. Last spring we planted, and everything we planted grew well. The white man gave us seed corn, beans, turnip seed. We planted all, and they grew very well. The corn grew taller than a man. My friends, we are very desirous of learning to read. We have heard that people who learn to read are well-off. We would value you very much if you would send someone to teach us to read."

We are very anxious to have someone come to these people. They are begging for teachers, and surely God would not have us neglect this opportunity to begin a work among a previously unreached people. The trader's cabin is sufficiently habitable to support two workers as soon as they could be assigned. Let us all pray for someone to hear the call of God to come to the Dakotas on the Cheyenne River.

Soaring Eagle read the letter slowly, taking in each line with a heart that began to pound with excitement. When he had finished the letter, he laid it on Dr. Riggs's desk with trembling hands, forcing himself to wait for Dr. Riggs to speak.

"It would appear, Jeremiah," said Dr. Riggs, "that God has answered Thomas's letter. I believe that your unhappiness in Boston was caused by God, because He is intending to call you away from those tearooms you mentioned to a trader's cabin on the Cheyenne River. Would you agree with that?"

"I don't know, Dr. Riggs. I hope that is true."

"Why do you hesitate, Jeremiah?"

Soaring Eagle looked soberly from Jim Callaway to Dr. Riggs and took a deep breath. "You may not think me qualified." He paused, continuing with difficulty. "In Boston there was, there was a woman named Julia, Julia Woodward."

Alfred Riggs sucked in air audibly before saying, "Go on, Jeremiah."

Jim Callaway steeled himself for the expected confession.

Soaring Eagle described Julia Woodward in great detail. He related their meeting and their subsequent friendship. Then he went on to tell of his last evening in Boston. He spoke in measured tones, trying his best to give a factual account uncluttered by excuses. He concluded in a miserable tone of voice. "And so I left. I was too weak to stay, Dr. Riggs. Too weak to stay and finish the classes. I was lonely and homesick, but that is no excuse for my behavior. I had to leave Boston to prevent the possibility of—"

"Yes, yes, Jeremiah. I see." Dr. Riggs interrupted Soaring Eagle with a wave of the hand. Reaching for the Bible that he always kept on the corner of his desk, he turned to 2 Timothy and read, "*Flee also youthful lusts: but follow righteousness, faith, charity, peace, with them that call on the Lord out of a pure heart.* Jeremiah, it appears to me that you did just what Paul instructed the young pastor Timothy to do. You recognized a dangerous situation and you fled." Dr. Riggs smiled at his prize pupil. "Jeremiah, I disagree with your evaluation of yourself. You did *not* fail in Boston. You recognized a temptation, and as far as I can tell, you responded biblically. Certainly you are now seeking to follow righteousness and faith, charity, and peace."

Dr. Riggs closed the Bible and returned it to the corner of his desk. He drummed the desk thoughtfully with his fingers before continuing. "I recall a moment in my own young life, Jeremiah." He paused. "Eons ago, of course, I was much younger and foolish. But I actually kissed a woman to whom I was not married." Dr. Riggs's eyes sparkled and one corner of his mouth rose in a smile. "I didn't think it disqualified me from ministry then, nor did the future Mrs. Riggs. On the contrary, it led to our sharing our life's work. I don't think one kiss disqualifies you from ministry, Jeremiah."

Soaring Eagle was quick to respond. "I'm not going to marry Julia Woodward, Dr. Riggs."

Jim Callaway spoke up for the first time. "How can you be so sure, Soaring Eagle? Didn't you say she's coming with the Committee to visit here at Santee? It sounds like she's honestly interested in the work here."

Soaring Eagle shook his head. "When you meet her, you will know, Dr. Riggs. She is not one to take into the west, to a log cabin." He sighed. "I have been praying that God would give me a wife, Dr. Riggs. And I think that God is calling me to the Cheyenne River. I don't know any women who would share such a life."

Alfred Riggs answered, "Then you must pray harder, Jeremiah. Scripture teaches that *a prudent wife is from the Lord.* The God who calls you to the west is also the God who created man and said it was not good for him to be alone. God can provide you with a wife who will share your burden for bringing your people to Christ."

As the meeting closed, the three men bowed their heads to pray. Dr. Alfred Riggs thanked God for his work in Soaring Eagle's life, and asked for guidance, and a wife. Jim Callaway thanked God for his work in Soaring Eagle's life, and asked for guidance, and a wife. Jeremiah Soaring Eagle King also thanked God and asked for guidance, and a wife, with the emphasis on the latter.

When the children and staff of the Santee Normal Training School filed into the chapel that afternoon for services, Dr. Riggs was already standing behind the pulpit. Soaring Eagle was seated to his right. He watched the schoolchildren file into the chapel and take their usual places, boys on the left, girls on the right. Scripture was read and then hymn singing began. Soaring Eagle joined in as the children's voices were raised in a song of praise, *Jesus waste made—hee waste, Jesus waste, Piwecida ya*. As he sang, his eyes gazed across the rows of children to the back of the chapel where Carrie Brown sat, trying her very best not to look at him. The song went on, *Miye awektonja nunu waun, Iye tehiya amkita ce, Heca nakaes owakida kta,* and finally the cornflower blue eyes glanced his way. When she saw that he was looking at her, Carrie pretended to drop something and ducked down in the pew.

The hymn ended and Dr. Riggs rose. "We have with us today, Jeremiah Soaring Eagle King, who is a graduate of this school. Mr. King has attended Beloit College in Wisconsin and John Knox College in Illinois. He has most recently been a student at Harvard in Cambridge. While there, Mr. King was an effective spokesperson for our school. He has now returned to us for a season of work, and I hope you will listen to what he has to say."

Soaring Eagle approached the lectern and began simply.

"When I first came to Santee, there were many difficult things that I had to learn. First, was a new language. Then," he glanced at the boys with a grin, "there were the awful lessons in geography and mathematics." The boys nudged one another and nodded in agreement. Soaring Eagle turned to the girls. "I was *very* glad that I did not have to learn how to sew." The girls giggled.

Soaring Eagle smiled, and then grew serious. "But the greatest challenge for me was to learn how to be a man. I remember telling James Red Wing that where I had come from, being a man was easy. I only had to hunt well and fight well. But when I came here, everything changed, and I no longer knew how to be a man." Opening his Bible, Soaring Eagle said, "But then I came to know Jesus Christ, and one day I was reading His Book, and I saw words that told me how to be a man. I was reading in the first book of the Kings, and there it was, what God says a man should do. Here is what it says." Soaring Eagle read:

Be thou strong therefore, and shew thyself a man; and keep the charge of the LORD thy God, to walk in his ways, to keep his statutes, and his commandments, and his judgments, and his testimonies, as it is written in the law of Moses, that thou mayest prosper in all that thou doest, and whithersoever thou turnest thyself.

"When I read those words, I knew that to be a man, I had to learn what God said in His Book so that I could walk in His ways, so that I could prosper—and be what God says a man is." He held up the Bible for the children to see. "When you look at this Book you see that the cover is worn. I have tried to study this Book. As I have read it, something has happened to me that happened to another man named Jeremiah. Jeremiah of the Old Testament said, '*Thy words were found, and I did eat them; and thy word was unto me the joy and rejoicing of mine heart: for I am called by thy name, O*

Lord God of hosts.' God has made me love this Book. When I read it, my heart feels joy and rejoicing and I want to study it more and more and to take it to my own people to show them all it says about God and His love for them.

"When I thought that God was telling me to take His Word to my people, I was afraid—just like that other Jeremiah, I said, *"Alas, Lord God! Behold, I cannot speak: for I am only a Lakota.* But then I read what God said to that other Jeremiah. He said, *Say not, I am a child—Soaring Eagle, do not say I am only a poor Lakota—for thou shalt go to all that I shall send thee, and whatsoever I command thee thou shalt speak."* Soaring Eagle looked around the chapel before continuing. "As I studied at Harvard, my heart grew heavy. I read of the needs among my own people, and I began to think that I should be with them, telling them of Christ. I have returned to Santee to ask God's guidance." Abruptly, Soaring Eagle stepped away from the podium. "Children," he said simply, "I ask that you pray for me. And I will pray for you, that you will continue your studies, that you will learn the ways of God, that you will learn to love His Book, and that you will return to your families and tell them of Christ." He stepped down, sitting in a front pew next to Jim Callaway.

Dr. Riggs rose. 'just this morning I have met with Mr. King. After a season of prayer, it has been decided that he will not be returning to Boston, as we had originally planned. We believe that God is calling our friend Jeremiah to a new ministry, and as soon as a partner is found and support is given, he will proceed to the Cheyenne River country with the hopes of establishing a permanent missionary station there among his own people. Let us pray for this new endeavor."

The moment Dr. Riggs made his announcement, Carrie, who had continued to study the floor at her feet, looked up sharply. If she had heard correctly, if the decision had been made, then Soaring Eagle's future would be drastically different from what she had envisioned. There would be no traveling the country to lecture and raise support for the Indian. There would be no admiring crowds, no newspaper publicity. She was ashamed to admit that she had lingered over the imaginary newspaper photos of Dr. Jeremiah King (also pictured: Mrs. King, the former Carrie Brown of St. Louis).

It can't be, Carrie thought. *He can't possibly mean it. He's so very good at lecturing. I saw those crowds in St. Louis, the way they responded to him. Surely he won't give that up for—*Carrie imagined Soaring Eagle in a sparsely furnished one room cabin, preparing a sermon by the light of a kerosene lamp. She tried, and failed, to add herself to the picture, living in the log cabin, seated in the front pew of a small church.

The service concluded with the singing of a hymn. Carrie followed Charity and the children out of the chapel, watching as two of the older boys almost tackled Soaring Eagle, begging him to come see the new wood shop and print shop. With a glance Carrie's way, Soaring Eagle put a hand on each boy's shoulder and followed them across the campus towards the shops. Carrie slipped back into the chapel and sat down in a back pew to think. *Everett was right,* she thought. *He told me I hadn't considered reality at all—that I was building a fantasy of traveling and being the wife of "Dr. Jeremiah King."* Carrie leaned her forehead on the pew in front of her. *My whole dream has been built around some romantic notion, not around the real man at all. He doesn't care about education, or newspaper articles, or money. He just wants to go home and preach to his own people. I haven't ever considered what Soaring Eagle might want—what God might want him to do. I'm no better than the people in St. Louis I used to get so angry with, the people who saw him as a curiosity, never as a real man, just as "the Indian." All this time I haven't really known him at all. Everett was right.*

"Is anything wrong, Carrie?" It was Jim Callaway.

Carrie jumped. "No, Jim, nothing's wrong. I just wanted to think about what Soaring Eagle said today. Did you, did you need something, Jim?"

"Soaring Eagle will be back in a few minutes. He asked me to make sure you don't go anywhere. He wants to say hello."

"He's changed."

"How do you mean?" Jim asked as he settled in the pew beside her. "He's more fluent, I guess, but I haven't noticed any real change, not in the man."

"What I mean is, he seems so single-minded about what he wants to do. So determined."

"No more determined than any missionary who's really committed to the Lord," Jim answered. "I think God has been leading him in that direction all along. It just took a while for Soaring Eagle to realize it."

Soaring Eagle's voice sounded at the door. "How is my little Red Bird? Are they teaching you good things at that university in Lincoln?" He touched her shoulder before seating himself in the pew in front of Carrie and Jim.

With Soaring Eagle's arrival, the conversation abruptly changed. Carrie commented briefly on the university and her work at the hotel, concluding with her plans to teach in a rural school for the fall and winter terms.

"How long will you be at Santee?" Soaring Eagle wanted to know.

Carrie looked at Jim, who said, "I need to get back for spring planting. I was hoping we could leave tomorrow, if that's all right."

"Tomorrow?" Carrie could not hide the disappointment in her voice.

Jim nodded. "I don't want to leave LisBeth—"

"Oh, of course, the baby."

Soaring Eagle's eyes sparkled with joy. "So. I am to be an uncle at last. When is this to happen?"

Jim grinned. "Just a few weeks away, we think; that's why I need to get back."

"Well, then, I am glad that I came today and was able to see my friend and my Red Bird." Soaring Eagle rose to go. He walked to the door and then turned back to Jim. "I think, Jim Callaway, that I would like to give this child a gift. When you return to my sister, I would like you to take the black mare with you."

Jim protested. "That's too generous, Soaring Eagle. She's to be the foundation for your herd."

Soaring Eagle shook his head. "No, I will have no need for a herd where I am going. It will please me to know that Lakota has a good home with my sister, my family. Tell the child that *leksi*, that is *uncle*, will come and teach him, or her, to ride."

He turned to Carrie. "Red Bird, you study hard at that university. Tell Everett Higgenbottom that Jeremiah King wishes him to watch over you well. And remember," he said gently, "you will always hold a special place in my heart."

CHAPTER 17

How long shall I take counsel in my soul, having sorrow in my heart daily?

Psalm 13:2

Sarah and Tom Biddle handled Abigail and David Braddock's death so well that no one in Lincoln suspected that their relationship had been anything but that of employer to employee. While Tom Biddle didn't quite understand his sister's insistence that her engagement to David be kept secret, he was proud that she had entrusted him with something so important to her.

Sarah had also sworn Dr. Gilbert to secrecy. "There's no need for anyone to know, Dr. Gilbert. It doesn't matter."

"But you've a right to at least part of the estate, Miss Biddle."

"I've no right that the surviving Braddocks wouldn't take into a court. I won't have that. I won't have David's name dragged into a court over things, Dr. Gilbert," Sarah insisted. "Mother Braddock told me about the others in the family. I don't want any trouble. I'll do my duty by David and Mother Braddock. I'll see that the house is cared for, and when the others arrive, I'll follow their instructions."

"And likely be out on your ear," Dr. Gilbert interrupted.

Sarah shook her head. "No, Dr. Gilbert. I'll go home to Aunt Augusta." Tears threatened. "As long as Augusta Hathaway is alive, Tom and I will always have a place to call home." Sarah regained her composure and continued. "Aunt Augusta is already assuming that we'll be coming back. Just last evening she said that she had two rooms waiting. She even apologized that she didn't have rooms near her own apartment. But there are two large rooms on the third floor. Tom and I will go there. Tom will have his inheritance."

"And you'll have nothing. Nothing for all the years of service. For the last months of hell."

Sarah's eyes softened as she disagreed. "Oh, no, Dr. Gilbert. It's not like that at all. I may have no things to show, but I've the memory of Mother Braddock's smile— and her belief in me. I've the proper grammar, and the knowledge of housekeeping, and all the things she taught me. I'll be able to get a good position soon, I'm sure of it. I've been thinking I might even look for a little house for Tom and me. As soon as I find suitable employment. Until then, we'll stay with Aunt Augusta."

Dr. Gilbert smiled warmly. "You've grit, Sarah Biddle, I'll give you that. You'd have been a fine wife to David Braddock. I hope he knew it."

"He knew it, Dr. Gilbert." Sarah didn't say more, for whatever had existed between her and David Braddock must be laid away forever. Sarah had already folded it neatly and stored it away where it wouldn't hurt quite so much.

And so Dr. Miles Gilbert kept his promise to Sarah and remained silent about her engagement to David Braddock. When the "other Braddock," Ira, arrived in Lincoln to settle the estate, Tom and Sarah Biddle had already moved their things back to the Hathaway House. Dressed in her finest suit, Sarah met him at the manse. Ira was the only one of the "other Braddocks" to make the journey west from Philadelphia to "close things up." When Sarah opened the door of the manse, she stifled a smile at the appearance of the first human she had ever seen to resemble a banty rooster.

With quiet and deliberate movements, Sarah showed Ira Braddock each room. When asked, she suggested how best to dispose of the fine things that she had lovingly dusted and arranged. With grace, she accepted Ira Braddock's snobbish disdain of Nebraska. With patience, she explained the things about Lincoln that had charmed Abigail and David Braddock. She didn't mention Abigail's interest in Tom, and she took great delight in the exclamation of shock that escaped Ira Braddock's lips when the will was read and Tom Biddle was the undeniable recipient of a generous gift which would easily pay tuition to a fine university back east, (although Tom stubbornly insisted that the University of Nebraska was the only school he'd ever attend). When the "other Braddock" had been assured by his attorney that Abigail's bequest was irreversible, he smiled indulgently, made a comment about his elderly relative's idiosyncrasies, wiped off his pince-nez, and resumed his superior position in the universe.

On the final day that Ira Braddock visited the manse, he made a grand display of offering Sarah a memento. "Anything you'd like from the house, Miss Biddle. Take something to remember the Braddocks by, dear." When he said it, he drew himself up to his full stature of 5' 4" and somehow managed to look down his nose at 5' 7" Sarah.

Sarah looked at him with steely gray eyes and said, "I'll be going now, Mr. Braddock." She took off her sterling silver chatelaine, and handed it to Ira Braddock. "All the door and cabinet keys are right here. I had the only complete set of keys, so be careful not to misplace these."

Sarah opened the front door, descended the wide stairs, and marched through the front gate, empty-handed. Heartily hoping that Ira Braddock was watching her go,

she forced her ___ ___alk north on 17th Street without a
backward gla___

Sarah Biddle managed to handle every decision that
arose over the next few weeks without a hint of the weight
of grief that had settled over her. Tom continued school at
Miss Griswall's and Sarah filled in for various absent hotel
employees, including Carrie Brown. She rode to Roca
often to help LisBeth stitch infant sacques and diapers, and
filled her evenings by helping Tom with lessons or working
on the baby quilt she had begun for LisBeth. She was
unusually quiet and introspective, but Augusta reasoned
that that was only natural. Sarah had, after all, been unusually close to Abigail Braddock.

Sarah requested Augusta's carriage often, and Augusta
readily assented, never suspecting that each carriage ride
ended with Sarah weeping over two headstones in Wyuka
Cemetery. David Braddock's body had been buried at the
site of the train accident, but Sarah had secretly paid to
have a headstone placed beside his mother's grave.
Augusta had attributed the second memorial to some previously unnoticed drop of compassion in Ira Braddock.
Sarah was grateful that no questions were asked.

But there came a day in Sarah Biddle's life when the loss
of both her fiancé and her benefactress nearly dragged her
into despair. There came a day when Augusta Hathaway
finally learned Sarah's most closely guarded grief.

Sarah returned one day from visiting the cemetery just
in time to see Asa Green drag a huge trunk through the
door into Augusta's quarters. Augusta hurried from the
kitchen into the hall and beckoned Sarah to follow her. "It
just arrived, Sarah. Fred over at the station sent a messen-
ger to ask me what I thought he should do with it. Said he

couldn't deliver it to the manse if he wanted to. Even the carriage house is locked up tight. Ira didn't leave instructions or keys, did he?"

Sarah shook her head. "Cropsey probably has a set at his land office. I think he's in charge of the sale. We could check."

"Sarah, it has David Braddock's name on it. And—" Augusta unfolded a sheet of paper. "Frank gave me this. It's an apology from the railroad. Apparently David Braddock had this with him on the train when—"

Sarah's face paled and she sat down.

Augusta continued. "It's David's, Sarah. Somehow it seems wrong to just deliver it to an empty house. And, frankly, Dear, I don't want Ira Braddock to have the satisfaction of getting his hands on anything else. Let's at least open it. As their housekeeper, you would have done that anyway. I know Abigail and David would approve if you decide about the disposal of whatever this is."

Sarah nodded and whispered, "All right, Abigail. Agreed. But there's no key."

With a glint of mischief in her eyes, Augusta removed one of her hairpins and knelt by the trunk. In only a moment she had it open. A faint scent of roses filled the room and Augusta bent to inspect the contents, let out an exclamation of surprise, and sat down abruptly.

Sarah, who was already seated, grew even paler. She stared at Augusta and then back at the trunk. Finally, with trembling hands, she reached towards the trunk and touched the most exquisite wedding gown she had ever seen. Only the bodice showed, but as she pulled it from the trunk, fold upon fold of heavy satin cascaded to the floor. The gown had been packed with dried rose petals. Speechless, Sarah clutched the gown to her, watching Augusta exclaim over the remaining items in the trunk.

"It's a trousseau, Sarah, a complete trousseau. David

Braddock must have had plans. I'm so happy he finally found someone." Augusta clucked, shaking her head, "Such a tragic end." Suddenly, Augusta realized that Sarah Biddle had had nothing to say for quite a few moments. Turning away from the trunk, Augusta was struck by an impossible possibility.

Sarah Biddle sat on the edge of Augusta's fainting couch. She had folded the wedding gown at the waist and smoothed the bodice so that it lay neatly across her lap, the sleeves stretching out on either side of her, the train pooling on the floor around her feet. Slowly, Sarah bent to pick up a pair of lace gloves that had dropped on the floor. With extreme care, she pulled on one glove, then the other. She held her hands in front of her, stretching out her fingers, inspecting the exquisite pattern of roses in the lace She ran her index finger along the high collar, down the rows of tiny pin tucks, to a cluster of soft pink ribbon roses at the waist of the dress.

"Oh, my dear." Augusta said softly. "My dear, dear, Sarah." Augusta sat down next to Sarah and laid her dimpled hand over Sarah's clasped hands. Putting one arm around Sarah's shoulders, Augusta drew her into an embrace that broke through the walls that Sarah Biddle had built around her secret.

"Why, Sarah?" Augusta asked gently. "Why didn't you tell anyone?"

"There was no need."

"But, Sarah, you were entitled."

"To nothing, Aunt Augusta." Sarah pulled away from Augusta and stood up, the wedding gown over her arm. Pulling off one glove, Sarah said wistfully, "Who would have believed it, Aunt Augusta? Mr. David Braddock of Philadelphia marrying an orphaned housekeeper." Sarah looked gravely at Augusta. "I told him that people would disapprove. Somehow I knew it wasn't meant to be. Tom and Dr.

Gilbert promised never to tell." Laying the wedding gown on the couch beside Augusta, Sarah knelt by the trunk and began to refold her trousseau. "No one must ever know."

Augusta frowned. "Sarah. You mustn't keep this inside. You've had a terrible loss. You must face it, and grieve it, and then get on with life. Don't try to say it doesn't hurt, Sarah."

When Sarah looked up from her place by the trunk, her eyes were brimming with unspilled tears. Tenderly she pulled the wedding gown towards her, clasping it to herself. Smoothing its wrinkles she folded it gently back into the trunk.

"I'm not saying it doesn't hurt, Aunt Augusta. I'm saying I won't have anyone know, because it was good and true and beautiful, and I won't have it brought out where strangers can discuss it and doubt it and laugh at it." Closing the lid to the trunk Sarah said softly, "I'd appreciate it if Asa could take this up to my room, Aunt Augusta." She smiled sadly as tears began to fall. Heading for the door, Sarah turned back to Augusta.

"I'm not denying the hurt, Aunt Augusta. I just can't—" she took a deep breath and stopped. She stood with her hand on the doorknob for a long moment before choking out, "I just can't find the right words. There *aren't* any words."

Sarah Biddle went up to her room. When Asa Green knocked, she had him put the trunk in the middle of the room. When Tom Biddle arrived home from school that day, he was met by Augusta and a list of chores that kept him hard at work all evening. "Just leave Sarah be, Tom. She wasn't feeling well this afternoon and I sent her to bed. It's nothing serious, but I don't think she should be disturbed." When it grew late and Augusta finally let him go upstairs, she did so with a reminder not to bother Sarah.

Tom crept down the hall towards his own room, but

couldn't resist checking in on his sister. He opened the door to her room without making a sound. Augusta had said she was in bed, but Sarah wasn't in bed. She was obviously deep in thought, unaware that Tom had opened the door. The deep sadness on her face made Tom frown with concern. *I don't think she should be disturbed.* Augusta's warning took on new authority, and something convinced Tom to obey her and leave his sister alone. Pulling the door closed, he left Sarah undisturbed, sitting by the window, staring at the contents of an open trunk.

CHAPTER 18

By love serve one another.

Galatians 5:13

Augusta Hathaway peered over her newspaper at Sarah Biddle. The two women had retired to Augusta's apartment, Augusta to read her newspaper, and Sarah to add to the ever-increasing pile of quilt blocks in her sewing basket. Sarah worked slowly, pausing often to lean back in her chair. She seemed half asleep, but Augusta knew that Sarah's weariness was the kind that more often prevented sleep.

"You haven't been sleeping well, Sarah," Augusta said quietly.

Sarah started at the sound of Augusta's voice. Looking up she replied guiltily, "I'm sorry, Aunt Augusta. Has my midnight descent to the kitchen been waking you?"

"Nonsense, Dear." Augusta folded her newspaper. "Not at all. I just know you haven't been sleeping. Cora says you're in the kitchen most every morning when she comes in. Says your sewing is usually always laid out, but you're not sewing when she comes in." Augusta paused and added gently, "I'm worried about you, Dear. Can't I do something to help?"

Sarah looked down at the sewing in her lap and smiled halfheartedly, shaking her head.

"That trunk in your room, Sarah, we should store it

somewhere, somewhere out of sight. It's not good for you see it day after day."

Sarah looked piercingly at Augusta. "I don't want that trunk moved."

Augusta unfolded her newspaper and Sarah picked up her sewing. After a few moments Augusta asked, "Sarah, would you ride out tomorrow and check on LisBeth for me? I've been out there three times since Jim left. LisBeth could do with some younger company."

"Oh, Aunt Augusta," Sarah protested, "I'm not fit company for LisBeth. Not now."

Augusta looked over the newspaper at Sarah. "Maybe not, Sarah, but she'll certainly be good company for *you*. Remember, Sarah, it wasn't that long ago that LisBeth was struggling with the same feelings. You must know that she will understand."

"I don't need understanding, Aunt Augusta," Sarah said softly. "I just need to forget."

"No," Augusta said firmly. "You do *not* need to forget. You need to remember every fine thing about David Braddock and Abigail. And, my dear," Augusta added, "you need to remember that while it may not *feel* like it at the moment, you are very much loved by the Lord."

Sarah was quiet, concentrating on stitching.

"Sarah," Augusta argued mildly, "you can talk to LisBeth. It will just be the two of you. No one else ever needs to know. LisBeth will be uniquely able to understand your heartache."

When Sarah remained unconvinced, Augusta changed her approach. "Sarah, I really do need to stay in town tomorrow. There's a board meeting for the Home for the Friendless after the Red Ribbon Club. Dr. Huff, the staff physician at the Home, is speaking at the club. She's asked me to lead the discussion of how we are going to make up the shortfall between the city and state support and what we need to actually run the home. We've nearly a hundred children living there now, and, as you know, private contributions just aren't keeping up with the expenses."

Sarah looked up from her sewing. "That's not fair, Aunt Augusta. You know I can't refuse when you mention the Home for the Friendless." She sighed. "All right, I'll go out to LisBeth's so you can stay here for the meeting. But don't expect me to bare my soul to LisBeth, Aunt Augusta. I really meant it when I said that I don't want to talk about it."

"You do what you think best, Sarah," Augusta said. "I can't force you." As Sarah wearily mounted the steps to her room, Augusta called out, "If LisBeth wants you to stay, don't feel you need to rush back. We'll manage just fine, and LisBeth has been lonely. These last few weeks of her confinement haven't been easy, especially with Jim gone to Santee."

Sarah forfeited attending church the next morning in favor of an early morning drive to the Callaway farm. The old horse Asa had hitched up for her plodded patiently along, and Sarah did nothing to hurry her. In spite of herself, she began to enjoy the view of the greening countryside, the smell of the warm earth, the songs of the birds that were just returning from the south to nest in the shrubs along the dirt road.

At some point along the road Sarah began talking to God. *You know, God, what hurts the most is that You let me have those expectations, and then took them away. When I was a homeless orphan I never expected to be loved or cared about. When Aunt Jesse and Aunt Augusta took me in, I never expected to be anything at all. But then I went to work for Mrs. Braddock, and a whole new world opened. I thought maybe I could do something worthwhile. Maybe I could even provide an education for Tom. Then David. Well, Lord, that was an expectation I never had. But he made me almost believe I could actually be a good wife to him, even if he was a leading citizen and I was only a housekeeper. I was almost getting used to the idea that maybe I really could be a lady. I liked it. If You weren't going to let that happen, why'd You let me build that dream and then tear it down? I don't understand it, God. Why couldn't You just let Tom and me be the Braddock's maid and houseboy? It was enough, God. It would have been enough.*

Sarah drove into the farmyard no less depressed than she had been when she left Lincoln. LisBeth waved to her from behind the picket fence that Jim had erected around the tiny burial plot just across the road from the house. "Sarah! It's wonderful to see you." LisBeth pressed a hand against the small of her back. "Think you could help a *very* indisposed friend finish weeding over here?"

Sarah climbed down from the carriage and joined LisBeth inside the picket fence where three rocks had been crudely engraved *Ma, Pa,* and *Mac.* "Augusta told me about this little plot, LisBeth, but I didn't realize Jim had put so much work into making it so nice."

LisBeth leaned against the fence. "The first thing he did when he came on this place was clean up Ma and Pa Baird's graves. MacKenzie would have appreciated knowing someone was taking care."

Sarah leaned down by the stone engraved *Mac.* "I remember Augusta telling me about that day you drove out with Mother Braddock and David. They drove in here and Jim had made that stone for MacKenzie even though his true resting place is out at the Little Big Horn."

LisBeth nodded and said softly, "Jim wanted to give me a place to visit Mac." LisBeth looked up. "Of course neither of us knew then I'd marry again, let alone marry Jim. But the day I saw that stone, I knew Jim Callaway was one special man."

LisBeth sighed, rousing herself from her own memories.

"Sarah, I'm so sorry about Mrs. Braddock and David. I wish I could have at least come to the service."

From where she knelt by the fence pulling weeds, Sarah managed a faint "thank you." Abruptly changing the subject she suggested, "Let me finish, LisBeth. You look worn out."

LisBeth answered honestly. "I am worn out, Sarah. Worn out with waiting. I guess it'll be worth the waiting, though, when the baby comes."

"You just settle there in the shade. There's not much left to do. I'll take care of it." Sarah bent to pull away the tall grasses that had grown around the three headstones.

"I hope you can stay, Sarah," LisBeth said hopefully.

"All day. Aunt Augusta said she wouldn't need me at all today. In fact," Sarah said, pulling out the last of the weeds and straightening up, "she even encouraged me to stay over—if you want the company."

LisBeth was adamant. "I'd love the company, Sarah. We've had so little chance to talk what with my, well—" she could not bring herself to say the word. "And then when Mrs. Braddock was so ill, then closing up the house and David's death." LisBeth didn't notice that Sarah turned abruptly toward the house. "It seems impossible that he's gone. That they're both gone." LisBeth followed Sarah out of the burial plot and towards the house. "I wonder who'll buy the house," she mused.

Sarah didn't answer, but turned instead towards the carriage. "I'll be in in just a moment, LisBeth. I need to unhitch Sadie, here, if I'm to stay the night."

Sarah unhitched Sadie and led her into the barn. Moments later she joined LisBeth, who was still rubbing her back while she heated water for coffee.

"It won't be long, now, LisBeth," Sarah reassured her. "I've almost got your baby quilt finished. I brought it along." She grinned. "Maybe I can even finish it while I'm here, if we talk half the night like we used to. Want to see it?"

LisBeth sat down at the kitchen table with a groan. "I'd love to see it, Sarah. But can we talk in my room? I've just got to lie down for a few minutes. My back is killing me." Without waiting for Sarah to answer, LisBeth made her way through the parlor and into her own room.

Sarah went to retrieve her satchel from the carriage. She had just started for the house when she heard a wagon coming up the road. Peering down the road, Sarah saw a rangy team of bays and a redheaded driver. She ran into the house calling out, "LisBeth, Jim's back!"

No answer came from the bedroom. Sarah smiled to herself. *She's fallen asleep.* But LisBeth was not asleep. She was curled up in bed, holding her back with both hands. She looked up at Sarah, fear shining in her eyes. "It's too soon, Sarah. But I think—" LisBeth squeezed her eyes shut and grunted. When the contraction had passed, she panted. "I think the baby's coming. Tell Jim—"

Sarah didn't wait for LisBeth to finish. Instead, she ran out to meet Jim, who was just getting down from the wagon, smiling a greeting. One look at Sarah's face, and Jim bounded into the house. He planted a kiss on LisBeth's cheek. "I'm on my way to get Dr. Gilbert, LisBeth. The team's worn out. I'll ride Buck. It'll be faster, anyway."

LisBeth grabbed her back and groaned again. "Hurry, Jim. Please hurry."

Sarah followed Jim to the back door. "Jim, it's the first baby. It will take a while. Always does. At least that's what Dr. Gilbert said. He often came by to check on Mrs. Braddock when he had another woman, in confinement. Just stay calm and don't break your neck between here and Lincoln. We'll be fine."

Sarah spoke with far more confidence than she felt. Still, her tone of voice had the desired effect on Jim Callaway.

Some of the worry went out of his lined face. He managed a smile. "I'm glad you're here for LisBeth, Sarah. Tell her I'll be back with Dr. Gilbert soon. Tell her—" Jim hesitated.

"Tell her you love her?" Sarah smiled.

Jim nodded, embarrassed. Sarah headed for the house. The moment the two separated, the calming effect they had had on one another was gone. Jim tore out of the farmyard on Buck, and Sarah rushed into the kitchen to heat water and ready clean linen.

Before the water was even lukewarm, LisBeth staggered into the kitchen. Her dark eyes were wide with terror. She blurted out, "No time, Sarah. There's no time for the doc—" She managed the last word and then was overcome by a contraction that left her pale and breathless, her knuckles whitening as she grasped the back of a chair.

As soon as LisBeth's grip on the chair relaxed Sarah helped her back to her bed. She barely had the quilts pulled back before LisBeth was struggling against another contraction. LisBeth fought against the labor. Sarah ran back to the kitchen for a knife and the kettle of warm water. She noted with dismay that she sloshed some of the water on LisBeth's new wool rug as she hurried through the parlor.

LisBeth was calling for her, and Sarah hurried back to her side. "LisBeth," she called out. Setting the kettle on the floor she dampened a cloth. "LisBeth!" Sarah called, turning LisBeth's face towards her and looking into her terrified eyes. "LisBeth, listen to me. There's nothing to be afraid of. I know what to do. I helped my mother birth my baby sister Emma. There's nothing to be afraid of. Do you hear me?"

LisBeth stopped moaning and a glimmer of hope came into her eyes.

"Listen to me, LisBeth. We can do this." Sarah paused and consciously forced confidence into her voice. "With

God's help, we can do it. You're young and healthy and there's nothing to birthing a baby. Just stay calm and hold my hand, LisBeth. I'm right here. I'm not going anywhere—" Even as she spoke Sarah prayed, *Dear God—let it be true. Let the baby come easy. Please God, help me know what to do. Help me remember what Mama had me do.*

There was no more time to pray, for even as trust shone in LisBeth's eyes and a faint smile played about her lips, another contraction came, and she and Sarah were carried into the world where birth and the valley of the shadow of death were often the same thing.

LisBeth Callaway was often to tease Sarah Biddle for saying "there's nothing to birthing a baby." Both women discovered in the next two hours that there was, indeed, a great deal to the process. LisBeth strained against it, clasping Sarah's thin hands until Sarah thought they would break. Between contractions, LisBeth grunted and moaned against her terrible backache, which Sarah tried in vain to relieve.

When the moment came to actually birth the baby, instinct did, indeed, take over, and LisBeth needed no instruction from Sarah on what to do. She strained and pushed and yelled with every ounce of strength while Sarah waited with outstretched hands to receive a miracle. The miracle arrived screaming lustily at his new surroundings. Sarah cut the umbilical cord with clumsy hands, tying it off with string and wrapping the baby quickly in a yard of hastily procured red flannel.

LisBeth's eyes shone with tears as she took her miracle from Sarah. She stared down into his face, fingering the cleft in his chin and murmuring, "You look just like your uncle, little boy—" At the sound of a familiar voice, the baby stopped screaming and looked up at his mother. LisBeth exclaimed, "Except for those beautiful gray-green eyes. Now *those* are from your daddy."

The baby flailed his tiny arms in the air, puckered up, and gave another yell. LisBeth didn't hesitate. Mimicking Sarah's gentle voice she said softly, "There's nothing to it, James Windrider Callaway." She put the baby to her breast.

When Jim Callaway and Dr. Gilbert rode into the farmyard some time later, Dr. Gilbert was just explaining, "I know you're anxious, Mr. Callaway, but, really, Sarah Biddle is a capable nurse, and, as I said, this is your wife's first child, and it will no doubt be some time this evening before—"

Dr. Gilbert's discourse was interrupted by a lusty yell that sounded suspiciously like the cry of a newborn. Jim jumped down from the still-moving carriage and ran into the house. Dr. Gilbert took time to pull his horse up. Leaving his black bag in the carriage, he followed Jim inside where he was met by Sarah Biddle.

"I'm so glad you've finally come. I think she's all right, Dr. Gilbert." Forgetting propriety, Sarah gave the doctor a thorough description of LisBeth's labor, the delivery, and what she had done in the absence of a doctor.

Dr. Gilbert was impressed. "We have a doting mother and a healthy child, Miss Biddle. I'd say you performed admirably." Proceeding to the bedroom, Dr. Gilbert was greeted by one of the promised moments that had led him to medical school—the view of a tired mother and an ecstatic father looking at the wonder of their love come to life.

After a thorough examination of both mother and child, Dr. Gilbert reassured Sarah Biddle that she had, indeed, performed admirably. "Miss Biddle," he said as he left later that day, "I don't know what your plans are for the future, but you would make a very good nurse. Lincoln is growing so rapidly with new families, I have often wished for someone reliable I could suggest when there is need for nursing care. If you are in the least interested, please come by the office when you return to Lincoln. I'd like to discuss it with you." Dr. Gilbert didn't wait for Sarah to reply before he urged his mare to a trot and headed for Lincoln.

Sarah Biddle remained on the Callaway farm for several days, caring for LisBeth and J. W. Callaway, cooking and cleaning. She did not immediately realize what her service to her friend was accomplishing in her own life until she returned to Lincoln. When Sarah drove into Lincoln, she turned Sadie east and then north along a familiar street, and finally to where a pair of massive iron gates were set into a high brick wall. Lingering for a moment before the iron gates, Sarah pondered the reality of losing access to the mansion on the other side of the wall. She was struck with the realization that, while sadness lingered, the sharpness of the pain had receded. In its place was the knowledge that in recent weeks she had participated in two wondrous events—*I helped Mother Braddock leave this world, and then I helped J. W. Callaway come into it.* Sarah looked up at the iron gates and smiled. *What I learned caring for Mother Braddock, losing David, and birthing J. W., I can use. I can use it all to build a future for Tom and me.*

The next morning, Sarah Biddle paid a visit to Dr. Miles Gilbert.

CHAPTER 19

Without counsel purposes are disappointed: but in the multitude of counsellors they are established.

Proverbs 15:22

I think you should go," Everett Higgenbottom said definitively. He was sitting across the table from Carrie Brown in the dining room at the Hathaway House Hotel. Carrie had just shared a letter from Charity Bond inviting Carrie to join her at the Dakota Missions Conference.

Carrie looked surprised. "You *want* me to go that far away?"

"Of course I, personally, don't *like* the idea of your traipsing halfway across the country to some church conference, but it's definitely in your best interest to go." Everett tapped the table with one slender index finger as he spoke. "Listen, Carrie, I'm your friend—right?"

"Everett, you've been one of the best friends I could ever have."

"You admitted to me that this notion of yours about your future had some sort of, well, setback."

Carrie pursed her lips. "What I *said*, Everett, was that you were right about my perception of Soaring Eagle. I was living a fairy tale. Now I've accepted that he's not going to be traveling around the east giving lectures." Carrie added earnestly, "That doesn't change my feelings for him. If anything, knowing his future more definitely has matured my feelings, made me accept a more realistic view."

Everett interrupted her. "Realistic. Right. Listen, Carrie, you haven't the slightest notion of what it's like on the frontier." Carrie took a breath as if to interrupt and Everett hurried on. "Now wait a minute. I know you grew up at Santee. I also know it was pretty well established before your mother went to live there. I don't know very much about missionary work, but it's pretty obvious that living at an established mission school and heading into uncharted territory to start a new work are two different things. How can you find out if you want to do that unless you attend this conference out west? At least you'll get to meet some of the people involved in the work. So, I say go with Charity Bond as she's asked, and learn everything you can."

Everett paused for a moment. "Carrie, there's something else."

"Go on, Everett, say it all."

"I'm not much of a Christian, but aren't missionaries supposed to receive some sort of 'call' or something? I mean, you're going about this thing as if it's a profession you can select."

Carrie squirmed uncomfortably in her seat. "Everett, I *am* a Christian. Am I such a poor one that you don't think I can do missionary work?"

Everett cleared his throat. "Carrie, you're a great girl." He grinned. "Why do you think I've followed you all the way to Nebraska and spent the last few years trying to get you to fall in love with me?" He paused. "You do everything right. You're kind, and honest, and all the things a Christian is supposed to be. There's just—" Everett hesitated.

"Just *what*, Everett?"

"Listen, Carrie. I went to a revival meeting last week over at the Methodist church with Myrtle Greer. It was great. There was a *passion* about that evangelist that I just can't describe. From what you've said, Charity Bond has that for working with those children. Soaring Eagle has it, too, or he wouldn't be turning his back on good hotels and the lecture circuit to head west to log cabins and poverty. But you, Carrie, you're different. You're approach to this thing is pretty clinical. It's as if your mapping out a strategy for investing in land. Buy this property. Build this house. Marry this man. But *then* what, Carrie? What if that all happens? Then you have to *live* the life of a missionary. It seems to me, that to live that life a person needs a call—a passion." Everett leaned back against his chair. "I'm sorry, Carrie, but you just don't have it for the work." He sighed. "So, I think you need to go back up there, go with Charity, and see what it's like." His voice was gentle as he added, "I care about you, Carrie. I don't want you to land a dream and then find out it's not what you wanted after all."

Carrie was quiet for a while, considering. "Everett, I'm not even sure it would ever happen. It's been a long time since that little girl fantasy began. Soaring Eagle has grown and changed since I first saw him. I'm beginning to think he'll never see me as anything but 'little Carrie Brown.'"

Everett grew suddenly earnest. "Listen to me, Carrie. I'm just a lowly university student, but I'll tell you something. I'm smart enough to know that when a girl like you pays attention to a man, he's going to notice. And if Soaring Eagle has a chance at you and doesn't take it, he's a fool."

Carrie laughed and feigned a bow. "Thank you very much, Mr. Higgenbottom!"

"Laugh all you want, Carrie. You can bet Soaring Eagle knows how you feel. In St. Louis you practically screamed it at him every time you looked at him."

"Then why didn't he—"

"Carrie, no man worth anything would make promises to a girl like you without a plan for how he could support you. And Soaring Eagle isn't exactly your average college graduate out looking for a job. Give the gentleman some credit, Carrie. Give him some time. Give yourself some time. Go with Charity Bond and see what happens. You'll either come back more determined than ever, or—" Everett grinned mischievously, "you'll come to your senses and realize that life with somebody like Everett Higgenbottom looks suddenly very appealing."

"You seem very willing to be rid of me." Carrie pretended to be hurt.

Everett was serious. "Carrie, I want you to be happy. That's all. I think we could be happy—you and me. But not if you take me because you gave up on something you think is better. I don't want a wife who spends her days wishing she was somewhere else. I'm not handsome or glamorous, Carrie, but I'm not stupid, either. I'm going to make a good lawyer. You could do a lot worse than marrying me. I'll wait. I still have three years at the university ahead of me. I'm not going anywhere. And you'll be back in the fall." Everett scooted his chair back and said casually, "I told Myrtle I'd be her escort tonight. Oscar Wilde is lecturing at the Opera House. Want to come along?"

Carrie shook her head. "No, thanks, Everett; I'd better write Grandmother and Grandfather about this and see what Mrs. Hathaway says."

Lucy and Walter Jennings wrote Carrie expressing doubts about her traveling so far from Lincoln. Knowing about Lucy's and Walter's doubts, Augusta Hathaway hesitated to encourage Carrie. But when LisBeth and Jim Callaway rode in to Lincoln to present J.W. to every available audience, Carrie gained support for her plan.

Jim stopped at Joseph Freeman's livery to unhitch his team for the day. Joseph emerged from his little room at the back of the livery, moving slowly. In spite of his advancing age, however, his voice was youthful as he boomed, "Finally! Let me get a look at that boy! My, my." His face wreathed in smiles, Joseph grabbed J.W., holding him close. "Now, LisBeth, you just go on in to Augusta and tell her I'll have this here boy in in a bit. His papa and me are gonna show him around the livery. Can't get too early a start on knowin' horseflesh."

LisBeth laughed. "Spoil him as much as you want. Then his *daddy* can sit up with him all night!" Kissing Jim on the cheek, LisBeth made her way down the newly constructed sidewalk towards the Hathaway House. LisBeth entered by the kitchen door, happy to find Sarah Biddle, her sleeves rolled up, her thin arms handling an enormous lump of dough.

"Where's that boy?" Sarah wanted to know.

"In the livery getting his first lecture on horseflesh." LisBeth grinned and changed the subject. "What about it, Sarah, are you going to listen to Dr. Gilbert? Are you going to nursing school?"

Sarah shook her head. "I've Tom to get through school, LisBeth. Then I'll think on it. In the meantime," she said happily, "I'm helping Dr. Gilbert when there's a case that needs in-home care. In fact, I just got back from a week across town with a new mother—of twins!"

"It's good to see you smile, Sarah. You've found the remedy for grief long before I did when Mac passed on." LisBeth took off her bonnet and smoothed her hair. "Well, are you joining Aunt Augusta and me for tea?"

"As soon as this bread is ready for rising. Go on in. Tell Aunt Augusta I'll be there directly. She's in a tizzy, LisBeth. Maybe you can settle her."

"About what?"

"Let her tell you about it. I'll be interested to hear what you think."

LisBeth frowned slightly and headed through the kitchen, into the front lobby, and on to Augusta's apartment. The two women were barely seated before Augusta said with concern, "LisBeth, Charity Bond has written Carrie. The Dakota churches are having their annual conference in Yankton in a few weeks. Charity has asked Carrie to go along. There's some committee from Boston to visit, and according to Charity, it promises to be an excellent week with all the native pastors, missionaries, teachers, helpers—everyone who is involved in the Dakota mission. If things go as planned, after the conference Charity will be heading up to the Cheyenne River territory to help get the work started there. She's going with James and Martha Red Wing. Charity wants Carrie to go along and help with the new work. They would be gone for weeks."

LisBeth didn't hesitate. "It sounds like a wonderful opportunity for her."

Augusta nodded. "Perhaps. However, there is a bit of a problem. Carrie has written to her grandparents and they are very much against it."

"And you're caught in the middle."

"In a manner of speaking, I am." Sarah slipped in while Augusta explained. "The Jenningses are counting on me to tell Carrie I can't do without her here at the hotel. They want her to finish her education and—"

"Forget the notion of missionary work," LisBeth finished the sentence for Augusta. A few moments of silence ensued before LisBeth spoke up. "Aunt Augusta, do you remember the night Agnes Bond charged into the kitchen demanding that we talk Charity out of being a matron at Santee?"

Augusta nodded.

"Well, Aunt Augusta, you're in the same spot now." LisBeth poured herself a cup of tea. "You're being asked to talk someone out of something they want to do. Carrie

Brown has said she wanted to come back to Nebraska and work with the Indians since she was a little girl. She's the same age Charity Bond was when she determined to serve the Lord in Santee. She's the same age I was when I married Mac and headed out west as a military bride. I think it is time we all stopped worrying so much about protecting 'little Carrie Brown' and let her find her own way in life. She's not going alone. Charity will be there. It's only a church conference, Aunt Augusta. She'll be in the very environment she's longed to be part of. Soaring Eagle will be there. He'd never let anything happen to Carrie." When Augusta was silent, LisBeth stopped short.

"Is *that* the problem, then?"

Augusta Hathaway poured her tea and said carefully, "I've a responsibility to the Jenningses, LisBeth. I promised them I would be a proper guardian."

"You *are* a proper guardian, Aunt Augusta. Carrie's blossomed living here and going to the university. She's matured and learned, and no doubt had a great deal of fun in the process. It's time to let her try out her wings. This is the perfect opportunity for her to see what it's like to be part of the mission. Let her go, Aunt Augusta. The Jenningses need to come to terms with the fact that their 'little Carrie' is very nearly a grown woman with a very distinct will of her own."

LisBeth grinned. "If you're concerned about something, be concerned for Soaring Eagle. I can't imagine how he's going to handle Carrie when she's on his home ground. It was difficult enough when they were in St. Louis."

Augusta looked shocked. "Relax, Aunt Augusta," LisBeth waved her hand in the air and shook her head. "I shouldn't have said that. All I mean is, I think we should all stop trying to interfere. The Lord has His will for Carrie and Soaring Eagle. Mama would be horrified that we are even thinking of trying to manipulate things. I think we should support Carrie in this and pray that God will lead."

LisBeth turned abruptly to Sarah. "What about you, Sarah? What do you think?"

Sarah thought for a long time before answering. "I think, LisBeth, that each of us here knows that God's will usually leads us into some places we never expected. But He does it for our own good. And I agree with LisBeth. Carrie has said that she has a dream of working among the Indians." Sarah looked up and her cheeks colored a little. "That dream also includes someone we all know. Both of these people are people we feel deserve our trust. We have no right to try to decide what is best for these people or to try to determine what will happen. We must pray diligently for God's will for Carrie . . . and this other person."

Augusta sighed with relief and interjected, "And help Carrie pack?" When Sarah and LisBeth both nodded, Augusta clapped her hands. "Praise be. Just what I thought you'd both say. Now, would either of you care to volunteer to write the Jennings?"

CHAPTER 20

The beginning of strife is as when one letteth out water: therefore leave off contention, before it be meddled with.

Proverbs 17:14

The Annual Conference of the Dakota Mission will take place at Yankton Agency, Dakota Territory, June 13–18, 1884. Julia Woodward read the headline in the *Word Carrier* as the train bearing the Boston Committee traveled west. *Its object is to advance the cause of Christ by stimulating native workers and increasing their knowledge, piety, and efficiency. The schedule:*

Friday, 3 P.M.
Opening sermon by Rev. John Thundercloud
Presentation of topics
Organization of conference
Saturday, 10 A.M.
Subject: "Pastoral Support"
3 P.M.
Subject: "Pastoral Visitation"
Sabbath, 9 A.M.
Model Bible Class
Monday, 10 A.M.
Subject: "Vernacular Teaching"
3 P.M.
Subject: "Iapi Oaye"
Reports from the committees and general business

Closing sermon by pastoral intern Jeremiah King

The Dakota Women's Board will also meet during the conference. A separate schedule will be available after the opening sermon.

Julia's interest in the remainder of the *Word Carrier* faded when her eyes read the name of the speaker for the closing sermon. She looked at her brother and Reverend and Mrs. Johnson. They were involved in their own reading material. Only R. J. Painter looked up when Julia folded the paper and laid it in her lap.

"Do you mind, Miss Woodward," Painter asked, indicating the newspaper.

"Not in the least, Mr. Painter." Julia handed it to him.

R. J. Painter casually opened the *Word Carrier* and began to read the back page, wondering why the announcement of a missions conference would make Miss Julia Woodward's lovely face take on new color.

"Welcome to Santee, ladies and gentlemen." Dr. Alfred and Mrs. Mary Riggs stepped across the porch of their home towards the carriages that had borne the Visiting Committee from Boston and journalist R. J. Painter to Santee. "Mrs. Riggs has prepared refreshment for you. Please, come and sit down." The visitors stepped onto the porch, grateful for both the shade and the tall glasses of water Mary Riggs quickly brought outside.

As soon as the visitors had settled into the chairs Alfred and Mary had dragged out of their dining room earlier that day, R. J. Painter began asking questions. Dr. Riggs explained, "Mrs. Riggs and I arrived in '69. Along with

James and Martha Red Wing, we erected a log cabin and a school. God has blessed us."

Dr. Johnson nodded appreciatively. "You have created a village, Dr. Riggs."

"The larger building is, of course, the school. Dakota Home, over there," Dr. Riggs pointed towards the east, "is our residence hall for girls. Birds' Nest, just a few rods farther east, is for the younger girls. You can also see a new building just begun for smaller boys. We've added two wings to the school and a chapel and workshop. The smaller buildings are the print shop, blacksmith shop, and cobbler shop. We are trying to teach our students useful manual skills."

Dr. Johnson nodded while R. J. Painter furiously scribbled notes. He had hastily sketched out the compound and was trying to label buildings as Dr. Riggs continued. "Growth has been steady over the past few years. Less than five years ago we had perhaps eighty students. Now there are over one hundred. In recent months some students have had to be turned away. We simply don't have the resources to provide for them all."

"Perhaps the Boston Committee can help rectify that problem," George Woodward offered. "What are the most pressing needs?"

"Three advanced pupils have been sent away to school for further study. You have had the pleasure of meeting one of the best—Jeremiah King," Dr. Riggs replied. "I was able to find monetary assistance for Jeremiah and two classmates, but we have dreamed of establishing a scholarship fund. Jeremiah has gone on to the conference site with Pastor Thundercloud. You may want to discuss this more thoroughly with him later. He can certainly give you the students' perspective of what would be most helpful."

Mrs. Riggs smiled sweetly at her husband. "And now, gentlemen, with your permission, the ladies will retire to their quarters and prepare for supper." Just then, Charity and Carrie emerged from the Birds' Nest. Mrs. Riggs called them over. "And here is Miss Bond and her assistant. They'll be happy to escort you over to the Birds' Nest where you can unpack."

Once settled in their rooms, Julia and Mrs. Johnson joined Charity and Carrie in the parlor of the family quarters at the Birds' Nest. Julia spoke up. "Please, tell us about yourselves, ladies. How did you come to be involved in the work here?"

Charity, her hands never idle, picked a dress off the basket of mending that sat by her chair and began to sew on a button while she answered, telling of her own conversion and growing desire for a life of service. "Every issue of the *Word Carrier* broke my heart. They were begging for help, and God used it to call me. I came in fear and trembling and found the most rewarding life a woman can imagine."

Julia Woodward looked at Carrie. "And you, Miss—?"

"Brown. Carrie Brown." Carrie retrieved a blouse from the mending basket and fumbled to mend an angular tear in the back as she spoke. "I grew up here at Santee. My mother was a matron. We lived here at the Birds' Nest. Then mother became ill and we were forced to leave."

Julia set down her glass of lemonade and leaned forward. "Why, Miss Brown, I feel as if I know you already. Jeremiah King spoke of you, surely it was you, in Boston one evening. We were having dinner. He was obviously very fond of 'little Carrie Brown.' How lovely to meet the very child he spoke of."

Charity offered, "Miss Brown is to accompany us to the conference, Miss Woodward. Then, Lord willing, she and I will be accompanying James and Martha Red Wing and Mr. King and another missionary up to the Cheyenne River villages to begin a work there. Carrie and I hope to establish a day school for the children. And perhaps a women's sewing society and a night school for adults as the Lord leads."

Mrs. Johnson broke in. "Tell me, Miss Bond, how does the Women's Sewing Society function here?"

"Our weekly meeting involves a prayer meeting and then a couple of hours in handwork. We make dresses, bonnets, aprons. Friends from many places send us patchwork already basted, which we can complete. The women are very ambitious. They sell their work to our own people or to others when the opportunity arises. Last year we were able to help support the publication of the *Word Carrier*. This year the project will help send Jeremiah King to the Cheyenne River country."

After a few minutes, Mrs. Johnson finally stood up. "Well, Miss Bond, Miss Brown, you've been very helpful. I commend you both for your dedication. Now you must excuse us. We are dining with Dr. and Mrs. Riggs this evening, and we should be making our way over there to see if we can assist Mrs. Riggs."

"I'll be along in a moment, Mrs. Johnson, " Julia Woodward said. "I'd like just a few moments to walk about the school grounds. If you'd be so kind, Miss Brown?"

"So, Miss Brown, this is to be your first conference as well?"

"Since I've returned, yes. Mother and I always attended the conferences." Carrie's voice was enthusiastic. "You'll enjoy it, Miss Woodward. I know it's a long way from Boston, and we don't have the conveniences you're accustomed to, but Indians will come from miles around. Young people taking the vows of church fellowship, singing, preaching. There may even be a wedding. It's a wonderful time. I know that Charity has often said that just when she was most discouraged last year, she attended the conference. Well, you'll have to get her to describe it. But I know it helped her."

"Is the work farther to the west very difficult, Miss Brown?"

"This will be my first experience in a new work, Miss Woodward."

"You must be very excited."

"I once promised someone I would come back to Santee. I've waited all my life for this opportunity. I'm not finished with the university yet, but when Charity invited me to accompany her, it seemed a wonderful opportunity to see if I'm fit for the life of a missionary. I've really never considered doing anything else—"

Julia stepped up onto the porch of the Birds' Nest and leaned against a porch rail. "If this is an accurate portrayal of the life, Miss Brown, I remain amazed at the dedication of young women like you who give up everything to adopt it. I can't imagine living in such a barren environment."

Carrie became animated. "Oh, but it isn't barren, Miss Woodward. Not when you come to know it. It's beautiful here. Just not in the same way that Boston and St. Louis are beautiful. In the spring, when the prairie comes alive, it just bursts into color. The girls bring in armfuls of wildflowers. And the sky! Sometimes you feel like you could just step right up into heaven from the top of the next rise. You take a walk, and the world opens up until you're forced to realize your place in the universe."

Julia laughed. "Well, you certainly are a good promoter, Miss Brown. You almost have me wanting to settle here! Jeremiah used to talk the same way about the land. He made a person want to come and see."

Carrie's heart dropped at the sound of Julia Woodward's voice trilling over the name "Jeremiah." Had she worked that into the conversation purposely, or was it just natural for her to speak of him in such a familiar tone? What exactly had he told Julia Woodward about "little Carrie Brown"?

"Yes, he has a way of doing that, of making a person respect his homeland and want to see it for themselves."

Julia smiled brightly. "I guess we'll both get the opportunity to do that in just a few days, won't we, Miss Brown? And just think, Jeremiah will be there to remind us of the beauty and the history behind everything we see."

CHAPTER 21

The sacrifices of God are a broken
spirit: a broken and a contrite heart,
O God, thou wilt not despise.

Psalm 51:17

Over one hundred people crowded into the little log church in Yankton, South Dakota, for the opening meeting of the 1884 Dakota Missions Conference. Only three of the congregation were aware of an undercurrent of emotion. Only one was miserable. Carrie Brown saw Julia Woodward arrive dressed in a stunning plaid silk gown with matching parasol. She saw Julia make her way down the center aisle of the church to the pew that had been designated for the Visiting Committee from Boston. Julia was on her brother George's arm.

Carrie watched as the Committee was introduced to the visiting missionaries and pastors. The reaction of one pastoral intern was all that mattered to Carrie. When Soaring Eagle caught sight of Julia Woodward, he bowed and shook her hand solemnly. But Carrie saw the light in his eyes and the faint curve of his mouth as he smiled.

She sunk into a back pew next to Charity Bond, watching as Julia stood by her brother, privy to the conversations of the pastors and the Committee. Suddenly Carrie realized that Julia would be at every meeting, every dinner, every event where Carrie could have had an opportunity to see and speak with Soaring Eagle.

Carrie watched as Julia nodded at something Dr. Riggs

had said. When she moved, the feathers on her stylish bonnet bobbed up and down. Julia leaned towards her brother to say something and then smiled happily at Soaring Eagle. Looking down at her plain blue calico dress Carrie noticed the dust that had collected around the hem and the dirt under her fingernails. She pushed at the red curls that had escaped from her prim hairdo to tickle her forehead.

Opening her Dakota hymnal, Carrie pretended to search through it. Her head stayed bowed, but her eyes looked up frequently, searching Soaring Eagle's face for his reaction to Miss Julia Woodward. The Committee was being seated. Julia Woodward scooted into a pew on the left, her brother George at her side. Soaring Eagle slid in from the opposite end of the pew to sit next to her. As they settled into their places, Julia glanced at Soaring Eagle. He returned the glance with a smile that made Carrie close her eyes and fight back tears. *I've never seen that smile.*

The meeting began with hymn singing. Julia Woodward shared her hymnal with Soaring Eagle. Soaring Eagle rose to introduce the Visiting Committee from Boston, taking the opportunity to thank the Reverend and Mrs. Johnson, and Mr. George Woodward and his sister Julia for their kind hospitality while he studied at Harvard. Pastor Thundercloud gave the conference schedule, reading the discussion topics, one of which was to be "The Marriage Covenant." He also announced that the Woodwards of Boston had offered to purchase New Testaments to be given to students at all mission schools who would commit to memory the first part of Christ's Sermon on the Mount. He introduced Jeremiah Soaring Eagle King as a pastoral intern who, along with David Gray Cloud, would be beginning a new work on the Cheyenne River.

"Miss Charity Bond and Miss Carrie Brown . . ." Charity nudged Carrie and pulled her by the arm. Pastor Thundercloud was introducing them as assistants to the Red

Wings who would be helping to establish a school in the new territory. "Miss Bond is well known to us for her work as a matron at Santee. Miss Brown has come to assist us for a short term before returning to Lincoln, Nebraska, where she will complete preparation for teaching."

As Pastor Thundercloud spoke, Carrie stole a glance at Soaring Eagle. He was whispering something to Julia Woodward. When he finally glanced at Carrie, he nodded at her briefly and then said something else to Julia. The exchange made Carrie even more miserable. Pastor Thundercloud's sermon was titled "The Call to Reach the Sioux Nation." The message stirred the hearts of those who listened, but Carrie Brown's heart was unaffected by the message as she sat in her pew fighting back tears, believing her heart was breaking.

Hundreds of Indians joined the conference as the week went on, riding in from as far away as 250 miles. Prayers and singing, preaching in the native tongue, women's meetings, discussions, and fellowship absorbed every participant. What should have been an uplifting time of revival among every attendee served to make Carrie feel more lonely, more alienated, and more depressed. After the first day, when Soaring Eagle said hello briefly, she avoided him, knowing that he was almost always in the company of the Visiting Committee from Boston.

Charity attributed Carrie's unusual quiet to her being overwhelmed by so many new faces and her struggle to remember the Dakota language. "It's been years since you've spoken Dakota. Just be patient, it will come back. Why, in only a few days I've seen vast improvement."

Carrie shrugged her shoulders and sighed. *"Jesus wastemada weksuya ye.* That's the only thing I remember for certain, Charity. Mother and I sang that song every morning. But all the other phrases and the grammar, they are buried awfully deep in this thick head of mine. I don't know if I'll ever get the words back."

They were sitting in their tent after an evening meeting. Charity was perched on her cot, brushing her hair. She began to sing the song softly, *"Jesus wastemada hee waste, Jesus waste, Piwecida ye."* She stopped abruptly. "Do you believe those words, Carrie?"

Carrie was unlacing her shoes when Charity asked the question. She pulled off one shoe and began to massage her foot. "Do I believe what, Charity?"

"That Jesus loves you. That He is good."

"What an odd question, Charity. Haven't I been taught that since I was a baby? Of course I know Jesus loves me. Of course I believe it. Why do you ask?"

Charity shot a prayer heavenward before answering. Then, she said slowly, "Well, Carrie, this week is usually quite an encouragement to those of us who work at the various stations. Especially seeing the native pastors and how they've grown. Take Pastor Yellow Hawk, for example. I remember when he gave his first message." Charity chuckled. "It was the most awful thing anyone has ever suffered through. Even now, his speech doesn't flow as smoothly as some. But it's apparent that he's very gifted in getting at the meaning of passages of Scripture. Pastor Riggs says it is because he is such a good Bible student. What I find most encouraging, though, is something his wife, Priscilla, said the other evening at a women's prayer meeting. She said that his life is conformed to what he teaches. He preaches nothing that he doesn't practice. Isn't that a wonderful thing for a wife to be able to say about her husband? It is such a blessing to learn how God is working in lives.

"Think of it, Carrie. Nearly 300 of these once wild people have sat down with us at the table of our Lord. And

He is their Lord, as well." Charity's voice was warm with emotion. "Last evening as I sat there looking about and listening to Pastor Yellow Hawk, I not only prayed 'Thy kingdom come,' but I added from the depths of my heart 'Hallelujah, it *is* coming. It has begun!' And to think, Carrie, that I am in some small way involved in the bringing of the kingdom to these people." Charity stopped abruptly, too filled with emotion to continue. After a moment, she moved to sit by Carrie and take her hand.

"But what about you, Carrie? You've been so quiet the entire week. You seem depressed. I thought there might be a spiritual reason." With a deep breath, Charity continued, "Carrie, I know you were raised to believe all these things you are hearing this week. But sometimes I wonder, do you believe it because it's part of your soul? Or do you believe it because you were raised to believe it? Do you know Christ in a personal way, Carrie? Can you really sing that little song knowing that He loves *you*. Is He real to you? Do you pray to Him, knowing He will answer? Are you seeking *His* will for your life?"

Tears ran down Carrie's cheek and dripped onto Charity's hand. Putting her arms around Carrie, Charity asked softly, "What *is* it, Carrie? Won't you tell me? I know something's wrong."

Carrie sobbed her way through her disappointment and heartache. "I thought that I was doing the right thing, Charity. Coming to see what missionary life is like, trying to prepare myself, trying to understand what the future would hold if—" Carrie pushed away from Charity and brushed away her tears. "Oh, it doesn't matter, anyway. It's not going to be that way, so I'd better just get over it." She leaned her head on Charity's shoulder, murmuring, "Everett was right. Again." With a little laugh she said bitterly, "I hate it when he's right. But, at least he doesn't gloat. When I get back home he'll say just the right things to make me feel better."

"Carrie, you haven't answered my question. About Christ. Your relationship with Him," Charity said gently.

Carrie sat up and answered without hesitation, "If you want to know if I'm a Christian, the answer is yes, Charity. I honestly do believe. But, I admit, I haven't spent much time thinking about what God wants me to do with my life." Carrie paused. "Funny, isn't it? I was raised by a missionary. Grandmother and Grandfather are active in evangelism. I've spent my whole life thinking I would be a missionary, too. I guess I have to face the fact that it's not going to happen."

Carrie looked at Charity, her blue eyes shining. "Soaring Eagle has been such a, such a *presence* in my life, Charity. He was my absolute hero when I was a child. What little girl wouldn't be in awe of a wild Sioux Indian who cares to be her friend. Pretty romantic stuff, isn't it." Carrie thought for a moment before continuing. "I've just always thought he would *be* there when I was ready. As I grew up, I made myself believe that I loved him. I couldn't imagine anyone else could love him as much as I—" Tears threatened, but Carrie swallowed hard and continued. "I didn't pray for God's will. I never considered His will could possibly be different from mine." Carrie bowed her head and whispered. "I've been a fool, Charity. All the time I've resented people calling me 'little Carrie Brown,' and that's exactly how I've behaved. Like a child who always gets her way. Soaring Eagle has never done one thing to indicate that he thinks of me in any other way than as his friend." Carrie looked at Charity soberly. "There, I've said it. I always knew it, but I never let myself think about it." She began to cry again. "This hurts, Charity. It really, really hurts."

Charity reached for her Bible, asking gently, "Carrie, may I share some verses that have really meant a lot to me?" When Carrie nodded, Charity opened to the book of Job and read,

> *"Behold, happy is the man whom God correcteth: therefore despise not thou the chastening of the Almighty: For he maketh sore, and bindeth up: he woundeth, and his hands make whole.*
>
> *Job 5:17–18*

"Carrie, I don't know anything about Miss Julia Woodward and Soaring Eagle except that she's beautiful and he does seem to like her. But I do know that God seems to be using Miss Woodward's presence here at the conference to speak to you. Perhaps you needed to be forced to contemplate something besides *your* plans, so that you could see *God's* plans for you." Charity patted Carrie's hand. "I've been where you are, Carrie. I know how it hurts."

When Carrie looked up at Charity, surprised, Charity smiled. "Did you think I came to Santee because I didn't have anywhere else to go, Carrie?" Charity looked away for a moment. "Well, Dear, that's not the way it was." She looked back at Carrie. "But God had called me to Santee, Carrie. I couldn't go anywhere else but where God had called. I would have been miserable. Carrie, if you belong to God, then you, too, will be miserable if you go anywhere but exactly where *He* wants you to be. You can't build your own dream, Carrie. God just doesn't allow it for His children. He knows what is best for you. Even when He tears something from our hands that we love, it is for our good."

Charity turned to another passage in her Bible and read aloud,

> *"Trust in the Lord, and do good; so shalt thou dwell in the land, and verily thou shalt be fed. Delight thyself also in the Lord; and he shall give thee the desires of thine heart. Commit thy way unto the Lord; trust also in him; and he shall bring it to pass. And he shall bring forth thy righteousness as the light, and thy judgment as the noonday."*
>
> *Psalm 37:3–6*

"Carrie, I've learned that these verses don't mean that if we do everything just right, God will give us what we want. They mean that if we concentrate on trusting the Lord and doing good, then He will shape our desires so that they are His will, which He can graciously bestow. *Bringing forth righteousness*, that's the result He wants. It's the result we should want."

Trust in the Lord, do good, dwell in the land, feed on His faithfulness. Delight in the Lord. Commit my way to the Lord. Trust in Him. As Carrie pondered the words her heart broke. *Lord, I've never really trusted in You. I thought I had to make things happen for myself. I've only wanted to do the kind of good that would bring me near Soaring Eagle. I've never really fed on your faithfulness or delighted in You, and I've never committed my way to You. I had my own way and my own plans. Lord, I don't know if I can trust You. I haven't done very much of it. Help me, Lord, to give it up. All of it. Help me to trust You. Show me where You want me to go to do good. Help me to dwell where You want me. Show me that You are faithful. Help me to delight in You, Lord, not in Soaring Eagle. I don't know if I can do it, Lord, but I want to try.*

That night, Carrie Brown slept the sleep of the emotionally exhausted. When the sun rose and she dressed for the final day of the Dakota Mission Conference, she was amazed to realize that her depression had lifted. She did her best to concentrate on doing good throughout the day, helping with meal preparation and organizing a game for the children. She forced herself not to look for Soaring Eagle and not to inspect Julia Woodward's wardrobe.

At the closing meeting, when Jeremiah Soaring Eagle King rose and left Julia Woodward's side to give his address, Charity reached for Carrie's hand. Soaring Eagle had chosen for his text a passage in 1 Samuel that read,

And turn ye not aside: for then should ye go after vain things, which cannot profit or deliver; for they are vain. . . . Only fear the LORD, and serve him in truth with all your heart: for consider how great things he hath done for you.

1 Samuel 12:21, 24

When he concluded his message and went back to sit by Julia Woodward, Carrie realized with a burst of emotion that God had done something amazing in her life. He had opened her heart and taken Soaring Eagle out. But He had filled the space with Himself, and joy—joy that filled her and flowed out in a burst of tears as she sang the closing congregational hymn.

Jesus wastemada—hee waste (Jesus loves me—that is good)
Jesus waste—piwecida ye. (Jesus is good—I thank Him)
Miye awektonja nuni waun (I forget Him—wander)
Iye tehiya amakita ce (He with difficulty searches for me)
Heca nakaes owakida kta (So indeed I Him will seek)
Jesus wastemade weksuya ya. (Jesus loves me I remember)

CHAPTER 22

Cast thy burden upon the LORD,
and he shall sustain thee.

Psalm 55:22

An early summer breeze swept down the valley of the Cheyenne River, causing the prairie grass to dip and sway in a rhythmic dance. Seated next to David Gray Cloud in an overfull wagon, Carrie Brown pushed her bonnet back away from her face. Lifting her chin, she closed her eyes and inhaled deeply. She gripped the edge of the wagon seat, trying to move with the rhythm of the jolting wagon. Up ahead, Martha Red Wing and Charity Bond walked alongside the Red Wings' wagon. Mounted on a spotted pony, Soaring Eagle rode far ahead of the two wagons.

"I think our friend Soaring Eagle would have these wagons fly, if he could find a way," David said.

"How many more days until we reach the trapper's cabin?" Carrie asked.

"From what Pastor Thundercloud told us, I'd guess we'll be there late tomorrow."

Up ahead, Soaring Eagle turned his pony around and cantered back towards the two wagons. Carrie fought the urge to call out to him, but he still pulled his pony alongside her wagon. "We call this the 'Good River,' Red Bird. To the south is *Shicha Wakpa*, 'Bad River,' overflowing with fresh water in the spring, but almost dry in summer. These plains," he gestured toward the south, "are green now, but soon they will become dry and brown. Then, later, the fires come to light the night sky. The prairie turns black, but out of the ashes comes new life."

Soaring Eagle paused and David Gray Cloud teased him, "Are you practicing the introduction to your first sermon among the Lakota? David clucked to his team and when they lurched ahead he grinned. "'New Life from Ashes.' I like it, my friend. And I think our Lakota friends will listen."

Soaring Eagle flashed a smile. "I pray that you are right, David." He rode along in silence for a few moments, and all the while Carrie prayed, *Dear Lord, the closer we get to the Cheyenne, the more he smiles and the younger he seems. Oh, Lord, he is beautiful, but he is not mine. Help me, Lord, to concentrate on serving You.* Carrie pulled her bonnet back in place and turned her head so that the brim hid Soaring Eagle from view. *Perhaps I shouldn't have come after all.*

The travelers stopped at noon. James Red Wing offered, "From what Pastor Thundercloud said, I believe we can reach the trapper's cabin by early tomorrow evening."

"Just what I told Miss Brown earlier," David agreed.

The group hurried through their meager meal and rested the teams less than an hour before starting out again. The Red Wings took the lead in their wagon, followed by Soaring Eagle and Charity Bond. David Gray Cloud rode the spotted pony, staying alongside the wagon and chatting with Charity.

Carrie walked alongside the Red Wings' wagon for most of the afternoon. Towards evening, Soaring Eagle called out to her. "Red Bird, would you like to ride to the top of the next hill with me? We can look for a place to camp."

The moment he spoke, David Gray Cloud jumped down from the pony and handed the reins to Carrie, climbing up beside Charity almost before Soaring Eagle had had a chance to vacate the wagon seat. Before Carrie could say anything, Soaring Eagle had lifted her onto the pony's back and jumped up behind her. With Carrie clutching at the pony's mane, the two rode up the next hill.

Soaring Eagle said, "White men wonder how we can live on these high, windy plains, Red Bird." As he talked, Carrie closed her eyes. *Peace, that's what it is. I hear a newfound peace in his voice. And joy, such joy.*

Carrie opened her eyes and looked over the vast prairie.

"Red Bird?" Soaring Eagle's voice brought her back to the present.

Carrie leaned forward, trying not to feel his closeness. She cleared her throat. "I was just thinking, Soaring Eagle, no matter what I write home to St. Louis, Grandmother and Grandfather will never know the feeling of this place. Unless you stood on this hill and looked at the miles and miles of grass stretching away as far as you can see." They had reached the top of a gradual rise, and Soaring Eagle jumped down and stood beside the pony. Carrie said softly, "It's barren and wild, and vast, and endlessly *endless*, but so very beautiful."

Watching Carrie's blue eyes gaze over the miles of horizon, Soaring Eagle knew that she meant what she said. He placed one hand on the saddlehorn and said quietly, "This was my home, Red Bird. What you see here and over the next rise, and the next, and the next. It is a hard country, where a man must be fully alive to avoid perishing." His voice tense with emotion, Soaring Eagle looked up at her and said, "And I have never felt more fully alive than I do at this moment."

True to James Red Wing and David Gray Cloud's expectations, the wagons trundled up to a dilapidated two-room cabin early the next evening. The trapper's cabin had been erected on a small rise that overlooked the fork of Cherry Creek and the Cheyenne River.

After only a brief look at the interior of the cabin, James directed a large tent to be pitched for the women. "The men will sleep by the campfire tonight. Tomorrow we'll get to work rechinking the logs." Turning to his wife, James smiled. "It's a good cabin, Martha. Two rooms and," he added, turning to Charity and Carrie, "a loft for the girls."

Rechinking and cleaning the cabin took only a few days. Soon the men were selecting timber for another cabin to be constructed just north of the trapper's cabin on Cherry Creek. When the first tree had been felled, the missionaries gathered around the site of the new school to pray God's blessing on Hope Station, the name Dr. Riggs had suggested for the new work. Six voices joined in song,

> *"Jesus Christ nitowashte kin*
> *Woptecashni mayaqu—*
> *Jesus Christ, The loving kindness*
> *Boundlessly Thou givest me."*

When a lone rider was spotted in the distance, Soaring Eagle walked out to meet him. The young brave made the sign of peace before commenting, "No white man has been there for a long time."

Soaring Eagle nodded. "We are teachers of the religion of Jesus. John Thundercloud was among your people in the month when the Deer Shed Their Antlers. He told us that you wished for someone to come and stay among you. We have come."

"I am Walking Thunder," the young man said. "I know this John Thundercloud. The people will be glad that you have come." He turned and rode away, but the next day he was back with several more braves. They sat on their ponies and watched while David and James and Soaring Eagle cut timber and built the new cabin.

"This will be a school for teaching," James explained, "and a place where you can come to learn of Jesus."

Walking Thunder called out, "Will the one with the hair like the setting sun be teaching? If she teaches, then I will come."

The day the school building was finished, Soaring Eagle and David Gray Cloud rode up the Cheyenne River to begin visiting in the villages. Carrie sighed with relief. *Now I can concentrate on the work here.* But without Soaring Eagle to *watch*, Carrie found there was Soaring Eagle to *ponder*. She turned her thoughts of Soaring Eagle into prayers for his work in the village. Paul's admonition to "pray without ceasing" took on new meaning.

David and Soaring Eagle were gone for days at a time, seeking those who had responded to John Thundercloud, encouraging all to attend the school. Wherever they were welcomed Soaring Eagle gave the same message: "Jesus was the Helper Man—the Son of God. He came to earth and died that man might once again belong to God. He made Himself alive again, and although men have destroyed themselves before God by their evil deeds, whoever knows the meaning of the name of Jesus, and fears for his own soul and prays, he shall find mercy and be brought near to God. Jesus the Helper Man saves all men, and He will save you."

The two young missionaries spent countless hours crouched around campfires. They talked of their time among the whites. They told the stories of their own conversions to Christ. They shook their heads in dismay at the mistreatment of their own people but stood firm in the gospel, insisting that the religion they had learned from the whites was true and the only way to freedom.

James Red Wing stayed with the women, preparing to

open the school and conducting intensive instruction in Lakota for Carrie and Charity. Lakota began venturing downriver to peer into the cabin and the school, to meet the newcomers, to ask questions. When the school finally met for its first session, the missionaries were thrilled to welcome a dozen students.

Carrie and Charity took the girls aside and began to teach sewing skills. While the girls eagerly accepted lessons in how to care for the clothing they had been issued at the agency, they howled with laughter when Carrie and Charity tried to speak Lakota. But only a few weeks had gone by before some measure of conversation could be held. Then the women began teaching music. Lakota translations of hymns had been prepared in advance. The girls found the cadence of the hymns attractive, and while they did not initially understand the impact of the words, it was not long before their voices were raised together singing,

> *Jehowa Mayooha, nimayakiye,*
> *Notowashita iwadowan.*
> *Jehovah, My Master, Thou hast saved me,*
> *I sing of Thy Goodness.*

The day after Carrie took over an English lesson for James, Walking Thunder appeared, sliding onto a bench at the back of the room. He had painted his face and sewed bells all the way up the sides of his leggings. Long plaits of sweet grass were looped up over one shoulder and across his body. He sat in rapt attention while Carrie tried to hide her amusement as he attempted to wipe the perspiration from his face without smearing his paint. When she introduced herself, Walking Thunder spoke out.

"My friend Soaring Eagle says that you are called Red Bird."

Carrie felt herself blushing. Clearing her throat she

answered, "Yes, I have been called by that name." Looking about the class she said softly, "You may all call me that name if you wish." And so "little Carrie Brown" became Red Bird to the people of the Cheyenne River country.

"I never should have come." Carrie lay on her grass-filled mattress in the loft of the Red Wings' cabin and spoke into the dark.

"What on earth do you mean, Carrie?" Charity asked.

"Just what I said, Charity. I never should have come."

"But, why?"

Carrie swallowed hard and whispered, "Because I've failed, Charity."

Charity sat up abruptly and peered through the dark at Carrie. "Nonsense, Carrie. You're much more fluent in Lakota than I. The children love you. Martha says she doesn't know what she'd have done without you—us." Charity lay back down, propping herself up on one elbow. "We haven't had any converts yet, but it's too soon, Carrie. You haven't failed. You've been a great help in starting a very promising work."

When Carrie was silent, Charity lay back down. She was nearly asleep again when Carrie said in a half-whisper, "But, Charity, it doesn't matter one bit how much I pray and how determined I am to grow out of it."

"Soaring Eagle." Charity interrupted her.

Carrie sighed. "Yes, Soaring Eagle. I *know* he means only friendship between us. I *know* he has plans with Miss Woodward. But—"

"He's admirable," Charity offered.

After a silence between them, Charity asked, "Carrie, what do you think of the mission work?"

Carrie didn't hesitate. "I love it. I love the children and

the challenge. I love the prairie, the wildness, the wind, I love it all. I can honestly say I know what Soaring Eagle meant when he said he never felt more alive than when he is here."

"He said that when he was looking at *you*, Miss Brown."

"He said it about being back here, where he grew up."

Charity didn't argue, but asked abruptly, "So what are you going to do?"

"I'm going back to Lincoln, where I belong, for now. I'm going to finish my studies. I'm going to wait for Soaring Eagle to marry Miss Julia Woodward. I'm going to pray for God to send me somewhere where I can be of use among the Lakota. And," she added miserably, "I'm going to make certain it's where I will *not* have to witness the wedded bliss of Mrs. Julia King." Unexpectedly, tears began to flow.

Charity heard Carrie stifle a sob and reached across to lay a hand on her shoulder. "'Delight thyself also in the LORD,' Carrie Brown, 'and He shall give thee the desires of thine heart.'"

Carrie muttered, "I used to think that meant I got what I wanted if I was an obedient girl. Now I know it means that when I put the Lord first, He changes my desires to match His." Stifling another sob she added forlornly, "I'm trying to delight in the Lord, Charity. So when will He change my desires about Soaring Eagle? When?"

Charity patted her on the shoulder. "When you get back to Lincoln it will be easier. You'll see." After a few more moments of silence, Charity offered, "They'll be gone most of the time over the next few days, Carrie. When they are in camp it shouldn't be too hard to avoid them. Offer to do most of the cooking, or to teach some extra lessons. Then you'll have a reason to be busy elsewhere. That's the only thing I know that might help."

In the darkness, Carrie Brown nodded wordlessly. She determined to follow Charity's suggestions to avoid Soaring

Eagle, to work harder than ever, to pray more diligently that her desires would match the Lord's—and to leave for Lincoln at the first opportunity.

"Red Bird, have I done something to anger you?"

Carrie jumped as Soaring Eagle's familiar voice sounded from the door of the little cabin. School had ended for the day, and when the children bounded out into the sunshine, Carrie had busied herself planning the next day's lesson. She looked up from her desk and answered carefully, "Of course not, Soaring Eagle. Why do you ask?"

"You have been here with Charity Bond for weeks. I know the work has been hard. David Gray Cloud and I have spent many hours in the camps. Still, it seems that when I come near—" he paused and then smiled at her. "Well, it seems that my little Red Bird flies away whenever I come into the camp."

"I'm sorry, Soaring Eagle. I didn't realize it." Carrie looked away briefly before adding, "You've done nothing to anger me, Soaring Eagle. It's been a very busy time, that's all. You have your work, and I have mine, with the children."

Soaring Eagle looked about the room. "You have no work now. Please, come outside. I want to talk with you."

Together they walked out of the schoolhouse and to a rustic log bench by the campfire where Martha Red Wing had been doing most of the group's cooking.

"You do your work well, Red Bird." He laughed softly. "I watched at recess one day. At times it was difficult to tell who was the teacher and who was a student." He folded his arms and leaned back to inspect Carrie. "I heard the children talking in camp one day. They love you."

Carrie laughed back at him. "The first day of school,

when I looked *up* at a few of those boys I was terrified. But they all seem to want to learn so much. It's been very easy to love them." Carrie sighed. "I'm going to miss them when I leave."

Soaring Eagle frowned. "Is it so soon?"

"Next week. James has to go back for supplies for the winter. I'll ride along."

"I thought that—" Soaring Eagle changed in midsentence. "It seemed that you were happy working here."

Carrie sighed. "Yes, I *am* happy here. But Charity and I have prayed about it, and I really think that God wants me to go back to the university for more schooling, more practical teaching. I'm still so inexperienced. I'll finish at the university. Then—" She paused. "Well, then I shall have to pray for God's guidance once again."

"There was a time when you spoke only of returning to Santee."

"There was a time when I was a very headstrong and foolish little girl who knew very little about living in God's will."

"The little girl is gone."

Carrie looked at him sharply. "Yes. I think so. And good riddance."

"When did this happen, Red Bird?"

"At the Dakota Missions Conference."

Soaring Eagle nodded. "That was a good time. Good fellowship. Good meetings."

Carrie laughed. "I didn't pay much attention to the meetings."

At his look of surprise, Carrie ducked her head. She formulated her next words carefully. "Soaring Eagle, I know you have had the experience of having the dearest things in your life ripped away from you, and then had them replaced with something far greater." Carrie lowered her voice. "That happened to me at the missions conference."

She looked back at him soberly. "It was very, very painful. But necessary."

"And whatever that was, that means that our friendship has changed."

Carrie laughed. "Don't you think it was about time for that to happen? You must have wearied long before that of the foolish little redhead who fluttered around you constantly." Carrie's cheeks reddened.

"I never wearied of it," Soaring Eagle said quietly.

"Well, Miss Woodward certainly must have."

At the mention of Julia Woodward, Soaring Eagle frowned. "Miss Woodward?"

"I know you haven't made an announcement yet, Soaring Eagle, but you said yourself that we are friends." Carrie cleared her throat. "I wish you well, Soaring Eagle. I hope you are very happy."

Soaring Eagle was truly amazed. "What are you talking about?"

"You and Miss Julia Woodward. It was apparent at the missions conference that you two think highly of one another. I just assumed—"

"So *that* is what you have been thinking. *That* is what has changed between us." Soaring Eagle shook his head and leaned forward, his elbows on his knees. With one hand he picked up a stick and began to scribble in the dirt. After a moment he tossed the stick aside and said, "Miss Julia Woodward returned to Boston with the Visiting Committee where I am certain she will continue to do very good work on behalf of the Indian. But Red Bird, think about it, Miss Julia Woodward in a *cabin* on the *prairie*." Soaring Eagle chuckled. "No, Red Bird, I am not to marry Miss Julia Woodward." He stood up abruptly.

Martha Red Wing came out of her cabin, wrestling a huge iron pot towards the campfire. Soaring Eagle hurried to help her while Carrie went inside the cabin and brought out a crock full of green beans. She sat on the bench and began to snap beans as Soaring Eagle set to work lighting a fire.

"This thing that you were forced to give up at the missions conference, Red Bird."

"Please, Soaring Eagle, don't embarrass me by talking about it."

Smoke began to curl from the chips of wood and Soaring Eagle moved quickly to encourage the flames. "Why should you be embarrassed by caring for someone? It was your caring for me that brought me to Christ, Red Bird."

"And resulted in my behaving like a fool."

"And you now believe that the dream to marry a much older man who wants to live among the wild Sioux is a foolish dream?"

"I realize that creating my own future without consulting God is folly. It has nothing to do with the age of the man or the life God has given him."

Soaring Eagle backed away from the fire and sat down next to Carrie. "Red Bird," he began, then stopped. "Let me tell you a story. One day I was in the village and Walking Thunder rode by. He had wrapped himself in plaited sweet grass and painted his face in a most amazing way. When I called to him, he said that he was on his way to school. I thought it an odd way for a boy to dress for school, and when I asked him if there was to be a celebration, he did not want to say anything. But then his friend spoke up and said that Walking Thunder had decided to woo the teacher. Walking Thunder was very angry when this was said, but then he looked at me and admitted that it was true. He said that he had decided that the best way to make a way in the new world was to take a white wife, and he had decided that the teacher would be a suitable candidate."

Carrie had stopped snapping beans and was listening

with honest amazement at the story. When Soaring Eagle paused, she spoke up. "I never, I never encouraged. What should I do?"

"You need do nothing, Red Bird. His attentions have turned to another girl in the village."

"Then why are you telling me this story?"

"Walking Thunder is a fine young man. He will make a good husband some day. He has a kind heart. But when he told me he was coming to court the teacher with the hair like the setting sun—" Soaring Eagle paused before continuing. "I didn't like it."

Carrie finished snapping beans before saying quietly, "And what does that mean, Soaring Eagle?"

"It means, Red Bird, that I saw you through the eyes of a young man who didn't know anything about 'little Carrie Brown.' He saw you as a young woman." He cleared his throat. "And when I thought of you in that way, then I really didn't like the idea of someone else courting you."

Carrie pondered the comment before saying, "Everett Higgenbottom never bothered you."

Soaring Eagle snorted. "Everett Higgenbottom is not for you, Red Bird."

"Yes," Carrie said quietly. "I know that. I'm going to tell him that once and for all when I get back to Lincoln." Carrie stood up, the crock full of prepared beans in her arms. "If I don't see you again before I leave, Soaring Eagle, please know that I'll be praying for you and the work here. You pray for me, too, won't you? That I'll have the strength to follow God wherever He leads me." She headed for the cabin, but he called her name.

"Red Bird."

When Carrie turned around, she saw Soaring Eagle standing in the middle of the path that led to his camp. He signed "friend." She returned the sign and hurried inside.

CHAPTER 23

The words of a wise man's mouth
are gracious; but the lips of a fool
will swallow up himself.

Ecclesiastes 10:12

So, Everett, you've been right—about everything. You were right when you said that I did-
n't have any understanding at all of Soaring Eagle. I saw
him as some hero I had created in my mind. When I saw
him as a man, I still loved and respected him. But then
came the second realization, that I didn't have a realistic
view of missionary work." Carrie paused to stir her coffee
before continuing. "But all that was masking the real problem, Everett. I didn't have a right relationship with God. I
knew all the right answers to every question, but I hadn't
really given my life to God."

Carrie had asked Everett to come to dinner the first
evening after her return from the Cheyenne River. She had
spent the entire meal asking Everett about school, telling
him about her experiences, and generally avoiding the
most important things she had to say. They had both finished dessert and were drinking coffee before Carrie had
the courage to launch the thing she really wanted to talk
about.

"And all that has changed?" Everett wanted to know.

Carrie traced the top of her coffee mug with one finger
as she thought about her next words. "It has. Oh, I don't
mean I have the 'meaning of life' figured out, Everett. But

I do know one thing. I had to give up my own plans and be willing to do what God wanted. Right now I feel certain He wants me finishing school. After that, I don't know. I did love teaching the Indian children. I won't pretend I didn't. I still think I'd like to serve somewhere in the Dakota Mission. But that's in the future, not now. For now, I'm content to be a student."

"What about Soaring Eagle?"

"I think he'll stay on the Cheyenne River for some time to come. The work suits him. He's a gifted evangelist, and the Lord is using him." Carrie looked up at Everett. "Before I left, we had a good talk about my foolishness and his forgiving it. I think we can still be friends. I'd like it to be more, but I don't know if it's ever going to be. He definitely thinks he's too old for me. He also has a reluctance to ask a woman to share his life because he's chosen a life that will undoubtedly mean poverty and hardship. I'm content to leave all that with God for now. But I didn't ask you here to talk about Soaring Eagle, Everett."

"Good, Carrie, because we have to talk about you and me." Everett leaned forward across the table. "Carrie, I know that I've been something of a nuisance, chasing you halfway across the country."

"You have *not* been a nuisance, Everett. Actually, you've been a great friend, even when I've treated you poorly. But, Everett—"

"Yeah, I know, Carrie. I've been a friend, and that's all." Everett cleared his throat. "Well, Carrie, I'm glad you asked me to dinner, because I have something to say about that." After a brief pause, Everett looked up and grinned. "I proposed to Myrtle Greer while you were gone, Carrie. We're getting married as soon as I graduate."

Carrie was stunned. "Myrtle Greer!"

Everett just sat grinning and nodding, giving Carrie time to absorb the news before he said, "She's a terrific girl, Carrie. I hope you can be happy for us. I know you never really cared about me that way. So I figured this wouldn't be too much of a shock for you, but I wanted to tell you myself before anyone else did."

Carrie sat back in her chair and contemplated the prospect of Everett and Myrtle Higgenbottom. After the shock subsided, she held out her hand to Everett. "Everett, I couldn't be happier for you. Myrtle is a terrific girl, and she deserves a better life than she has had to date. I hope you'll be very happy."

"Thanks, Carrie. I knew you'd feel that way."

"I'll miss you, Everett. You always gave me very good advice."

"Which you rarely took, Miss Brown."

"Well, I'm older and wiser now, Everett. I have taken all of your advice from the past few years all in one giant dose. I believe I am healed of the illness, Dr. Higgenbottom. Selfishness and strongheadedness. Is that a word? And lots of other things. I'm trying hard to overcome them all."

Everett stood up to go. "You've started well, Carrie. I wish you the very best. And now, I have to excuse myself. I'm taking Myrtle to the Opera House this evening to celebrate our engagement. Myrtle will be relieved to hear that you're happy for us."

Carrie didn't hesitate to reply. "Indeed I am. Please tell Myrtle that for me. I only reserve the right to one thing, Everett. When you're a famous lawyer, I get to tell everyone that you honed your debate skills with me!"

Throughout the fall and winter sessions at the university Carrie Brown threw herself wholeheartedly into her study and her work. She recited at 9 o'clock every morning in mathematics, at 10 o'clock in history, and at 11 in languages. No afternoon classes were scheduled so that she could work at the Hathaway House. Evenings and Saturdays were reserved for preparation. Carrie quickly learned that for every hour of recitation she had to spend two hours preparing. She was expected to virtually memorize her professors' lectures and regurgitate the information perfectly.

Somewhere in her store of boundless youth, Carrie found the energy to join the Palladian Society, which had been founded "to help build up and perfect the moral and intellectual capacities, and in like manner the social qualities" of university students. The society's Friday evening meetings involved orations, recitations of original poetry, and debates. Carrie especially enjoyed participating in the latter. She developed positions on everything from "Resolved, That the University Should Forbid the Formation of Secret Fraternities" to "Women's Suffrage—a Simple Matter of Justice." Debating helped her to establish her own opinions and to found them on something besides her emotions.

The engagement of Everett Higgenbottom and Myrtle Greer left Carrie without a regular escort to evening lectures. She was rescued by "the slate," a small book bearing the names of the female members of the Society. The book was circulated throughout the week by an official "slate-bearer" until some gentleman had written his name by every young woman's name on the slate, thereby promising the necessary escort for every female who wished to attend the Friday meetings.

Early in January, Carrie was escorted to a debate by Charles E. Field, who was to oppose Carrie in the evening's debate: "The Indian Question—Resolved, That the Indian Must Be Christianized and Civilized." Charles E. Field gave the negative argument against the Christianizing and civilizing of the Indian, concluding with the comment that the

Indian was, by nature, uncivilized and savage and was best left in his natural and godless state, which would eventually lead to the demise of the Indian nation and, therefore, a bloodless and natural end to the Indian Problem.

When it came time for her to present her position, Carrie rose, so angry she could scarcely speak. She went on to present her affirmative argument, ending by saying, "It is obvious to this debater that her opponent would be hard pressed to distinguish between a Sioux Indian and a snapping turtle." The audience dissolved into nervous laughter whereupon the master of ceremonies directed Miss Mollie Runyan to quickly rise and present the musical portion of the program. Mr. Field found no trace of Carrie when the evening concluded and he was to have escorted her home. Miss Brown had marched back to the Hathaway House in record time, awakening her Aunt Augusta with a resounding slam of their apartment door.

At Augusta Hathaway's invitation, Jim and LisBeth Callaway drove in one spring Friday to attend the "Fifth Annual Exhibition by the Palladian Literary Society." The exhibition had been planned as an official ending for the school year and Carrie was to be involved in a debate on women's suffrage. When the program concluded, Carrie accompanied the Callaways and Augusta back to the hotel where the political discussion continued and eventually turned to the problems faced by Nebraska farmers.

Jim shook his head. "Deflation just has to be stopped, Augusta. I don't know what it'll take, but when we're paying our bills with dollars worth a lot more than the dollars we borrowed to buy our land, it's hard to see our way out of the credit crunch. Thank God LisBeth and I don't owe the bank. But plenty of our neighbors do. Ben Carter told me that if this year's wheat crop isn't better than last, he's done for."

Augusta interrupted him. "I know Ben Carter. He stuck

it out through the grasshopper plague. Nebraska needs to keep men like that."

"Well, Ben Carter has ten boys to provide for, and the strain is beginning to show. The district is so broke they're losing their school teacher after this term. The last time Ben and I came into Lincoln to deliver hogs he made it for Bassett's Hall and downed half his money in liquid form before I could convince him to head for home with me."

Augusta shook her head. "I hate to see that. I'll drive out tomorrow and see Mrs. Carter. Maybe I can be of some help, somehow. What can we do to help the farmer, Jim? J.W. Callaway is the nearest thing to a grandchild I've got, and I want to do whatever I can to assure his future. He *is* going to be a farmer, isn't he?"

Jim grinned. "I'm feeding him an ounce of Nebraska earth a day just to make certain he gets it in his blood!"

"What about a debate or a lecture at the Red Ribbon Club?" Carrie offered. "Why not bring the problems of agriculture before the public? I know there would be interest. The proposal for an agricultural college at the university has been a topic of late. The students at the university think the idea is ridiculous. So many of them left the farm to get an education, and I don't hear anyone wanting to go back. A debate could remind people that farming is an honorable way to live and that some people choose it because they love it, not because they can't do anything else. It could also remind them that Nebraska farmers are an important part of this nation's economy."

"That's a wonderful idea, Carrie. I'll propose it." Augusta turned to Jim and LisBeth. "Will you two come?"

Jim nodded immediately. "We *do* need an agricultural college. Farmers need help. Most of the ones I know weren't born here. They all came from back east where there are plenty of rivers and trees and springs and practically no grass. Now we're battling prairie, little water, no timber, and grass so thick you can build houses from it. We can feed the world someday, but not without help: help from the banks to control deflation, help from the railroad to get our products to market at a fair price. And we need an agricultural college to research and teach the best ways to farm this land."

"You talk like that, Jim Callaway, and we'll get something started. Bring Ben Carter and a few more of the homesteaders near you." Augusta turned to LisBeth. "And you be sure that Ben Carter's wife comes with him. I'll plan a reception for farm women after the meeting. We need to put faces onto the discussion topic. Let a few influential people see the young men and women who are struggling to build this state."

LisBeth nodded. "I'll be there, Aunt Augusta. And I'm sure Mrs. Carter will come, too."

"Good, LisBeth," Carrie said earnestly, "'The hand that rocks the cradle is the hand that rules the world.' That's a direct quote from one of our suffrage debates not long ago. What *women* care about is what *gets* cared about. We may not be able to vote yet, but that doesn't mean we can't participate in government."

Augusta was already shuffling through her desk, locating pen and paper and making plans for her reception. She was discussing tea blends and cake selections when Jim began to chuckle. "If women do ever get the vote, heaven help us all. They already run things, anyway. Why bother with marching to make it official?"

LisBeth flushed angrily. "Jim Callaway! Shame on you! I've heard you say time and again that it's a crime that Joseph Freeman can't vote. You were so upset at Carrie's debate tonight, you almost stormed the platform to take over for Carrie on behalf of the Indian. Why don't you think women should vote? It's a matter of simple justice, Jim. Just as Carrie said tonight."

Carrie joined in. "Are women so inferior that you think different rules apply for them?"

"Don't get steamed, LisBeth, Carrie. I didn't mean it."

LisBeth snorted, "You *did* mean it, Jim Callaway."

Jim abruptly changed the subject. "Carrie, we forgot to ask you. Would you be interested in teaching a term next fall at the district just north of our place? Ben Carter said the present teacher has accepted a position back in Missouri. Like I said, the district can't afford to pay much."

Carrie interrupted. "The pay doesn't have to be a lot, Jim. I've missed teaching. And I could use a change from the university. I'll have to pray about it, but it sounds terrific."

"You can board with us, Carrie," LisBeth offered. "We'd love to have you."

LisBeth was unusually quiet for the rest of the evening. She went upstairs to bed long before Jim had concluded his agricultural discussions with Augusta. When Jim slipped into bed beside LisBeth, she kept her back turned to him and inched away towards the edge of the bed.

Jim put his hands behind his head and lay staring at the ceiling for a long time before saying, "I was glad to hear Carrie say she'd love to come to teach in the fall. She certainly has matured this past year. It was good to hear her talking about praying about a decision instead of just rushing into it. School has done wonders for her. She was superb at that debate tonight. I was as proud of her as if I were her older brother."

Silence.

"She presented her case very well."

Silence.

"She seems to have mellowed somewhat on the suffrage issue. Last year I thought she'd be out marching in the streets of Lincoln. She's more settled, seems to have a better idea of what she wants for the future and seems really committed to following the Lord."

Finally, Jim reached out to stroke LisBeth's hair. "I'm sorry, LisBeth. What I said about the women's vote was patronizing and hypocritical. Forgive me?" There was no response from the far edge of the bed. Jim moved closer. "I can only manage one cause at a time, though. Could women's suffrage wait until we get support for the agricultural college? Then I'll lead the parade through Lincoln if you want me to."

He sensed a softening of the iron will lying at the edge of the bed. "I'll write a confessional for the *State Journal.* 'Idiotic Husband Sees the Light. Realizes Wife Has Brains. Desires to Borrow Some.'"

Muffled laughter made the bed shake slightly. Sensing victory, Jim laid a hand on LisBeth's shoulder and moved closer. He whispered in her ear, "You can run for governor if you want to, Lizzie. Only forgive me." He kissed her ear. "Let's have a planning meeting." He kissed her neck. "Tomorrow."

CHAPTER 24

Trust in the LORD and do good. . . .
Delight thyself also in the LORD;
and he shall give thee the desires
of thine heart. Commit thy way unto the LORD;
trust also in him; and he shall bring it to pass.

Psalm 37:3-5

Miss Brown!" Silas Kellum called to Carrie, "There's a letter here for Mr. and Mrs. Jim Callaway. Guess whoever wrote it didn't know to send it to Roca. They have their own post office now. Aren't you going down that way soon?"

"I'm leaving tomorrow, Silas," Carrie answered, reaching for the letter and catching her breath when she saw the handwriting. "I'll be happy to deliver it." Carrie took the letter into her room, sitting on the edge of the bed with the letter in hand for a few moments before opening the lid of her trunk and laying it on top of the pile of books she had just recently packed.

The next day about noon, Jim Callaway arrived to take Carrie south to Roca. Sarah Biddle and Augusta Hathaway were on hand to bid Carrie good-bye.

"Now don't you forget, Carrie," Augusta said. "Joseph or Asa will come whenever you want and fetch you back to Lincoln. If it doesn't work out, you just get word to us and we'll bring you right back here."

"I'm sure it'll work out, Mrs. Hathaway. If I can handle an overgrown bunch of half-wild Sioux, I can surely meet the challenge presented by the agricultural community of Nebraska."

Jim chuckled. "You're beginning to sound mighty capable—and almost trail-worn, Miss Brown."

Carrie kidded back. "As long as all they throw at me is garter snakes and toads, I'll do fine, Jim. At least I think I will."

"We'll be down next weekend to visit," Sarah said shyly. "Can't stay away from J.W. Callaway for long. He's growing up too quickly and we want to witness every new trick firsthand. Letters just don't suffice."

"Letters! Jim, there's a letter from Soaring Eagle in my trunk. Silas Kellum gave it to me yesterday. Soaring Eagle must not know that Roca has its own post office. Does he write often?"

Jim shook his head. "Hope nothing's wrong. Can't remember the last time he wrote. LisBeth keeps him up-to-date on our news. But we don't hear from him more than twice a year, if that."

Carrie moved to climb into the wagon and get the letter, but Jim stopped her. "No need, Carrie. I wouldn't read it without LisBeth, anyway. Letters are special to LisBeth. We'll read it together when I get home. Just let it be."

After a round of hugs and more promises to keep in touch, Carrie climbed up beside Jim for the two-hour ride south to the Callaway farm. Jim stopped on the way to show Carrie the schoolhouse, which was situated at the base of a hill. "Folks are gonna drag it to the top of that hill before fall," Jim said.

When Carrie asked why, Jim shrugged. "I told 'em it's a mistake. Too windy up there. But they want the schoolhouse up where the sound of the bell carries better. And," he added with a smile, "the Smiths have all the money in the district and they've decided their kids have to walk too far. Said it'd be more 'equitable' if we move the schoolhouse a half mile southeast."

The remainder of the ride to Roca was spent with Jim telling Carrie about the students she would likely see on her opening day at school. He ended his monologue with a warning about Ned Carter, Matthew Glenn, and a student named Philip, whose last name Carrie couldn't remember.

As soon as they arrived at the homestead, Jim hurried inside to share Soaring Eagle's letter with LisBeth.

Carrie followed him inside, calling out, "I'll just get settled in my room, LisBeth—if Jim will carry the trunk in for me."

"Nonsense, Carrie. You're going to be part of our family. You don't need to leave just because we're reading a letter from Soaring Eagle. Heavens, he's practically family to you too. Just sit down here and relax." LisBeth waved Carrie into the parlor and began to read.

> *"The people grow dearer to me every day. The village has changed somewhat. A number of the people have moved farther up the river, and some of Walking Elk's people have moved in. There are not so many people as there were earlier, but the village is still a large one. All seem very glad to have us here. We thank God for what He has done and pray that our light may so shine that many more of the people may see our good works and glorify our Father who is in Heaven.*
>
> *Charity Bond has gone back to Santee, so that the work among the women is left to Martha Red Wing, which is a great burden to her. We pray that another woman will come soon to join Martha, who is very busy all the time.*
>
> *If Carrie Brown comes to stay with you when she is teaching, please tell her that she is to ride Lakota so that the way is easier for her. Lakota is a very intelligent mare. She will learn the way to school and home quickly, so that if there is snow or rain, Red Bird can always trust Lakota to take her home.*
>
> *I would like to see James Windrider. If God wills it I will come to you next spring so that he can see his Indian uncle and hear stories of his people."*

Jim spoke up. "When he comes in the spring, he'll have a new foal to train. Lakota should foal in April. Be sure to let him know when you write back. In the meantime," Jim looked over at Carrie, "it looks like you won't be needing to walk to school, after all—as if we would have expected you to."

Carrie answered quickly, "It's really kind of Soaring Eagle to think of me. I hope I can handle Lakota. I'm not the best rider. If you'll excuse me, I need to get unpacked so I can help LisBeth with supper." Carrie pushed herself away from the table and retreated to her room, sincerely hoping that her red cheeks had escaped LisBeth's notice. *Goodness,* she thought, *I thought I was over this foolishness. I haven't really thought about Soaring Eagle for months, now.* Carrie stopped in midthought. *Not true, Carrie Brown. Not true. You haven't spoken of Soaring Eagle for months. But you have thought about him—a lot.*

Far to the north, in the Cheyenne River country, Soaring Eagle was also doing a great deal of thinking about a great many things, not the least of which was Miss Carrie Brown.

Her first day of school, Carrie once more looked *up* at more than half the class as they filed past her into the one-room school. Standing behind her desk, she surveyed her class with honest terror, realizing that several of the older boys were not only much taller than their teacher, they were very nearly her age. They sat in the back row, obviously regretting their presence in school. Two older girls whispered quietly, alternately nudging one another and giggling at the faces made by a half-grown farm boy who sat across the row.

When Carrie cleared her throat to speak, the room grew deadly quiet. One of the boys scraped his heavy boots across the floor, barely managing to crowd his long legs under his desk. Carrie opened the drawer to her desk to retrieve a class roster and jumped backwards with a little "Oh!" The back row grinned in anticipation of the new teacher's imminent demise.

"*Thamnophis sirtalis sirtalis,*" Carrie said matter-of-factly. "Garter snake. Indigenous to the area." Picking up the foot-long snake, Carrie let it curl around her fingers, slithering from one hand to the other and back again while she walked around her desk, relaxing visibly and smiling at the back row. "Non-poisonous. Excellent deterrent to insect pests in the garden." Pausing, she surveyed her students. "Whose mother has the biggest garden?"

A hand went up, not surprisingly, in the back row. The male voice cracked in midsentence, precipitating a chorus of giggles from the female ranks. "Mine, ma'am. There's ten of us boys. Takes a lot of garden to feed us."

Carrie proceeded down the center aisle towards the back row. "Ten—*all boys?*"

"Ten boys. One girl. My sister, Tess. She don't come to school yet. Ma says she's too little."

"And what is your name, young man?"

"Carter. Ned Carter."

"Well, Ned Carter, suppose you take this fellow home to your mama's garden. When we've time to build a proper cage, perhaps you can bring him back and we'll do a study of snakes. It's called herpetology, and I'm sure *all* you older boys will enjoy it. When the time comes, you'll have to bring us *Pituophis melanoleucus sayi.* A bull snake. A big one. Maybe three- or four-feet-long. I'll let you know when."

Ned Carter accepted the snake from Carrie's outstretched hands. "Keep him in your desk, Ned. He'll be fine until school lets out. Now," Carrie turned and made her way back to the front of the room. "Just so you know," she said, "My name is Miss Brown. I grew up among the Indians, and I learned to *love* snakes, and frogs, and mice.

Love to play with them. In fact, I love just about everything that's supposed to scare a teacher."

She scowled briefly at the back row, and then broke into a radiant smile. "Now, I'm certain we're going to get along fine. I don't believe in whipping students, and I'm equally certain *you* young gentlemen don't really believe in bullying young ladies. I'm sure we'll get on. Let's do roll call. I'm first. Miss Carrie Brown, teacher. Present."

By noon, Carrie had learned her fifteen students' names. She knew where they lived, what level they had reached in their lessons, and how many brothers and sisters they had. She *didn't* know that during the lunch break, Ned Carter collected his cohorts Matthew Glenn and Philip Damrow and vowed to protect the new teacher from any more foolishness.

Swallowing a huge chunk of his lard sandwich, Ned said, "She'll learn us good. Besides, we never had a pretty teacher before. Let's keep her."

Matt and Phil nodded their agreement and the club that had planned various acts of terrorism against the new teacher was summarily dissolved.

District 117 had children in every grade except one until the fourth week, when a towheaded little girl was dragged to school with her older brother. Ned Carter passed along his pa's message. "Larn 'em and make 'em tough. If you have to, lick 'em, but larn 'em."

Carrie welcomed Tess Carter warmly and soon discovered that no "lickings" would be necessary to "larn" the sweetest child she had ever met. Tess, age six, settled quietly onto the front row, unable to reach the floor with her feet until Carrie set the dictionary on the floor as a lift.

"Thanks, ma'am," Tess whispered sincerely. Carrie

leaned over and whispered back, "I learned to keep a dictionary or a step-stool in just about every room when I was growing up!"

"You ain't growed up much, Teacher," Tess said honestly.

Carrie grinned back. "You're right about that, Tess. And I still keep dictionaries and footstools about!" Carrie winked at her new charge and called the first-year scholars to recite. When they stepped forward, she realized that Tess was mouthing everything with them. When questioned, Tess said, "Ned teached me my letters, ma'am. He draws 'em in the dirt and then I learns 'em." Carrie made a mental note to work on grammar with Tess and Ned Carter, and then went on with the school day.

As the weeks passed, Carrie learned something about herself. She was a born teacher. She loved her students and loved preparing lessons. The few parents who had grumbled about Carrie's lack of a university degree began to see the results of loving instruction and to dread the end of the term when Miss Brown would return to Lincoln.

When the fall term ended the students of District 117 invited their parents to an evening of recitations to exhibit their accomplishments. Carrie and the children worked together all day, cleaning and sweeping, making paper chains and adorning the room with bittersweet.

The evening of the program the students and their families filled every available inch of space inside the tiny schoolhouse. Each child presented a brief recitation. To close the evening, the students sang several Christmas carols. When Tess Carter got up and recited the entire first chapter of Luke, everyone burst into applause.

Jim Callaway leaned over to Carrie and whispered, "You larned 'em real good, Miss Brown."

Carrie beamed with pride. *Lord,* she prayed silently, *I think I finally know what I want to be when I grow up. I want to be a teacher.*

CHAPTER 25

 God thundereth marvellously with his voice; great things doeth he, which we cannot comprehend. For he saith to the snow, Be thou on the earth . . . And it is turned round about by his counsels: that they may do whatsoever he commandeth them upon the face of the world in the earth. He causeth it to come, whether for correction, or for his land, or for mercy.

Job 37:5, 6, 12, 13

January 12 dawned warm and beautiful. Huge flakes of snow drifted gently to the ground, but it was not cold, and Carrie decided to ride Lakota to school. The little mare snorted and shook her head playfully as Carrie saddled her.

"We'll have a fine ride this morning, Lakota," Carrie said. "And then I'll get to hear Tess Carter recite. You should hear her, Lakota. She already knows the entire Gettysburg address. She stands with her hands clasped in front of her, so serious you'd think she was ending the war herself by what she says. She's just too adorable for words."

Riding out of the farmyard, Carrie urged Lakota to a gallop. The mare responded willingly to the idea of a morning run, making her way down the road until Carrie impulsively urged her to hop a board fence and take the remaining two miles to the schoolhouse through pastureland.

Lakota trotted to the top of the hill where the schoolhouse had only recently been moved. Carrie dismounted, surprised to see smoke emerging from the chimney. At the sound of Lakota's stomping and snorting, Ned Carter came to the schoolhouse door. "I'll hobble Lakota for you, Miss Brown," he offered. "I came early to start the fire."

"Thank you, Ned." Carrie slid down off Lakota's back smiling. "Are you trying to get on the teacher's good side? If you are, starting the fire is a great way to do it!"

Carrie went inside, hanging her coat just inside the door and proceeding to her desk where Tess Carter had left a slate bidding "Miss Brown, Good morning." Carrie looked up from her desk just in time to see Tess scamper outside. She began to ready the day's lessons. Only about a dozen children came that day.

"Pa said we might have a storm," Matthew Glenn offered, "but he let us come anyhow, since we live so close. Bet the Millers and the Dawsons stayed home 'cause of the weather."

Carrie wisely refrained from criticizing the Millers and the Dawsons aloud, but inwardly she wondered at their keeping their children home. *It's Nebraska, for heaven's sake,* she thought. *Eight or ten inches of snow shouldn't keep them from school.*

Ned had pulled his sister, Tess, to school on a sled that day, and at lunchtime the children coasted down the hill into the draws. Carrie watched them wistfully, and when recess time came early in the afternoon, they invited Carrie to join them.

"Aw, come on, Miss Brown," Ned wheedled. "You ain't, I mean, you're not *that* much older than us. You *got* to like coasting."

"Well." Carrie hesitated. It took only a little more encouragement from the children to make her admit, "Coasting *is* one of my favorite things." Carrie pulled on her felt boots and headed out the door. She ran across the ground, flopped on the rickety sled, and headed down the draw. She hit the bottom breathless and laughing.

Carrie was barely back on her feet when Ned called down the hill, "Miss Brown, you better come look at this."

Carrie trudged up the hill and looked to the northwest. The sky was dark. It had been snowing all day, huge flakes almost the size of walnuts. But since lunch the snow had stopped.

Carrie looked up at Ned. "What's it mean, Ned? You've grown up here. I'm new to the west."

Ned looked worried. "I think it may be a good old-fashioned blizzard, Miss Brown. Wind's been from the south all day. Could blow it all north of us. But it's so quiet now. The wind can change fast."

"Well, we'd better get a good fire started. There's plenty of coal in the coal shed."

"We can keep warm, Miss Brown. That ain't the problem. The wind comes up, it just might blow that schoolhouse right off those blocks. Then we'd all freeze."

Carrie looked doubtful. "You really think it could be that dangerous?"

Two or three of the older students gathered round. "You ever seen it snow *sideways*, Miss Brown?"

No sooner had Carrie dismissed school than parents began arriving to collect their children. "You done right, Miss Brown," one father commended. "This could be a bad 'un. I don't like the look of those clouds one bit. You get home as quick as you can, you hear?"

In less than an hour the children had all been collected. All save Ned and Tess Carter. The black wall seemed to be approaching more quickly from the north, and Carrie grew concerned.

"Pa was headed up to Lincoln today to take some hogs," Ned explained. "He went with Jim Callaway. Didn't know when he'd be back. Told us to get our own supper." Ned reassured Carrie. "We can make our way home, Miss Brown. It ain't—isn't—that far. You go on. We'll be all right."

Carrie had heard about Ben Carter's visits to Lincoln before. They usually began with the selling of something, and ended in one of various "establishments" the temperance leagues were doing their best to close down. "Ned, you're a strong young man, and normally I'd let you go, but I just can't take responsibility for your being out alone. Not when you have to head right towards that wall of clouds. What if you two come home with me? You can stay at the Callaway farm tonight. I'll leave a note on the blackboard for your father so he'll know you're safe." Carrie added, "Besides, Ned, I'd feel better about having company on the way home in case I get caught by my first Nebraska blizzard."

At the thought of becoming protector for Miss Brown, Ned quickly agreed to accompany her to the Callaway farm. Carrie insisted that Ned and Tess ride Lakota. "She knows me better, Ned. If it starts to snow, she'll follow me home with no trouble. She might not want to follow you." As if to agree with Carrie, Lakota nodded her head.

Ned reluctantly pushed Tess into the saddle, climbing up behind her and taking hold. The trio headed south towards the Callaway farm, and had just reached the road when the storm hit.

Suddenly a terrific wind crashed through the osage hedge on the west side of the road, scooping up snow off the ground and swirling it in the air. It was as if a great white curtain had been dropped over the road. Carrie turned to encourage the children, but the wind ripped the sound of her voice away before the children heard her. Laying a hand on Lakota's nose, Carrie reached towards the children. She could no longer see them. She felt along Lakota's neck towards Tess.

Ned leaned towards her to hear. Carrie screamed up at him, "Ned, unbutton your coat and wrap it around Tess, too. Hold on tight. Don't you fall off. Whatever you do, don't fall off."

Carrie stumbled back to Lakota's head and they plunged ahead. They were lost in a thick, enveloping whiteness, a cloud of vapor that shut Carrie off from everything around her. Fear clutched at her as she wondered, *How can it be dark—and yet everything be white.* She struggled to hold onto Lakota's reins while holding a scarf up to her mouth. Lakota's nostrils were caking over with ice. When Carrie turned into the wind to claw the ice away, snow covered her own face so quickly she feared her eyes would freeze shut.

Her only sense of direction came from the wind. She knew the storm had come from the northwest, so she turned her back to it, praying that they were going in the right direction. The osage hedge had disappeared from view long ago. They were surrounded by a high, white wall. Already it was a struggle to move through the deepening snow.

They struggled on for only a few moments when Lakota began pulling at the reins. Finally, with a shrill whinny, she stopped dead, bracing herself against Carrie. *Trust the horse, Red Bird. The horse knows the way home.* Who had taught her that? Soaring Eagle. Surely he knew more about Nebraska blizzards than she. He had broken Lakota himself. He had said she had good sense. *Trust the horse.*

Her mittens were frozen to the reins. She pulled them away and draped the reins about Lakota's neck. Making her way along the little mare's side, she touched the legs of the half-frozen children and screamed through the wind. "I can't see the way. Lakota will take us home. I'm going to hold onto her tail and let her take us home." Making her way to the back of the pony, Carrie grasped her tail and hung on. The minute she was given her head, Lakota turned them in the opposite direction and began to pick her way through the ever-deepening snow.

Jim Callaway had left Lincoln with a load of supplies as soon as he saw the clouds to the north. His traveling companion, Ben Carter, had been located—dead drunk—in a local saloon. Slamming two quarters on the table at the saloon, Jim had asked the bartender to give the man a bed for the night. "This looks bad. I've got to get home to my wife and baby. Tell Ben I stopped at the school for his kids. They can stay at my place until he comes for them."

The wall of snow hit Jim when he was only a half mile north of the school. It was directly in his path for home, and he rejoiced to read the note Carrie had scrawled on the blackboard. "All children sent home before storm hit. Ned and Tess Carter with me. Went to Callaway's, three miles south." *Good girl, Carrie. At least I know LisBeth's not alone.*

A mile south of the school, the wind lifted Jim's wagon like a toy and tossed it on its side, covering the supplies with snow almost immediately. Jim struggled out of the snowdrift he had been tossed into and tried to help his big, rangy team right the wagon. When it became obvious that they couldn't do it, he quickly unhitched the team. With numb fingers, he used the long driving reins to tie himself to his horses, yelling at them to "giddap," following them into the white night, trusting them to take him home.

On the road only two miles ahead of Jim Callaway, the little mare Lakota was doing her best to break a way through the huge drifts. The two children perched on her back hunched over against the wind, clinging to her mane, half unconscious from cold and terror and weariness. Behind Lakota, Carrie floundered through the snow on numb feet, grasping the black tail with one increasingly numb right hand. The hem of her dress was decorated with a double row of pleats and braiding. Snow had been driven through her coat and lodged between the rows of braids, making a huge roll of frozen snow about her ankles. Walking was nearly impossible unless she held up her skirt. The snow changed from wet flakes to dry powder, but intense cold had frozen Carrie's clothing, damp from sweat, into a solid armor about her. She had stopped shivering long ago, stopped thinking, stopped praying. Now all she could do was concentrate on the unbelievable effort it was taking to put one foot before another—one more step—one last step.

Suddenly, Carrie was floundering in a huge drift. She reached out feebly to catch Lakota's tail, but the tail was gone. The white wall had closed her in and she was alone. She called for the children, screamed for them, but there was no answer. *Move on, Carrie, move on.* With supreme effort, Carrie got her feet beneath her and managed, somehow, to walk a little farther. She no longer knew if she was headed toward the farm or not. She stumbled on through the swirling snow for what seemed like hours until she ran into something. Thinking she had at last found Lakota, she began to cry with relief, but the animal she had run into was a lone cow huddled up to a haystack. Hay! With the last of her strength, Carrie made her way inch by inch to the south side of the stack where the snow was not quite so deep, the wind not quite so strong. Desperately, she clawed her way toward the middle of the haystack. Once she was buried in the middle of the stack, she began to cry. *Dear God, Dear God, the children! The children! Tell Lakota how to find the way, God.* She sobbed and prayed aloud until her frostbitten cheeks began to hurt too much. Then she prayed inwardly until the muffled roar of the wind lulled her into an unnatural sleep.

Jim Callaway's team found their way home. They ran straight into the west wall of the barn and stopped in their tracks. Staggering between them, Jim reached out to feel the wall of the barn and shouted praises. He felt his way along the barn to the corral gate. It was already open. Jim lead his team away from the northerly wind and inside the barn. Snow was being driven through every crack in the barn, piling up in the corners, covering the hay, sprinkling the stock with a fine dusting of powder.

Jim pounded his hands against his knees, trying to get circulation back so that he could tend his team. He had his back to the other stalls, but the sound of a low nicker and a human-like whimper made him turn around. Lakota was peering at him from the last stall at the far end of the barn. Still clinging to her back were two half-frozen children.

The moment the storm began, LisBeth Callaway had lit several lamps and placed them in every window in the house. She worried and paced, praying that Jim had stayed in Lincoln and that Carrie Brown had had the good sense to keep her students at school. J.W. spent the evening playing happily, until the wind tore a shutter loose. Then he whimpered while his mother opened the door to refasten the shutter. The force of the wind threw her back into the parlor, and it took all her strength to reclose the door. In the few moments the door was open, snow flew in and over the floor. Once the door was closed, LisBeth scooped the snow into a cook-pot and set it on the stove to melt, afraid to open another door. She dragged a thick comforter off the bed and nailed it over the window with the missing shutter before picking up J.W. to comfort him.

Sometime after the baby had gone to sleep, LisBeth made coffee with the snow water and sat down at her kitchen table with her Bible. She was trying to read and pray when a strange sound made her go to the back door. It was flung open and Jim staggered in with two children in tow.

Relief, tears, and praising lasted only a few seconds. As the children were being freed from their frozen coats, Ned stammered, "Miss B-B-Brown. She, she's lost. She had Lakota's tail, said she would hang on, said Lakota would bring us home."

"I'm going to find her," Jim said grimly. "Keep those lamps lighted, LisBeth." Hurrying into the bedroom Jim threw off frozen clothes, dressed in layer after layer of dry clothes, and pulled on his old buffalo coat and fur mittens. He grabbed a fur-lined hat from a hook by the door, loaded his rifle, and went back out the door into the storm.

LisBeth worked to calm the children's fears while she tried to thaw them out. The wind abated long enough for her to bring in two crocks full of snow. "You children put your hands and feet in this snow. We must thaw you slowly and carefully. Are you hungry?"

Tess whimpered with pain as her fingers and toes began to thaw. Still, her eyes sparkled when LisBeth brought out bread and butter and cold chicken. Tess and Ned ate heartily and drank nearly a quart of warm milk each while LisBeth replenished the crocks with snow.

LisBeth kept the two children awake as long as possible, thawing them out carefully, but it wasn't long before exhaustion set in and they threatened to fall out of their chairs. Then she put them to bed buried under a mountain of quilts and comforters. They both fell into a deep sleep, their cheeks having taken on a rosy glow that told LisBeth that somehow they had managed to escape the savage storm with no frostbite.

She returned to the kitchen, washed dishes and crocks, made more coffee, and settled again by the window to wait for Jim. *Please, God, let him find her. You know where she is, Lord. Help Jim to find her.* LisBeth prayed over and over again. She was jolted awake by the opening of the back door. An unrecognizable form entered the kitchen. Only when she had broken through the solid crust of ice that coated the man's entire body, including his face, did LisBeth recognize Jim.

His voice was filled with despair. "I can't find her, LisBeth. Not a trace. Can't see anything. Can't make a way through the snow. Wind must be fifty miles an hour. It feels like it's fifty below."

LisBeth looked into the gray-green eyes. They were angry, hurt, and afraid—the same eyes she had seen when Jim first came to this farm, haunted by his past. LisBeth wrapped her arms around her husband. "You did what you could, Jim. God knows where she is. Now we must wait upon Him." Her own sobs were joined by Jim's and the two stood for a long time in the kitchen of the old farm house, clinging to one another.

The storm lasted until daylight. As soon as the wind stopped, the silence woke everyone on the Callaway farm. Ned and Tess got up sleepily, rubbing their eyes and staring about them stupidly, having forgotten how they got wherever it was they were. J.W. crawled over to the bed where he pulled himself up to stand and pound on the quilts. He blinked at Ned and Tess, amazed that two strange faces confronted him. Looking about the room, he saw his mother come to the doorway and gurgled happily.

"Good morning, you three," LisBeth murmured. "Storm's over. Come and see." LisBeth scooped up the baby and beckoned to Ned and Tess. "You'll be all right. You can stay here until your pa comes for you."

"Where's Miss Brown?"

LisBeth stopped in the doorway and looked back at the two pairs of eyes that looked at her soberly before Ned repeated, "Where's Miss Brown?"

LisBeth cleared her throat. "Well, Miss Brown didn't—" a lump formed in her throat. "Mr. Callaway couldn't find Miss Brown."

The full meaning of the statement sunk in. Tess blinked a few times, and began to cry. Ned wiped his own tears away to comfort his sister. "Aw, Tess, it'll be all right. She probably just sat it out in somebody else's place, that's all."

Tess looked up at her brother. "There's no other place between the school and here, Ned. You know that."

LisBeth interrupted. "Mr. Callaway has gone out this morning to look for Miss Brown." LisBeth swallowed hard. "I'm sure he will bring her home to us."

Ned and Tess Carter were sitting at the kitchen table eating breakfast when Jim Callaway kicked open the door and rushed inside with what looked like a bundle of rags in his arms. Without a word, he rushed passed LisBeth and into their bedroom. LisBeth followed him, coming back quickly to the kitchen for a pair of scissors. Tersely, she ordered the children, "You stay in this kitchen where it's warm. Ned, you keep an eye on J.W. for me."

LisBeth and Jim had to cut Carrie's frozen clothes off her. As they worked, they exchanged glances. "She was crawling through the snow, LisBeth. Couldn't walk," Jim explained.

Carrie's cheeks and nose were black with frostbite. She

seemed unable to speak, and her hands and feet were ominously dark. But her blue eyes watched them gratefully as they worked. Jim hauled a huge washtub into the bedroom and filled it with snow. They plunged Carrie's frozen feet and hands into the snow, trying to thaw them slowly. The pain began as circulation returned to her face and hands, and Carrie bit her lips to keep from crying out.

LisBeth worked for hours until Carrie fell into an exhausted sleep. Still, LisBeth continued her ministrations, bathing Carrie's feet in kerosene, trying to remember every remedy she had ever been told for frostbite.

Ned and Tess Carter proved to be very capable children. They entertained J.W. and made their own lunch. They played quietly in the parlor and looked out the kitchen window towards the barn. Snow had drifted against the entire north side of the house so that the windows and door were completely blocked. A drift at the front of the barn would have made it possible to step out of the haymow in the loft and slide to the ground unharmed. Jim tunneled his way to the well and the barn. He and LisBeth held a whispered conference in the kitchen after which Ned and Tess saw Jim go outside again. They went to the kitchen window and saw Jim mounted on his buckskin gelding, headed toward Lincoln. To their amazement, he rode the horse up and over where the farmyard fence stood, without breaking through any drifts.

"Mr. Callaway has gone to Lincoln for Dr. Gilbert," LisBeth explained. "He'll come and check on Miss Brown for us. Mr. Callaway will also let your father know that you are both safe. Your pa stayed in Lincoln during the storm."

Tess and Ned Carter looked at each other in a way that told LisBeth no further explanation was necessary.

"Can we see Miss Brown?" Ned wanted to know.

"She's sleeping, Ned."

"She gonna be all right?"

LisBeth answered honestly, "I don't know, Ned. I hope so. It was terribly, terribly cold last night, and she's had her hands and feet frozen. We'll just have to see what the doctor says."

When Dr. Gilbert arrived from Lincoln, what he said changed Carrie Brown's life.

CHAPTER 26

For I know the thoughts that I think toward you, saith the LORD, thoughts of peace, and not of evil, to give you an expected end.

Jeremiah 29:11

No. You can't. I won't let you." Carrie Brown pulled the quilt on her bed up under her chin and looked past Dr. Gilbert to where Sarah Biddle stood, her hand on the door. "Sarah, you're a good nurse or Dr. Gilbert wouldn't have brought you out here to see about me. You and I can take care of my hand."

But Carrie's hand was beyond anything medical science knew to do. By the end of the day, Carrie had lost two fingers from her left hand. Dr. Gilbert performed the surgery quickly and efficiently. With a few instructions to Sarah Biddle, he was gone, having bundled up Ned and Tess Carter to deliver home on his way back to Lincoln.

While Carrie slept, LisBeth and Sarah sat in the kitchen, drinking coffee and whispering. "Does she know? Did Dr. Gilbert discuss—" LisBeth could not bring herself to say the words.

Sarah shook her head. "No. He thought it might be too much for her, today. He said there's time to wait. There are a few things I can do over the next few days. She's in much too poor a condition for us to transport her to Lincoln, and if he has to do further surgery, he'd prefer to have her there where he can check in more often."

LisBeth patted Sarah's hand. "I'm so glad to have you here, Sarah. It's a great comfort. I know God gives grace where grace is needed, but I'm glad I don't have to do this kind of nursing alone. Do you think she realizes how badly frozen her feet are? Do you think she suspects?"

"I imagine she thinks that the surgery that was needed is done, and that with time everything will return to normal."

"When will Dr. Gilbert know?"

"He told me what to look for. He'll be back in a few days."

"Then we must try to prepare Carrie for the worst and hope it doesn't happen."

But the worst that LisBeth and Sarah could imagine did happen. When Dr. Gilbert returned to examine Carrie's hand, which was healing nicely, he unbandaged her feet and shook his head sadly. Sitting down beside Carrie's bed, Dr. Gilbert rewrapped her hand, struggling with how to tell his patient what needed to be done.

"You're trying not to tell me something, Dr. Gilbert." Carrie watched him carefully. Sarah slipped into the room while Dr. Gilbert rummaged in his medical bag for nothing. LisBeth brought in a tray of soup and tea, but instead of leaving the room, she settled on the corner of the bed.

Looking from Sarah to LisBeth, Carrie leaned back against her pillow. With a pathetically brave voice she said firmly, "Tell me."

Dr. Gilbert sighed. Placing his hands on his knees he began. "Miss Brown. I've done everything I know to do about your feet. Miss Biddle and Mrs. Callaway have followed my instructions to the letter. You have been an excellent patient. However, the circulation seems to have been permanently impaired."

"It won't get better?" Carrie wanted to know. "With time, won't there be healing?"

"I'm afraid not."

Carrie pondered the information, her eyes growing larger as the import of what she was being told sunk in. She barely managed to choke out the question. "Are you telling me that you must—amputate?" Once said, the horror of the word nearly overwhelmed her. She caught her breath. Her chin began to tremble. Sarah moved across the room, taking her right hand and squeezing it gently. LisBeth laid a hand on Carrie's knee and bowed her head to hide her own tears.

"Not entirely, Miss Brown." Dr. Gilbert focused on the clinical information he had to impart. "Just the front portions."

Carrie peered at him with angry, horrified eyes. "They'll heal. Get better. The blood will flow again. Things will get better." Wincing with pain, Carrie struggled to sit up.

Dr. Gilbert shook his head sadly. "No, Miss Brown. I think not."

"How can you be so certain?" The voice was trembling with a mixture of anger and near panic.

Sarah broke in. "Listen to Dr. Gilbert, Carrie. He's the best doctor we have in Lincoln. He wouldn't do anything unless he was sure."

Dr. Gilbert continued, "If we delay any longer, Miss Brown, we risk gangrene. At the moment, the living tissues are healthy." Doctor Gilbert's face was a mask of compassion as he hastened to explain things to his young patient. "You are a very brave and determined young woman, Miss Brown, but you are in a great deal of pain. The medical term is *ischaemic rest pain*. That means that the blood vessels in the tips of your feet were frozen and they are no longer able to carry blood into the tissues. Where there is no blood flow, Miss Brown, the tissue dies. We must act to preserve the healthy tissue in your feet, and to remove what cannot live before inflammation spreads." Dr. Gilbert paused before continuing, "We have waited as long as we dare, Miss Brown. I had hoped for better things, but there is what we call a 'dry, demarcated gangrene.' There is no active inflammation. The skin is healthy above that line. But we must act before your condition deteriorates."

"No—no—no!" Carrie wailed. She turned away, tears pouring down both cheeks.

Sarah reached out again. "I'll help you, Carrie. We all will. We are so grateful that you survived, Carrie. The stories are beginning to pour in of so many others who didn't. It's been a tragic, tragic, storm."

The doctor added, "You're young, Miss Brown. Strong. You'll be walking in no time, and able to carry on a useful life."

Carrie moaned, "I'll be hobbling about on crutches. Is that what you mean? Stuffing cotton into the tips of my shoes and hobbling like an old woman." Wincing with pain, she pleaded, "Go away. Leave me alone."

Putting his hand on Carrie's shoulder, Dr. Gilbert tried to console her. "Life is hard, Miss Brown. It has a way of throwing things in our way that we don't want. I do understand how you feel. But I am not going to let you die. You have too much to live for. I know that somewhere deep inside you, you know that too. I also know that you have the courage to overcome this." Dr. Gilbert retreated to the door. Before leaving the room, he added, "You must be brave, Miss Brown. Many others caught in the blizzard were not as fortunate as you. Many will lose more than fingers and toes. Many others died."

From the depths of the pillow came a muffled response. "And I wish I had died, too, Dr. Gilbert." Carrie raised her head up from the pillow and peered at him, angry tears spilling down her cheeks. "I don't know why God didn't just let me die. It would have been better than this."

Dr. Gilbert shook his head. "That's where you're wrong, Miss Brown. I'm convinced that God has a great plan for you. He gave you the strength to find that haystack. He guided Jim Callaway to you when you couldn't walk. And He saw to it that you got very good care from people who love you. God went to a lot of trouble to see that you were saved, Carrie. I'll be watching to see what He does through you when you get well."

Carrie had turned her back and covered her face. Dr. Gilbert could see the bed shaking as she sobbed. He went back and sat beside her and tried to reassure her again. "You will have to walk with crutches, but only at first. You may learn to do without. I'll help you. And Miss Biddle and Mrs. Hathaway will help, too. Think about it, Miss Brown. Pray about it. I want to move you to Lincoln so that I can perform the procedure there. Mrs. Hathaway is almost beside herself with worry, and she wants you back at the Hathaway House." Dr. Gilbert stood up. "Now, you get some rest while we make the appropriate arrangements to transport you to Lincoln. Sleep if you can, Miss Brown. Then I will come back and we'll talk further, if you like."

Jim had been standing at the door, trying to be invisible, while the rest of the group clustered about Carrie. At the first mention of Carrie's being moved, he motioned to Lis-Beth, who got up and went to the door. "Tell Dr. Gilbert I'm hitching up the wagon, LisBeth. I've already put the runners on, but I'll put a thick layer of hay in the bottom and that old buffalo robe."

LisBeth nodded. "Then we'll take J.W.'s feather bed. I'll open the trunk and get some of Mama's quilts out and heat some bricks in the oven. We'll make her as comfortable as possible." Jim left for the barn as Sarah and LisBeth followed Dr. Gilbert into the parlor, closing the door to Carrie's room and moving to the far end of the parlor where they sat in a close circle, talking with lowered voices.

"Carrie could stay here, Dr. Gilbert," LisBeth protested.

"And she would be well cared for here, Mrs. Callaway,

but you have a young child to care for and a farm to run. Mrs. Hathaway has already wired Miss Brown's grandparents, and they are coming as soon as the rails are cleared. It would be far better to move Miss Brown now. The bitter cold may not subside for weeks. The sun is shining today and as long as we can keep her warm, the fresh air will do her good. She's been very brave, but I know she's in a lot of pain. She'll be amazed by how much better she feels physically once this procedure is over. Being surrounded by her university friends and family will be the best emotional treatment for her recovery."

"Will she be able to—" LisBeth bit her lip, not wanting to continue.

"If she cooperates with her recovery, Miss Brown should be able to do everything she did before the surgery."

"Except wear a wedding ring." Sarah Biddle interjected. "That's the first thing she mentioned when she woke up from the first surgery."

Dr. Gilbert went on. "She will be able to walk, perhaps even without canes after a little practice. If all goes well, we will have her up on her feet and learning to walk in two weeks. Cases like this usually heal very well and offer an excellent prognosis. I understand from Miss Biddle that she was making plans to teach. I see absolutely no reason that she cannot become an excellent teacher. If she enlists this trial for her good, it will make her a stronger person. We must pray that she allows that to happen. You—" he looked seriously at LisBeth and Sarah, "You must do all in your power to help her resist bitterness and self-pity. We really have no choice in the matter of treatment."

Dr. Gilbert went outside to help Jim with the wagon, and Sarah and LisBeth went to prepare Carrie for the trip to Lincoln. Jim Callaway lifted Carrie out of bed effortlessly, but the weight of the blankets on her frozen feet caused

Carrie to grip Jim's shoulders tightly. Despite herself, she cried out in pain.

Dr. Gilbert spoke up. "There will be very little pain after tomorrow, Miss Brown."

Through clenched teeth Carrie muttered, "That's little comfort at the moment, Dr. Gilbert." She buried her face in Jim's shoulder and hung on tightly as Jim transported her to the back of the wagon where she was nearly buried beneath a mound of quilts.

"Can't I sit up, Dr. Gilbert?" she asked.

"Of course you may, Miss Brown."

Sarah helped Carrie, piling hay and feather pillows behind her until she could just peer over the edge of the wagon box. Sarah climbed up beside Dr. Gilbert. Just before they were to leave, LisBeth hurried out of the house, J.W. on her arm and a book in her hand.

"When we unpacked Mama's quilts, it came to me to give you this, Sarah. It's my mama's own Bible, with all the verses she liked underlined. Soaring Eagle sent it to us when J.W. was born. He thought we should hand it down to the oldest son. I think Soaring Eagle used it a great deal when he was first learning." LisBeth's voice faltered as she tucked the Bible into the folds of the quilts.

"Carrie, this quilt on top, this raggedy one. It's the one Mama made when Rides the Wind died. Ask Augusta to tell you the entire story, it might bring you some comfort. And I know this Bible will, if you read it." LisBeth choked back tears. "Oh, Carrie, just don't give up. Not for a minute. I *know* God loves you. I *know* He cares. It doesn't feel like it right now, but He does."

"Thank you, LisBeth," Carrie murmured. "I don't know what else to say right now but thank you."

"Don't say anything, Carrie," Jim said gently. "You just do everything you can to get well, and know that we are praying for you every day. The children of District 117 will be wanting their teacher back as soon as possible."

Dr. Gilbert slapped the horses with the reins and the wagon slid gently into motion. LisBeth, with J.W. in her arms, stood next to Jim, waving until the wagon was out of sight. Carrie closed her eyes tightly against the bright sun, drinking in the cold, fresh air and listening to the chirping of birds. They hadn't gone far when she heard a familiar call. Carrie could almost hear her mother's voice say, *Hear that, Carrie? He's telling you you're pretty-pretty-pretty.* Squinting against the bright sun, Carrie caught a glimpse of brilliant red. The cardinal flitted from branch to branch of a copse of bushes along the road, eagerly devouring a few sun-dried chokecherries. The memory of her mother struck Carrie. *Mama, you lost your beauty, your health, but you still served God.*

Looking down at the ragged quilt that covered her, Carrie thought, *LisBeth's mother, Jesse King, I remember Soaring Eagle telling me about you. You buried your first child and your husband, lost Soaring Eagle, and yet you still loved God.*

As the Callaway farm disappeared in the distance, Carrie thought *LisBeth, Mac died but you came home and went on with life. And Augusta Hathaway came to Lincoln before it was anything. She was already a widow. She made a way for herself.* All the way to Lincoln, Carrie Brown was assaulted with the realization of the disappointments and griefs that everyone around her had endured. *I bet Dr. Gilbert has a few disappointments of his own, only we just don't know about them. Everyone I know has had trials, but most haven't let the trials ruin their lives.* Carrie blinked back tears. *Why should I expect that I wouldn't have any trials?* The red bird twittered again, landing momentarily in the snow. *I have to decide. I can let this turn me into a bitter, hateful person, or I can just cope with it and get on with life. Dr. Gilbert says I can still teach. That's something good. He says I'll be able to walk. What if I couldn't walk? Think how terrible that would be.*

Under the quilts, Carrie moved her hands together and felt the bandages on her left hand. The image of no wedding ring finger loomed. *Well, I just have to face the fact that I may not*—Tears threatened again. Carrie willed herself not to think about it. *One thing at a time, Carrie. Today you are facing surgery and learning to walk again. Today has enough sorrow. Let's take it one day at a time. Isn't that what Dr. Gilbert has said, and LisBeth, and Sarah.*

Carrie called up to Sarah. "Sarah, could we maybe sing or something, to pass the time?"

Sarah looked at Dr. Gilbert in amazement before answering, "Of course, Carrie. I thought you were asleep. What shall we sing?"

"Oh, anything. No, not anything, Mama's favorite hymn. Let's sing 'Rock of Ages.'"

Sarah's uncertain voice joined Carrie's as they softly sang,

> *"Rock of Ages cleft for me, let me hide myself in thee;*
> *Let the water and the blood, from thy riven side which flowed,*
> *Be of sin the double cure. Save me from its guilt and pow'r.*
> *Nothing in my hand I bring; Simply to thy cross I cling;*
> *Naked, come to thee for dress; helpless, look to thee for grace;*
> *Foul, I to the fountain fly: Wash me, Savior, or I die."*

When the song was finished, Carrie asked Dr. Gilbert to explain the surgery to her again. She kept her mind busy asking questions and anticipating her recovery, talking until the steady plodding of the horses and the monotony of the snow-drifted landscape lulled her to sleep.

When Jim Callaway's team pulled up to the kitchen door of the hotel, Silas Kellum was waiting to transport Carrie to her room in Augusta's apartment. Augusta fluttered and fussed, smoothing Carrie's pillow, unpacking her things, promising the best supper that Cora Schlegelmilch could produce.

"Sarah," Carrie called out. "Sarah don't forget the quilt from the wagon, and the Bible LisBeth gave me. I'm not really sleepy." Carrie turned to Augusta, "I slept halfway to Lincoln. I think I'd like to read some."

When Sarah came through the door to Carrie's room carrying Jesse King's ragged quilt and old Bible, Augusta exclaimed with amazement. "How'd LisBeth come to think of that?"

"She was pulling every available quilt out of the house, so worried about keeping me warm," Carrie explained. "She said to ask you to tell me the story of the quilt. Do you think you could, before—?"

Augusta plopped down in the rocker by Carrie's bed. "Of course I can, dear. It began back in '43, when Jesse King was traveling across Nebraska with her husband, Homer, and their baby, Jacob. Now Homer King was a stubborn man. . . . " Augusta spent the next half hour re-telling everything she knew about Jesse King and the creation of the quilt that now lay over Carrie Brown's bed. When she concluded, she wiped away the last of her own tears and said softly, "So you see, Carrie, this quilt has left quite a legacy. Why, it's just a rag, of course, but it represents heartache and healing. I'm sure that's what LisBeth wants you to understand, Carrie. That's what we're all praying. That this heartache in your life will be healed and that you will go on to be a blessing to others, just as Jesse King was."

Carrie thought hard before saying, "I'd say I have a lot of good examples to follow when it comes to dealing with tough times, Augusta. I'm going to try to make you all proud of me."

Augusta Hathaway stood at the foot of Carrie's bed, nodding with satisfaction.

"I am a little afraid about tomorrow." Carrie looked up at Augusta. "But worrying won't change anything, will it?" Carrie sighed. "So that's that." With an attempt at a smile, Carrie asked, "Can I have some supper?"

Augusta went to the hotel kitchen where Dr. Gilbert was giving last minute instructions to Sarah. "These are the times I desperately wish for a hospital. By next year I'll have my clinic built. But, for now, Miss Brown will have to convalesce here. Thankfully my office isn't far and the patient is easily moved." Dr. Gilbert turned to Augusta. "Since Miss Biddle has made herself available to do extended nursing care, we can bring Miss Brown back here as soon as the procedure is completed and I am certain there is no profuse post-surgical bleeding. If things go as planned, Miss Brown will be back in her own quarters by late tomorrow afternoon."

Sarah took Carrie her supper and settled into the rocker by Carrie's bed while both girls ate. Abruptly, she said, "You seem to be doing very well with all this, Carrie, but I still won't leave you alone. Not tonight. You don't have to say a word to me if you don't want to. I'll bring in some needlework and be quiet as a mouse. And if you need to talk, I'm here. I won't presume to tell you that I know exactly how you're feeling, Carrie. I don't. But I do understand loss and hurting."

Augusta checked in before retiring. Sarah brought in her sewing basket and drew out a pile of half-finished quilt blocks. Lighting the gas lamp on Carrie's small desk, she sat, quietly stitching, while Carrie slept.

As the night wore on, Carrie began to toss and turn. Her dreams became her enemies and she woke, terrified, crying, trembling. Sarah held her gently. "It's all right, Carrie. It's all right. You're a brave girl—we all know it—but even the bravest know fear. Tell me about it, let me help you."

"I can't talk about it," Carrie sobbed. "I can't. I'm really trying to trust, Sarah. I really am."

"You *are* trusting, Carrie. That doesn't mean you shouldn't shed any tears or be afraid."

Carrie looked up at Sarah. "Thank you for staying with me. Would you read to me? From that Bible LisBeth sent, just something to fill the silence. Something to keep me thinking the right things."

"You don't want to tell me what it is that's bothering you?"

Carrie was quiet for a while. Sarah took up the Bible and had it open to a favorite passage before Carrie spoke. "People will stare at me."

"Yes, I expect they will. But don't they already stare at you, Carrie? You're a beautiful young woman."

"It will be different."

"Yes, it will."

"It will hurt."

"I suppose so."

After a long silence, Carrie asked quietly, "Do you think that a man could—love—" She stopped abruptly. "Never mind."

"I think," Sarah answered promptly, "that a man who had the good fortune to be loved by you would be a fool to let anything keep him from you."

"How has it been for you, Sarah? I mean, is it so terrible being alone?"

"No, Carrie, it's not terrible. It's different. But it's not terrible. It's a wonderful thing to assist Dr. Gilbert in a confinement, or to help someone convalesce after a serious illness. Those things bring me great joy. I have learned that there are other things besides marriage, Carrie, that can fulfill a woman." Sarah insisted, "But, Carrie, you should never assume that this unfortunate incident means that you can never marry. You are going to have a complete recovery and be able to live a very normal life."

Carrie shook her head slowly. "Yes, I hope so. And I suppose I'll deal with everything in time. There's no use dwelling on it. Please, Sarah, just read to me." Carrie burrowed into her pillows while Sarah began to read softly,

> *"This I recall to my mind, therefore have I hope. It is of the LORD's mercies that we are not consumed, because his compassions fail not. They are new every morning: great is thy faithfulness. . . . But though he cause grief, yet will he have compassion according to the multitude of his mercies."*
>
> *Lamentations 3:21–23,32*

As Sarah read, Carrie's face relaxed and she fell back to sleep. Sarah continued to read, passage after passage of the Bible, wherever there was an underlined verse or a passage smudged with paint. Long into the night, Sarah read aloud, her soothing voice filling the silence in the room, keeping back the dreams that had haunted Carrie Brown, dreams of rejection, dreams of a life with no husband, no children, dreams of a life lived alone.

CHAPTER 27

LORD, make me to know mine end, and the measure of my days, what it is; that I may know how frail I am. Behold, thou hast made my days as an handbreadth; and mine age is as nothing before thee.

Psalm 39:4-5

The same blizzard that changed Carrie Brown's life tore into the Cheyenne River valley with screaming winds and so much snow that signs of civilization were almost totally obliterated. Soaring Eagle and David Gray Cloud sat out the blizzard with James and Martha Red Wing in their cabin, grateful for ample firewood and food. When the storm abated, the Sioux living in the village dug paths through the snow from one tent or tepee to another, but from a distance these tunnels were invisible. Only the thin lines of smoke rising from campfires gave any evidence of life.

Two days after the blizzard, Soaring Eagle and David Gray Cloud rode north to the village. They found an enemy that was to take a much worse toll on their potential congregation than any blizzard ever could. Smallpox had come to the village with a newcomer from Fort Randall. When He-Who-Roars first took to his bed, complaining that his bones were on fire, no one worried. He-Who-Roars had always been a complainer. His woman cared for him slavishly. She had begun to feel that her own bones were on fire when she noticed that her husband's face was covered with red spots. The spots spread and grew, filling with putrid fluid and then scabbing over. He-Who-Roars died, but not before infecting his entire family. The disease spread quickly throughout the village. Those who were not sick began leaving. Family members who were already ill were left behind to fend for themselves.

In the midst of the terror and chaos, James Red Wing rode for a doctor. Soaring Eagle, David Gray Cloud, and Martha Red Wing, who had been vaccinated against smallpox at Santee, did their best to comfort the dying and ensure that they entered the next life as Christians. They set up a clinic of sorts in one of the larger tents that had been abandoned. The sick and dying were carried in, quickly filling the tent. They moaned with pain and cried out for help while Soaring Eagle and David Gray Cloud worked feverishly, trying to save them all, knowing at last that they would save pitifully few.

Days went by and there was no word from James Red Wing. When an ancient woman feebly offered her bag of medicine, Soaring Eagle was thrilled to find that it contained *Peshuta natiazilia*. "We boil this, David, then bathe the aching limbs in it. I wish we had more. This one, we call *poipie*, it will help the fever. We make tea from it. I hope the doctor arrives soon. Perhaps he will have something better. Until then, we go back to the old ways."

But the old ways did little to relieve the suffering caused by a disease the Sioux had never had to battle. With no immunity and no vaccinations, they were easy victims for the smallpox virus. Day after day, more died. Day after day, more left to get away from death. Soaring Eagle and David Gray Cloud worked through initial fatigue into exhaustion, sponging fevered limbs, praying, trying every home remedy Martha could remember.

Walking Thunder followed the two men everywhere,

trying to be of some help. "I am not afraid to die," he explained. "I have met Jesus and He will come for me if it is my time to go. I think I would like to go to heaven. It is very sad for my people now."

When Soaring Eagle heard the simple speech, he got up from the bedside of his patient and stumbled outside. Half-consciously he crashed through the snow until he had reached the little schoolhouse he had helped build across the trail from the Red Wings' log cabin. He stumbled inside and lay prostrate on the cold floor, crying out, "God, my God, they are my people and they are dying." He began to sob. "Help me save them, my God. Can You not see into my heart? It is breaking! Can You not see what is happening here, God? Or do You not care for a few Sioux up here on the Cheyenne River? They are sick, they are half-starved. How can I tell them You love them when you let them die?"

Soaring Eagle sat up, leaning against the wall of the schoolroom. "Spirit, intercede for me. I have no more words." He stayed there, seated on the floor for what seemed like hours. He wasn't sure he had been sleeping, but he was unaware of time passing until he heard horses stomping, bridles rattling, and voices. Looking across the path, he saw that James Red Wing had at last returned, apparently with a doctor, for he was accompanied by a man who led a pack mule well laden with boxes and odd-shaped bundles.

Soaring Eagle trudged across the path and followed James Red Wing inside the cabin. "Ten have died since you left," he said dully. "There are at least thirty more who suffer."

One look at Soaring Eagle told James Red Wing that his friend was at the end of his strength. "You have done well, Soaring Eagle. Dr. Harvey and I will ride up to the village. We'll send David Gray Cloud back as well. You must rest."

"There are the dead to be cared for."

"We'll take care of that, Soaring Eagle. You stay here. Get some sleep."

Soaring Eagle didn't argue. As the doctor and James left for the village, Martha bustled about preparing a meal for Soaring Eagle and David Gray Cloud. They ate mechanically and climbed the ladder to the loft. David dropped onto his hay-filled mattress with a groan. Soaring Eagle leaned over to remove his fur-lined moccasins. The next thing he knew he was waking up to the aroma of frying meat and boiling coffee. Beside him David Gray Cloud stretched and grunted, sitting up and asking, "Do you know the time of day?"

When Soaring Eagle shook his head, David called down to Martha. "You both climbed the ladder to the loft yesterday morning. It is the next day and the sun stands overhead," she answered.

David and Soaring Eagle looked at one another in disbelief. Rising slowly, they made their way down the ladder. It was bitterly cold, but the sun had begun to shine, and in the distance they could see smoke rising from the village.

Soaring Eagle sat down at the table and asked, "What has been done to help the people?"

"The doctor vaccinated everyone who was left. He brought medicines to try to make the rest comfortable."

Martha set two mugs of coffee down before the men. "Ten more died in the night. Many more have left. The only ones remaining are the sick and dying. In a few more days they will be dead, or ready to follow their families. James has said that we will stay to see that they are cared for. Then he thinks we should go back to Santee until spring. James believes that in the spring, people will begin coming back. This is a good place to camp and to live. When they know the sickness is gone, they will return. We all need rest and time to plan."

At the prospect of returning to his room at the Red Wings', Soaring Eagle experienced a sense of relief. "I thought I was about to lose my faith in God," he said quietly.

"That was exhaustion talking, my friend," James Red Wing's voice sounded from the door. "Even Christ withdrew to rest and to spend time alone with His Father. You have had no time for that since coming here. Faith waivers when the body is not refreshed. None of us is invincible, Soaring Eagle. Martha always reminds me that fatigue makes us vulnerable to the roaring lion." James sat down beside Soaring Eagle and patted him on the shoulder. "God is mindful that we are but dust. He does not wish that we wear ourselves out with overwork. You must remember this."

Martha Red Wing spoke up. "Or get a wife who will remind you!"

David Gray Cloud and Soaring Eagle smiled at one another sheepishly. Thankfully, Dr. Harvey entered the cabin at that moment. "We've done what we could," he said. "I have to head back south to the fort. I'll give my report, and the recommendation that a physician be appointed to work here full-time beginning in the spring."

With a few last suggestions to the four missionaries on how to treat the handful of remaining villagers, the doctor urged his horse into a lope and rode away towards the south.

In the next few days, the Red Wings, David Gray Cloud, and Soaring Eagle completed their first season of work among the Sioux of the Cheyenne River. The village of nearly a hundred had dwindled to nothing. Soaring Eagle and David Gray Cloud wrapped the bodies of the remaining dead and found places for them high in the trees that overlooked the river valley.

"The army would not approve of this," Gray Cloud

observed as he pulled the last body up into the fork of a tree.

"The army would want us to leave the bodies for the wolves, or burn the entire village," Soaring Eagle muttered. He looked up at David Gray Cloud. "Praise be to God that we don't work for the army."

The two worked together in silence. Finally, Soaring Eagle said, "I don't understand anything that has happened here this winter. I thought we had established a work that would continue. But an unseen enemy came and snatched the souls away. I don't understand it. I never will."

"Of them which thou gavest me have I lost none," Gray Cloud quoted back. "We'll come back to the Cheyenne River, Soaring Eagle. And when we return, there will be souls just waiting to hear about the Savior. We'll begin again."

Soaring Eagle turned to go. "I don't know if I have the strength to begin again," he said quietly. "Right now, all I can think about is going back to my little room at Santee."

As the two walked back towards the Red Wings' cabin, Soaring Eagle said, "In Boston I hated being surrounded by buildings. Never seeing the sky, the prairie. All I could think of was coming back to what I know. I never thought I would look at this," he included the vast river valley in one sweeping gesture, "and feel alone. I know these hills, these trees and valleys. I know where it is good to winter, and where it is good to hunt." He stopped on the trail. "Tell me, David Gray Cloud. Why do I feel as I did in Boston? I have returned to the land of my youth and yet I am not satisfied."

Coming to the cabin, the two men mounted horses and, along with James and Martha Red Wing, began to make their way along the valley. When the trail widened, David Gray Cloud urged his horse alongside Soaring Eagle. "I know things have not been as you had planned, my friend. We are both disappointed. But the work will continue.

What is wrong with us is not the difficulty of the work." Soaring Eagle frowned and said nothing. David Gray Cloud smiled and continued. "Dr. Riggs has told us both what we need to do. And Martha Red Wing has added her advice. I think we both should admit that we have an absolute and most urgent need for wives."

Soaring Eagle opened his mouth to answer, but David interrupted him. "You told me you had been thinking about it. Stop thinking so hard, my friend. *Do* something about it. Or did you think that God would put a woman on the trail with a sign on her forehead 'For Soaring Eagle'?"

Soaring Eagle grinned reluctantly and shrugged.

They rode along in silence for a while before David Gray Cloud offered, "It shouldn't be too hard for you, Soaring Eagle. I can name at least three willing candidates at various mission stations between here and Santee in case you need help. And," Gray Cloud added, half-joking, "when Charity Bond and Carrie Brown were here in the fall, I did notice that Carrie Brown seems to have grown up quite acceptably."

At Soaring Eagle's look of surprise, David laughed again, rich, booming laughter that filled the valleys and echoed from the ridges above them. At the sound of David's laughter, a herd of elk drinking from a river less than a mile away raised their regal heads as one and listened. An eagle soaring overhead peered suspiciously across the canyon. And the missionaries from Santee rode along, tiny dots moving along the edge of a creek while the sun sparkled on the pristine snow.

CHAPTER 28

Whoso findeth a wife findeth a good thing, and obtaineth favour of the LORD.

Proverbs 18:22

When the travelers from the Cheyenne River rode into Santee, they dismounted in front of Alfred Riggs's home and filed wearily inside. Dr. Riggs praised them for their faithful service, and agreed that after a season David Gray Cloud and Soaring Eagle would return, perhaps with more help.

"In the meantime," Dr. Riggs said, "go home and rest. James and Martha, we will pray for another couple to continue the work you began. Your farm will need your attentions this spring. Jeremiah has said that he would like to visit his sister and meet his nephew. I think that is a fine idea. Would you be willing, if it could be arranged, to speak at one or two churches in Lincoln, Jeremiah?"

Soaring Eagle nodded. "Of course. Do you have nothing for me to do here at Santee?"

"I think, Jeremiah, that you should take the time to rest and spend time in God's Word. Everyone needs times of refreshment. I can only imagine the physical exhaustion that you have experienced. You must guard against a similar spiritual exhaustion."

The missionaries joined Dr. Riggs in prayer and rose to go. As they filed out of his office, David Gray Cloud turned back. "Dr. Riggs, if you have a moment, might I ask you something in private?"

Soaring Eagle and the Red Wings mounted their horses and prepared to ride home. As they filed past the Birds' Nest, Charity Bond came running out. "Soaring Eagle! I just happened to look out. There's a letter here from Lis-Beth. It's been here for a while. There was no way to get it to you." Charity reached up and handed it to Soaring Eagle. "I've heard from LisBeth since this letter was posted. I want you to know that everything is all right. You may read some things that worry you, but things are on the mend. I won't say any more." Charity turned to go and then stopped and said, "I'm glad you're all back safely. We've been praying for you. Please, Martha," Charity called, "let me know if there's anything I can do to help you get resettled. There's a Sewing Society meeting Friday. If you can join us it would be wonderful."

Martha Red Wing assured Charity of her presence at the meeting and followed James and Soaring Eagle up the trail to the Red Wings' home. They found that a raccoon had taken up residence in their absence. It took the better part of a day for the three to rediscover the neat cabin that Martha had left a few months before. It was evening before Soaring Eagle lighted the lamp in his own little room and, lying back on his cot, opened LisBeth's letter.

He had read only a few lines before he sat up abruptly, frowning and grasping the letter tightly, reading and re-reading.

We pray that you were safely indoors when the blizzard struck. Please try to write as soon as you can and let us know if you are well. Jim was halfway home from Lincoln when the storm hit, but by tying himself to his team, he made his way home unharmed.

Carrie Brown was not so fortunate. She managed to get two of her students to safety, through the wisdom of your mare, Lakota, who brought them home. But she herself was lost in the storm, spending the night in a haystack that God miraculously provided just when her strength had failed her.

Dr. Gilbert and Sarah Biddle have given her excellent care, but it was necessary—

Soaring Eagle blinked his eyes, and read again. He laid the letter down and wiped tears from his eyes. *Red Bird— caught in the storm. Red Bird—afraid and alone—hurt—and now, recovering, but never the same.*

Charity Bond had said that things were all right, that he would read some disturbing news, but that things were all right. How did she know? It was late, so Soaring Eagle waited through a sleepless night before riding back to Santee He was watching when a lighted lamp appeared in the kitchen at the Birds' Nest.

Charity jumped at the sound of a knock at the door. He didn't wait for her to answer, but opened the door. "You said that it is better now. What is better? Tell me what you have learned." His face was lined with sadness, his voice tinged with something Charity had never heard before.

"LisBeth has written that Carrie is back in Lincoln. The surgery was a success. She is doing very well, Soaring Eagle. You don't need to worry. LisBeth says that her progress has been remarkable. She's planning to return to the school to teach as soon as possible."

Charity had been building a fire to begin heating water for coffee. At the earnestness in Soaring Eagle's voice she paused and looked at him. He was standing just inside the back door, with a look on his face that Charity had never seen. "Sit down, Soaring Eagle, please. I'll make you coffee."

Soaring Eagle obeyed mechanically. While Charity tried to collect her thoughts, Soaring Eagle said, "It was her caring that brought me to Christ."

"Yes, I know," Charity said softly.

"Her spirit has always—" he fumbled to explain, "has always been here." He indicated his heart. "Somehow she has always been with me, a little girl who looked past the wild Indian." He stopped and looked at Charity. "It is foolish for me to speak this way." Standing up he said, "I only wanted to know that she was all right."

Looking at Soaring Eagle, Charity Bond knew what she must say. "Soaring Eagle, I think that you should go visit Carrie and see for yourself how she is doing. LisBeth wrote that you had mentioned going to meet your nephew. He's probably walking by now. Perhaps it is time you went to see him," Charity added with meaning, "and Carrie."

"Yes. I think you are right." Soaring Eagle left as abruptly as he had come.

As soon as he had gone, David Gray Cloud bounded up onto the porch and invited himself in for coffee. "Since your first suitor didn't stay for coffee, may I join you?"

Somewhat flustered, Charity invited David in and poured coffee. "There goes a tortured man," David said, indicating Soaring Eagle.

"Tortured?"

"Needs a wife and can't seem to realize it. I, on the other hand, am wise with the wisdom of my people." Setting his coffee cup down, David Gray Cloud looked up at Charity. "Please, Miss Bond, won't you be seated?"

Charity sat down, a quizzical expression on her face.

"Did you enjoy your work on the Cheyenne River, Miss Bond?"

Charity smiled sincerely. "Oh, yes."

"And would you be interested in returning in the spring for a further season of work?"

"Has Dr. Riggs said that I might go? I'll have to write Carrie and see if she can come. We work so well together."

"Miss Bond, I had another partner in mind for you."

"Who?"

"Me."

"You?"

"Me."

Charity looked at David Gray Cloud in amazement. "But—"

"Does the idea revolt you?"

Charity blushed. "Far from it, but—"

"Can we pray for a season and see what God will do?"

Charity hesitated. "I don't quite know what to say, David."

"Don't say anything, Charity. Just pray. Dr. Riggs told me long ago to get myself a wife. This is a rather unromantic way to begin, but good marriages have begun in much stranger ways."

"Yes. I suppose they have." As a single woman and a matron at Santee, Charity Bond had long ago learned to conduct herself with irreproachable inattention to the men she encountered. Suddenly she looked at David Gray Cloud as a woman observing a man. She liked what she saw. She had always liked what she saw when David Gray Cloud entered a room, but she had never allowed herself to admit it. But David had given her permission to admit it. She realized that she should, indeed, pray about things for a season. Still, she had the distinct impression that it would be a very short season before she realized that she could love David Gray Cloud.

CHAPTER 29

 We glory in tribulations also: knowing that tribulation worketh patience; And patience, experience; and experience, hope: And hope maketh not ashamed; because the love of God is shed abroad in our hearts by the Holy Ghost which is given unto us.

Romans 5:3–5

Carrie Brown woke early after a nearly sleepless night and made her way slowly into the Callaway's kitchen, where she tried in vain to start a fire and boil water for coffee without waking LisBeth. No sooner had she settled in a chair than LisBeth stood at the door asking, "Are you all right, Carrie?"

Carrie looked up from the Bible that lay open on the table before her and sighed, "I'm sorry, LisBeth. I didn't mean to wake you."

"A mother's ears, Carrie. Actually, it wasn't you I heard first. J.W. must have been having a bad dream. He's back asleep now." With a smile, LisBeth looked out the window towards the east. "It's near daylight now, anyway. Time I was up too." She poured herself a cup of coffee and sat down opposite Carrie. "Are you nervous about today?"

"Scared to death," Carrie admitted. "More frightened than I was that first day last fall." She took a gulp of coffee. "I wish I could have learned to do without the canes sooner. It would have been easier for the children, and," she admitted, "much easier for me. We could have pretended nothing was different for a few minutes."

"Carrie," LisBeth said sincerely, "if *you* don't act awkward about the change, then the children will follow your lead. Take all the mystery out of everything. Just be open and honest. Let them ask questions. You're going to do fine."

LisBeth reached across the table and patted Carrie's hand. "And don't forget, Carrie, you *are* our local heroine. You saved Tess and Ned Carter's lives."

Carrie shook her head. "I think that honor goes to Lakota. That little horse just wouldn't give up. When I headed the wrong way, she threw a fit. I really had no choice but to let her lead." Carrie smiled. "Who would have thought God would use that little mare in such a way?"

Carrie looked out the window at the pink-tinged sky. "I could almost hear Soaring Eagle's voice saying *follow the horse, Carrie, follow the horse.* I never would have thought to do it. We'd have floundered around in the blizzard and likely died. I'll have to write him and thank him for that."

"You won't need to write it, Carrie. You can tell him yourself. He'll be here any day."

Carrie's face remained expressionless, but she pulled her left hand away from LisBeth and put in her lap, shifting nervously in her chair.

LisBeth explained, "You got in so late last night from town, I forgot to tell you. Jim had a letter from Charity with him. She said that Soaring Eagle and the others had just come back from the Cheyenne River." LisBeth got up and left the kitchen, returning momentarily with a letter in hand. "Thank God now we know they are all safe. Here, Carrie, you need to read this."

Carrie read Charity's account of the trouble at the Cheyenne River and the plans to return in the spring. Her heart ached as she thought of Soaring Eagle and the others working so hard and losing so many to smallpox. Then she read something that made her heart beat a little more quickly.

They came in late in the morning and met with Dr. Riggs. I gave Soaring Eagle your letter just as they road out toward the Red Wings'. I told him that I would write you and let you know that he was safe. But he was waiting outside the Birds' Nest when I lit the lamp in the kitchen the next morning. He must have been waiting for me to get up. I've never seen him so upset. I actually think he had tears in his eyes when he spoke of her.

I hope I didn't misspeak, LisBeth, but I encouraged him to come to you and to see for himself how Carrie is doing. His face shows the effects of his season's work. It is lined with care and, somehow, he doesn't look healthy. I'm glad he is coming to you. A few weeks with J.W. and your cooking, some time working out-of-doors with Jim away from the cares of a missionary can only have a positive effect.

You will, of course, want to prepare him for the physical changes in Carrie, but the spiritual changes I read in her letters encourage me so much. It is such a blessing to know that she has adapted without bitterness. I know this is in at least some way due to your sharing your mother's Bible with her, LisBeth. Praise be to the Lord who put it in your heart to turn Carrie's attention from herself and to her blessed Lord.

This morning I read 1 Peter 4:19, "Wherefore let them that suffer according to the will of God commit the keeping of their souls to him in well doing, as unto a faithful Creator." *We have all seen that verse lived out in Carrie Brown, and I hope you let her read this letter so that she will know how much I am encouraged by her testimony. I am still praying that she will be able to return with us to the Cheyenne River in the spring.*

With us, you say? Well, that is the other news that I have to share. Just after Soaring Eagle left the Birds' Nest, who should come into my kitchen but David Gray Cloud. And what do you suppose he wanted? He had been to talk with Dr. Riggs, and apparently Dr. Riggs had encouraged him. LisBeth, he has asked me to consider returning to the Cheyenne River with him in the spring—as his wife!

Now if you are amazed, you are no more amazed than I. I had always thought that my life would be spent among my children here at Santee. I stopped dreaming of being a bride long ago. Isn't it amazing that just when we have given up our own plans, God pours out "exceeding abundantly beyond all that we ask or think"? Do you suppose that He only wants us to let go, and stop trying to make things happen for ourselves, and then He can pour out blessings? I do not understand it all theologically, but I am once again humbled and amazed by His workings.

You will be even more amazed to hear that I have agreed to consider. It isn't very romantic, I know, but I think many happy marriages are made between good friends, and David Gray Cloud is quickly becoming my very good friend. We have many months to build this friendship. And yet I admit that when I see him coming up the trail to join me for coffee (in plain view of everyone, of course), something does happen to this old maid's heart. He makes me laugh. He has even said that he admires me.

I have thought often of the night that mother demanded that Lis-Beth and Augusta talk me out of coming to Santee. Had she known then that I would live to be courted by a Santee Sioux, she probably would have tied me to the bedstead! But God has His time for everything, and when I finally got the courage to write her about David, she only asked if there was a possibility that she, too, could come to the Cheyenne River. She worded it this way: "Do you suppose that an old woman could be of any use in such a work? It breaks my heart to think of you so far away and me alone here in Lincoln. I am still in good health, and perhaps I could help with things like the sewing society—or even the garden."

Can you believe it? My mother who never weeded her own garden and never wanted to let her child go away from Lincoln, is now offering to follow her daughter and Indian son-in-law into the wild west, and to keep their garden! I think perhaps God has done a miracle in us all, hasn't He? Please pray for us as we call upon God for His direction. I am already beginning to have a bit of difficulty praying objectively. David Gray Cloud may not be as handsome as Soaring Eagle, but there is a light in his eyes, and something about his smile.

Carrie handed the letter back to LisBeth without making any comment. Jim came into the kitchen and she asked, "Jim, as soon as you can, if it isn't too much trouble, I'd like to get to the school before the children." She looked at LisBeth and continued, "I wanted to be seated at my desk for the first day, let them get used to things."

Jim interrupted, his voice encouraging, "Why, Carrie, you don't have to worry a minute about those children. You're a heroine to every one of them. What you did for Ned and Tess, sacrificing yourself that way."

"Just the same, Jim, I'm a little nervous, and I'd feel better about doing it this way."

Jim nodded and made his way to the door. "It'll only take a few minutes to get the team hitched up. I'll do chores when I get back."

"Thanks, Jim." Carrie sat at the table, rubbing the back of her hand, absentmindedly tracing along the neat scar where Dr. Gilbert had had to remove two frozen fingers. She didn't want to admit it, but a knot was beginning to form in her stomach at the prospect of seeing Soaring Eagle again. *Why'd he have to hurry so fast? If he'd only waited until later in the spring, I could have been without the canes.* She cross-examined herself. *And why should that matter? He's just a friend coming to see a friend, so why should it matter?*

The sound of the wagon rattling up to the house brought her out of deep thought. She made her way to the back door and pulled on her coat and mittens.

"It's going to be a nice day, Carrie," LisBeth offered. "Don't be afraid. It's going to be fine."

Carrie nodded wordlessly and hobbled slowly out the door and across the porch. Jim lifted her up onto the wagon seat. She took a deep breath. "Thanks, Jim. Wish I ould figure a way to get up on a wagon without help."

"A gentleman always helps a lady in and out of wagon, Miss Brown." Jim slapped the team with the reins and they jolted off towards school. Three miles of nearly spring air did much to relax Carrie. She looked at the schoolhouse smokestack and was relieved to see that no one had come early to surprise the teacher by building a fire.

"Do you mind carrying in some firewood, Jim? I'll get a student to volunteer after today."

"My pleasure. No problem at all." Jim pulled the wagon up to the school door. "You know, Carrie, if it really bothers you, let me see how close I can get to the steps. Maybe if I pull up just right—" Jim maneuvered the wagon so that Carrie was able to get down herself, landing on the second step from the top.

She smiled gratefully. "Thank you, Jim."

Only a few moments before Carrie descended from Jim's wagon Ned Carter had called out from his place at the schoolhouse door to warn his classmates of Miss Brown's arrival. "They're coming!" he had called, rushing away from the door and taking his place at the front of the room where his classmates already stood in two rows, stretched out behind the teacher's desk.

Miss Brown was concentrating so much on managing her canes and her coat, her bonnet and her mittens, that she didn't glance towards the front of the schoolroom. She took off her cloak and managed to hang it up before something made her look towards the desk. There were two rows of beaming faces looking back at her.

Carrie blushed furiously and wobbled about, trying to get her skirt out of the way so she could position her canes properly. Before she could get turned all the way around, the students burst into song. The young voices warbled uncertainly and finished on a decidedly flat note, but never before had Carrie Brown heard more beautiful music. She blinked back tears and mumbled nervously to thank the children, but they didn't hear, for they were flocking down the center aisle of the schoolroom and around her, eagerly offering help.

Tess Carter reached out and covered Carrie's hand with her own. "Can I help you walk up front, Miss Brown?"

"No!" said Matthew Glenn. "You're too little. I'll help her."

"No, let me."

"You said *I* could help!"

"Children!" Carrie almost shouted in mock anger. When they quieted she said softly, "Thank you very much, Matthew, Philip, Tess, Ned. But if you will all be seated." She hadn't even finished her sentence before every child had obediently taken his place at the desk. They turned sideways, watching Carrie.

Carrie took small steps down the aisle, keeping her back erect and her head up, placing the canes carefully. When she finally reached her desk, the children sat quietly, waiting. Peering down at the drawer in her desk Carrie asked suspiciously, "Ned Carter, if I open this desk drawer is there going to be a surprise in it?"

The children giggled and Ned blushed, standing up. "No, ma'am, the snakes are all still hibernated, ma'am."

When the laughter subsided, Carrie grew suddenly serious. "I am so grateful to the dear Lord that each one of you has come back to our school. That day of the blizzard, as I was falling asleep in the haystack, I was praying that God would take care of each one of you." Carrie swallowed hard. "Now, you all know that I had to have some surgery after the storm. I am still walking with canes, but the doctor says that if I work hard, I should be able to throw them away soon. I hope you can all be here the day I burn them in that stove. Which reminds me, no one has started a fire yet."

Jim came in the back door with an armload of wood just as Carrie said, "Ned, would you do the honors today? Then I need volunteers."

Several hands shot up and the schedule of fire tending was easily arranged. From the back of the schoolroom, Jim tipped his hat and nodded at Carrie, going back outside and heading back to home and morning chores.

Carrie asked, "Now, if there are no more questions—"

Tess Carter raised her hand.

"Tess, you have a question?"

Tess nodded somberly and slipped out of her seat. Approaching Carrie's desk, she looked with wide eyes at Carrie's left hand. Carrie resisted the urge to curl her hand into a fist and shove it into her lap. Clearing her throat, she said quietly, "What did you want to ask, Tess? It's all right. You don't have to be afraid."

Gently Tess reached across the desk to pat Carrie's hand. Her eyes welled up with tears and her little chin trembled as she whispered hoarsely, "Does it *hurt*, Miss Brown?" She looked up with loving eyes and waited for Miss Brown to answer. Carrie's throat grew tight as she managed to answer, "Oh, no, Tess. It doesn't hurt at all." Tess was not satisfied. She nodded, but one tear spilled down her cheek. "I was thinkin', Miss Brown, if Ned and me hadn't had to ride Lakota that day, you would have, you would have—" Tess lowered her head and began to sob. "I'm sorry, Miss Brown. We didn't mean for you to—"

Carrie was nearly overcome with emotion. She reached out for Tess's little hand and clutching it, pulled Tess around the desk and into her arms. "Oh, Tess. Dear, sweet, little Tess. Don't you think for one moment that I have ever regretted having you and Ned with me. Didn't Ned keep you good and warm inside his coat? And didn't Lakota take us all home? Why, it wasn't your fault I was too silly to hang on to Lakota's tail. And didn't God provide a haystack when I needed it? Why, Tess, I can still walk and I can still teach, and, look, Tess—" Carrie held out her hand and ran Tess's finger along the scar. "See, Honey. It doesn't hurt at all. I can still walk and I can still do just about everything with this hand that I ever could. I can do what's most important too, Tess. I can still hug my schoolchildren!" Carrie hugged Tess. Looking up at the rest of the class she said, "I have learned that the best way to deal with fear is to talk about it. So if any of you other children want to talk about things, you just ask me. Don't be afraid to ask."

No hands were raised, and so Carrie stood up and began the day of school.

"This morning," she began, "I think we will begin by writing a composition. It shall be called 'The Blizzard of '86,' and I want each one of you to write down everything you remember about the blizzard: what it felt like to you, how it affected your families, everything you can remember. We're going to put our papers into a book, and then someday, when someone wants to know what it was like, they will have our memories. You may begin now. We will work for the next twenty minutes, and then have a brief recess before going back to our study of the Revolutionary War." A groan went up from the back row. Carrie looked at Philip Damrow. "Which reminds me, Philip, you were to recite the preamble to the Constitution for me that day when we had to dismiss school early. You must work on that. Be prepared to recite on Friday."

School District 117 in Roca, Nebraska, was back in session.

CHAPTER 30

Surely as I have thought, so shall it come to pass; and as I have purposed, so shall it stand.

Isaiah 14:24

Jim Callaway was forking hay into Lakota's stall when he saw the mare jerk her head up from where she had been snuffling through the fresh hay. She stopped chewing for a moment. Her small ears pricked forward and she listened carefully. Jim stopped forking hay and cocked his head, listening. A horse was coming up the road. The sound of hoofbeats grew louder as the horse turned in at the farm. Jim went to the barn door and peered out just in time to see Soaring Eagle dismount and lead his horse to the well.

At the same time Jim stepped out the barn door, LisBeth emerged from the house. "How did you find us? How did you know where to find us?"

"I found the livery in Lincoln. Joseph Freeman told me where to find you."

"But how did you find Lincoln?"

Soaring Eagle finished drawing the bucketful of water up the deep well. He set the bucket down for his horse and leaned back against the side of the well, pushing his hat back on his head and wiping some grime off his forehead with the back of his hand. "The salt flats," he said matter-of-factly. When LisBeth looked confused, he shook his head. "Did you think the white people who began that city of Lincoln were the first ones to see those salt flats? The Sioux, and other tribes, came there long before any white man ever knew they existed. I knew the way to the salt flats. After that, I followed the rails of the train to the train station and across the street to the livery. From what you said about Joseph Freeman, I knew he would help me find you."

Jim reached for the horse's reins. "I'll see your horse gets bedded down, Soaring Eagle. You go on with LisBeth. I know you want to see J.W." Jim headed for the barn and Soaring Eagle followed his sister into the house and through the kitchen to the bedroom where J.W. lay sleeping.

"He still takes a morning nap," LisBeth whispered. "But he'll be awake soon."

Soaring Eagle looked at the sleeping baby and murmured, "He has our father's chin."

The two went back into the kitchen before LisBeth answered. "Yes, I thought so, too, from what you've told me. His eyes are gray-green, like his pa's."

Soaring Eagle went to the door. "I will help Jim with the horse." He went outside without waiting for LisBeth to answer.

In the barn, Jim had already unsaddled Soaring Eagle's horse and was rubbing it down. In the walkway just outside the stall sat an old carpetbag and a parfleche. When Soaring Eagle came into the barn, Jim nodded. "Looks like you're planning a good visit. I'm glad."

"Dr. Riggs thinks that I need what he called 'a time of refreshing.'"

"From what we heard from Charity Bond about your time up on the Cheyenne River, Dr. Riggs is right," Jim offered. He was currying the horse's tail and just escaped a kick. He grinned. "Tell me you didn't break this horse, Soaring Eagle. 'Cause if you did, you're slipping."

Soaring Eagle smiled in spite of himself. "No, I didn't break this one. But I intend to break his habit of kicking while I am here." He sat on a pile of hay bales in the walkway.

Jim began to meticulously comb the horse's mane, fingering at imaginary cockleburrs until he picked up a brush and began to rub the already shining coat. When he could find no other reason to continue grooming the horse, Soaring Eagle still had not moved from the hay bales.

Jim headed back toward the barn door. "Come on down here, Soaring Eagle. Let's work on the tack a bit." The two men walked to the open area at the east end of the stalls where sunlight poured in the open door. Jim pulled down a pile of harnesses and, opening a tin of saddle soap, began to work. Soaring Eagle joined him.

Abruptly, Jim offered, "You're welcome for as long as you want to stay, Soaring Eagle. I could sure use the help on the place."

Soaring Eagle looked up, surprised.

Jim shrugged and said, "It's been a long time since I stumbled onto this place, friend. But I remember needing quiet—a place to just *be* for a spell, until I sorted things out."

"I would sleep in the barn."

"Stay as long as you can, Soaring Eagle. If you've a mind to, you can help with spring planting. Lakota's due to foal any day. Joseph Freeman will be bringing out a string of prospects for his livery next week. I promised I'd help gentle 'em, get 'em ready for city streets."

Soaring Eagle broke in abruptly, "Is Carrie Brown all right?"

Jim laid aside his harness and leaned forward. "She's fine, Soaring Eagle. Really. She's amazed everyone with her reaction to things. She rehabilitated faster than the doctor thought possible. Sent her grandparents back to St. Louis in only three weeks. She was already walking by then."

"But in here." Soaring Eagle looked at Jim, touching his chest. "In here?"

Jim rubbed the back of his neck with his hand. "As far as anyone can tell, Soaring Eagle, she's doing great. Why don't you ride over and see for yourself? She started teaching school today." At the look of amazement on Soaring Eagle's face, Jim smiled. "Yep. That's right. In fact, you probably rode right near the schoolhouse where she's teaching. Go on over."

"Which way?" he wanted to know.

Jim pointed. "Three miles straight north. The school's at the top of a hill just after the creek takes a turn back to the east. There's a hedge along the road."

Soaring Eagle rummaged in his parfleche and then went to the door.

Jim offered, "Take Lakota there, she's yours anyway."

Soaring Eagle shook his head. "No. I'll walk." He stopped to get a drink at the well and headed back out onto the road, towards the school.

LisBeth saw him heading up the road and came to the barn. "Is he all right?" she wanted to know.

Jim shook his head. "I don't know, LisBeth. He's going to stay awhile. Help me work the place."

LisBeth smiled with pleasure. "Wonderful. He'll get to know J.W." She walked down the walkway to the end of the barn and opened a door. "Do you think we can fix this tack room up for him, Jim?" she called out.

Jim nodded. "You bet. I'll get it cleaned out and we'll set up a cot."

LisBeth was inspired with plans. "I'll get some of the gingham, tack up some curtains. The little stove we packed away should be just right for this corner. Then he can make his own coffee if he wants it." She headed back towards Jim, almost tripping over the parfleche. "What's this?"

"Soaring Eagle brought it. He didn't explain. Guess it's important to him."

LisBeth resisted the urge to open the parfleche. Instead, she headed for the house to retrieve a bucket and mop, a scrub brush and soap, to prepare a room in the barn for her brother who was at that moment walking down the road towards a schoolhouse, with a small bundle under his arm.

During recess at the schoolhouse, Carrie had been surprised to see a wagon approaching. Ben and Ellie Carter hopped down and approached the school, where Carrie sat on the edge of the porch. "Hello, Miss Brown," Ellie said shyly, handing Carrie a basket. "I brung these to say thankee—fer what you did fer Ned and Tess." Ellie backed away, nearly hiding behind Ben. Carrie peeked under the napkin and pulled out a garland of strung dried apples and green beans.

"Why, thank you, Mrs. Carter," was all she got a chance to say, because suddenly another wagon was approaching.

Ben Carter explained. "Us parents decided we ought to give you a proper welcome back, Miss Brown. If you got no objections, we'd like to have a little picnic lunch here—for you and the children."

Carrie smiled and nodded, and before long there were several wagons lined up at the schoolhouse. The wagons held planks and sawhorses, and tables were set up and a feast spread for parents and children alike. When Carrie Brown slowly made her way down the stairs of the schoolhouse and across the short distance to the place of honor at the table, the parents and children applauded. Carrie blushed furiously, not knowing what to say.

Ben Carter spoke up. "This here is a good day for

District 117. We got our teacher back, and every child that was caught by the storm made it home to safety." Ben shifted his weight from one foot to another before continuing. "Miss Brown, some amongst us had things to say when we got a teacher without her college degree." He squinted meaningfully at Philip Damrow's parents. "But, fact is, Miss Brown, we want to keep you. The school board has authorized me to offer you a raise if you'll stay on next year."

Caught by surprise, Carrie didn't know how to respond. She had already discussed her options with Augusta Hathaway, and worked out a plan for finishing at the university in spite of the new physical challenges. Now she wasn't so certain she needed that plan.

"Thank you, Mr. Carter. I'll—" Carrie paused. "I'll certainly consider your offer." *Maybe I could attend the summer session, take double hours.* She was already considering how she might finish her university degree and at the same time continue to educate these children.

For another hour the children played and Carrie visited with their parents. Then, as if a bell had been rung, the parents rose and cleaned up the picnic, packed the tables into the backs of their wagons, and trundled towards home. Wagons headed in every direction as Carrie mounted the steps and rang the school bell to resume classes.

She smiled with pleasure at the presence of yet another surprise on her desk. But as she made her way up the aisle her heart began to pound. It looked like—it couldn't be—and yet, it was. A little bundle wrapped in soft elkskin, tied with thongs. As quickly as she could, she rushed back to the doorway of the little schoolhouse while the children filed inside and settled into their desks.

Carrie stepped outside the door and searched the schoolyard, the trees, the horizon. There was no one visible. Still, it seemed that there must be some one there—watching, waiting.

"What 'cha doin', Miss Brown?" Tess Carter's voice called from the doorway. "You all right, Miss Brown?"

Carrie turned around. "Yes, yes, Tess. I'm fine. I was just—" Without finishing her sentence, she turned to go back inside. At her desk, she heeded the children's curious questions and said simply, "This is something from my childhood." With trembling hands she unwrapped the skins and held up Ida Mae. "This was my first doll. I gave her to a friend," Carrie stopped. "I really can't explain it, children. Let's go on with our lessons. First grade come forward for arithmetic."

When Soaring Eagle returned to the farmstead and went into the barn, he heard a child laughing. The sound came from a little room at the far end of the walkway. And just as he started down the walkway, a little boy emerged, toddling carefully along, clutching a scrub brush in his hands. He looked up at Soaring Eagle with great, dark eyes, and studied him carefully. Soaring Eagle didn't move toward the child, but crouched down and looked at him without moving. With only a moment's hesitation, the child smiled brightly and toddled toward him. Stopping by the parfleche he leaned over to bang on the stiff rawhide top. It gave way, and J.W. tumbled into the hay, bumping his head on a stall board. Smiles instantly became tears of rage.

LisBeth hurried after J.W., but Soaring Eagle had already swooped the boy up and whispered something in his ear. The child stopped crying immediately, grabbed his uncle's long hair, and pulled ferociously. Soaring Eagle laughed. J.W. giggled back.

LisBeth folded her arms and leaned back against the doorway. "You've charmed him already."

"He's a fine boy, my sister."

"Just like his uncle, and his father and grandpa too."

Jim came in. "Time to hitch up and go get Carrie. Want to ride along?" He looked at Soaring Eagle, who surprisingly, shook his head. Puzzled, Jim made his way into the corral where the team was waiting hitched to a post. Soaring Eagle carried J.W. outside. "They had some kind of picnic at the school."

Jim nodded. "The parents told me about it. They wanted to surprise her. A welcome back."

Soaring Eagle put J.W. up on one of the horse's backs.

"What is it, Soaring Eagle. What's eating at you?"

"She's doing well?"

"I told you she was. Didn't you talk to her?"

Soaring Eagle shook his head and Jim ducked under one of the horse's necks and checked the harness on the off side. He stood up abruptly. "Why not?"

"I left a gift on her desk, but she didn't see me." Soaring Eagle put his own hands over J.W.'s little fists and opened his hands, encouraging him to hang on to the horse's mane. Jim pretended to adjust a harness that needed no adjusting and Soaring Eagle continued, "Everything that has happened to me happened for a reason. I can accept it. I can endure it. I read the Bible verses and I know they are true. *All His ways are justice. Righteous and upright is He. He wounds and He heals. It is good for me that I was afflicted, that I may learn thy statutes.*" Soaring Eagle looked up at Jim with a pained expression. "I accept His chastening of *me*, His direction for *me*. I humbled myself and have tried to learn from the Cheyenne River, to grow, and to be better equipped for the future. But I cannot—" he hesitated briefly, but then allowed the words to flow. "I cannot bear to think of my little Red Bird—" the words came out choked with emotion. Soaring Eagle brusquely pulled J.W. down from the back of the horse and turned away. "I cannot bear to think of her suffering, and—" he looked at Jim with eyes that shone with tears. "I do not know if I can bear to see her now. I have come all this way to make certain that *her* soul is well, that *her* heart is right. And I find that my own soul and my own heart are aching."

"You need to see Carrie right away, friend," Jim urged, "because when you talk to Carrie, you'll know that you don't have to wonder why God allowed her to get caught in that blizzard. The answer is written all over her face, Soaring Eagle. LisBeth used to worry about the way Carrie used to pout and scheme to get her way. Now, she's happy and content, she's closer to the Lord than ever." Jim shook his head, searching for words. "She's just quite a little woman, Soaring Eagle." He tossed Soaring Eagle the reins. "See for yourself." Taking J.W. from Soaring Eagle's arms, Jim walked away.

Reluctantly, Soaring Eagle climbed into the wagon box and headed for the schoolhouse.

CHAPTER 31

A gracious woman retaineth honor

Proverbs 11:16

She saw who was driving the wagon and wanted to flee. She had shoved the little bundle that held Ida Mae under her arm, pressing it against her side to free her hands for the canes. She could feel it slipping, but she didn't want to drop a cane and let him see.

As the wagon trundled up to the front of the schoolhouse, he held up one hand in a halfhearted greeting. He climbed down slowly from the wagon. Reaching into the back of the wagon, he hefted a huge log to the side where Carrie would have to climb up. He put it down on the ground and looked up at her. "Jim said that you don't like having to be lifted into the wagon. I can't drive as well as he, to bring the wagon up so close for you. But this way—"

Carrie shook her head. Her heart was pounding. "Yes, yes. I see. It's a good idea. Thank you." She began to descend the stairs and he climbed up beside her, awkwardly trying to take her arm, not knowing what to do. "If you'll just take Ida Mae from under my arm, I can manage the rest just fine."

Soaring Eagle took the bundle and put it under the wagon seat. He turned just as Carrie was stepping onto the log. It wobbled a little, and when he reached to steady her, he knocked one cane away. To keep from falling, she laid her hand on his shoulder. When she had climbed into the wagon box, she smiled down at him. "Thank you, Soaring Eagle. You're very patient."

Soaring Eagle retrieved the cane he had knocked away, tossing it into the wagon box. He walked back around and got up beside her. He picked up the reins and urged the team to a walk. "Thank you for bringing Ida Mae. It was a lovely surprise."

"I didn't want to interrupt the picnic."

"How did you ever manage to get her on my desk without being seen?"

"The window."

Carrie nodded. The wagon passed the osage hedge along the rode and crossed the creek before Carrie said, "Charity Bond wrote that you might be coming. I didn't think it would be until later this spring."

"I wanted—" He stopped in midsentence. "Dr. Riggs thought I should come now."

"I'm sorry about the Cheyenne River work. I'm sure it will go better this spring."

He shrugged. "I have given up trying to understand God's ways."

Carrie was quiet. It was a warm afternoon and she felt her palms sweating. She pulled off her mittens, hiding her hands by gripping the edge of the wagon seat.

"Isn't J.W. a wonderful child?"

Soaring Eagle nodded. "He likes to pull my hair."

Carrie chuckled. "Mine, too. LisBeth is such a good mother—" She broke off, suddenly uncomfortable mentioning motherhood in his presence.

"You seem well."

"Yes, I'm fine." She tried to fill the silence between them. "Except for riding Lakota, I seem to be able to do just about everything."

"Why can you not ride Lakota?"

Carrie regretted having said it. Now she had to explain. She bit her lip. "I'm not strong enough to pull myself up. And with the fronts of my feet—" she stopped and then added. "Well, I just can't seem to balance properly to mount. Anyway, if I ever fell off, which is a distinct possibility since I'm not the best rider, I'd be stuck, and," she laughed nervously, "as you saw back at the school, I'm not quite ready for a three-mile walk."

Soaring Eagle thought for a moment. "I can teach you to ride better."

"Are you staying, then, at the Callaways'?"

"For a while. To help Jim with spring planting. To see Lakota's foal."

Carrie said softly, "I'd like to be able to ride better."

Soaring Eagle began to think of a way to help Carrie Brown mount a horse without help. Conversation ended abruptly, but communication did not, for as they rode along, Carrie Brown and Jeremiah Soaring Eagle King were well aware that the space between them was filled with unspoken words.

Soaring Eagle began working with Lakota the next morning. He was up at dawn, putting the little mare through her paces until she flawlessly switched from one gait to another, changing leads on command, stopping, trotting, galloping at the first command she received.

On Saturday morning Carrie walked to the barn breathless with excitement. When Soaring Eagle lifted her into the saddle, she fumbled awkwardly with the stirrups, trying in vain to get her feet positioned correctly. Soaring Eagle draped the stirrups over the horn of the saddle. "I have been told it is not proper to say this word," he smiled, "but

I must. Grip with your *knees*, Carrie. Learn to ride without the stirrups."

After the first lesson, Carrie groaned when she hobbled back to the house, but she was happily exhausted. As time went on, her young muscles responded to the new demands, and she found that she could, indeed, ride without stirrups, which meant that the problem her surgery presented in balancing her weight in the stirrups was solved. She barely put any weight in the stirrups, compensating instead with newly strengthened leg muscles.

"But I still have to have help to mount," she said to LisBeth one evening after supper. "I don't quite know what to do about that."

"Jim doesn't mind taking you to school, Carrie. By next year we'll have a carriage. Then you can drive yourself."

Carrie shook her head. "I know, I know, but I'd still like to be able to get myself there and back. I want to be useful, LisBeth, not a burden."

"You're *not* a burden, Carrie."

At that moment Jim came to the kitchen door. "Come outside, ladies. We have something to show you."

Soaring Eagle and Jim stood at the back door, with Lakota saddled and bridled. Carrie and LisBeth went outside. Jim motioned to Carrie. "Come over here Carrie, on this side, where you mount."

Jim handed Carrie a riding crop. "Now, Carrie, touch her on the foreleg and say, "Down, Lakota, down." Carrie complied and to her amazement, Lakota bent her foreleg and knelt down.

"Can you pull yourself into the saddle by yourself, Red Bird?" Soaring Eagle asked gently.

Carrie nodded and did just that.

Jim said, "Now, when you're ready, touch her flank with the crop and say, "Up, Lakota, up " The moment Carrie said the words, Lakota got up.

LisBeth clasped her hands under her chin and shook her head. "I never would have believed it! How did you ever get her to do that? Carrie always said Lakota was so stubborn!"

Soaring Eagle smiled. "I am more stubborn than Lakota. She didn't like learning it, but she learned it. And she will do it, whenever it is needed." He patted Lakota and looked up at Carrie. "Now you can ride to school. You don't need help—except from Lakota."

Carrie was fighting back tears. "I don't know how to thank you," she said in a half whisper. Abruptly, she bent over and kissed Soaring Eagle on the cheek. "Thank you, Soaring Eagle. Thank you." Taking Lakota's reins in hand she said, "Will you ride with me?" Soaring Eagle nodded and went into the barn. Quickly putting a bridle on his horse, he jumped astride bareback and joined Carrie for an evening ride.

When Carrie Brown and Soaring Eagle came back from their ride, Jim and LisBeth had gone to bed, leaving a lamp lighted in the window and hot coffee on the stove. Soaring Eagle reached for Lakota's reins, but Carrie shook her head. "No, if you'll give me time I'd like to brush her down myself."

Together, they led their horses into the barn, currying and brushing and cleaning hooves without saying much, until Soaring Eagle went to check Bear's hind feet. With one swift motion, Bear lifted Soaring Eagle off his feet and sent him flying. He landed with a thud and a look of surprise on his face that sent Carrie into gales of laughter.

"I'd say you've spent too much time teaching Lakota to kneel and not enough time breaking Bear's bad habit."

Soaring Eagle got up, rubbing his back and laughing.

Carrie perched on a bale of hay and watched while he insisted on picking up Bear's foot, again and again, until Bear stopped trying to kick.

Together they walked back to the house. "They've gone to bed," Carrie said quietly. "The lamp's in the window."

"Sit here with me," Soaring Eagle invited, sitting down on the porch and leaning against the railing.

Carrie settled opposite him. Once again, unspoken words hung in the air. Soaring Eagle pulled a few down and said, "I have been angry with God about you."

"About *me*?"

"I didn't think it was right for Him to let that happen—in the blizzard."

Carrie was quiet for a long time before she said anything. Finally, she answered, "I was angry for a while too. I didn't think it was fair."

"But you are no longer angry."

In the gathering dark, Carrie shook her head. "No. I'm not."

"Why?"

She gathered her thoughts and said carefully, "Well, ultimately, of course, because of the Lord. But getting over the anger began with your mother."

He was amazed. "My—mother?"

Carrie nodded and began to tell Soaring Eagle about her ride into Lincoln for her surgery, the realization of everyone else's trials, and, finally, reading Jesse's Bible. "Would you like to hear some of the things that spoke to me the most?"

It was Soaring Eagle's turn to nod in the half-light. He was watching her with a curious look in his eyes. It made Carrie's heart beat a little faster. She looked away and began to recite. *"Who hath made man's mouth? Or who maketh the dumb, or deaf, or the seeing, or the blind? Have not I, the Lord?'* I really didn't like that verse. But there it was. I had to deal with it. Was He the Lord or wasn't He? Could He have rescued me from that blizzard? Absolutely. But He didn't. Why didn't He? I don't know. But I do know that He *is* Lord. He has a purpose and He is not obligated to tell me His purpose. If He didn't explain the 'why' to Job—the most righteous man on the earth—He certainly doesn't have to explain anything to little Carrie Brown.

"A passage that really challenged me was in Romans. It says, *'Who are you, O man, who answers back to God? The thing molded will not say to the molder, "why did you make me thus?" Will it? Or does the potter have a right over the clay.'"* She laughed nervously. "I may have given up that ridiculous notion of the wild Sioux and the little redhead, but there was still a lot of Carrie Brown's will that needed to be kicked out of me, I guess." She reflected for a moment before saying softly, "It's such a *battle* being pleasing to God. After the blizzard, I looked around me and there stood a multitude of people who had each one faced trials just as difficult as mine—if not more so—and come out victorious. They picked up the pieces of their lives, they sang praises to God, and they went on to live useful lives. I decided I wanted to be one of those kinds of people. So I'm trying to 'humble myself under the mighty hand of God' and get on with serving Him in the best way I can."

Soaring Eagle reached across and took her hand. It was her left hand—without two fingers—and she unconsciously made a fist and tried to pull it away. But he didn't let go and she stopped resisting. Gently, he pulled her fist open, bending to kiss each finger, and the scar. "Carrie Brown," he said softly. "Jim Callaway was right. You are quite a little woman."

He reached down and cupped her chin in one hand. "The man who finally wins your heart will have won something to be treasured." Backing away from her, he turned and walked toward the barn.

Carrie made her way slowly to her room and stretched out on her bed. *Why, Lord, is it happening now? Just when I was content to be a teacher. Just when I could say to his face that I had given up the notion of the wild Sioux, he kisses my hand, and my heart beats faster, and I still feel there is so much to be said. But the words just hang there. I can't seem to gather them.*

In the barn, Soaring Eagle picked up a curry comb and began to groom Lakota. When he had finished, he stepped out to look up at the stars and pray.

CHAPTER 32

 My beloved spake, and said unto me, Rise up, my love, my fair one, and come away. For, lo, the winter is past, the rain is over and gone; The flowers appear on the earth; the time of the singing of birds is come, . . . Arise, my love, my fair one, and come away.

Song of Solomon 2:10-13

ell, are you?" Jim asked Soaring Eagle. They were working together on the team's harness, preparing to plow a new field.

Soaring Eagle looked up. "Am I what?"

"Are you going to marry Carrie Brown?"

Soaring Eagle looked down at his work. He smiled. "The better question is, is Carrie Brown going to marry me?"

"No problem with that one, my friend. You ask. She answers yes."

"Are you so certain?"

"You know, Soaring Eagle, at times I can't decide if you're trying to be the stoic, noble savage—trying to wait upon God—or just plain slow. You've been here for three weeks. You think I'm blind? You're in love with her, Soaring Eagle. So get on with it," Jim grinned and tossed him a rag, "and get out of my barn. Unless, of course you were planning to wait and see J.W. graduate from school."

Soaring Eagle was suddenly very serious. "I am much older than Carrie."

"And my father was older than my mother. And Rides

the Wind was older than Jesse. It doesn't matter. She loves you, Soaring Eagle. I can see it. And if I were stupid enough *not* to have noticed, LisBeth has confirmed my suspicions."

"Well," Soaring Eagle offered, "I have been praying.'

"And how do you expect God to answer your prayer unless you ask some worthy female to marry you? Listen, Soaring Eagle, Carrie Brown has loved you since she was a little girl. She lives, eats, drinks, breathes, and dreams you. She's grown into a beautiful woman who has a sincere love for the Lord and a desire to serve Him. Now just what, exactly, is she lacking that you've been praying for?"

Soaring Eagle grinned. "A suitor with the courage to ask her."

Jim grunted. "Let me get this right. You jumped off a cliff trusting two eaglets to land you safely. You fought alongside Sitting Bull. You went to school in Boston. You've stood before congregations made up of retired military men who hated you. But now, you're suddenly afraid to ask a little redheaded girl who weighs less than a hundred pounds to marry you?" Jim tossed his rag down and stood up. "I give up, my friend. You're going to die a lonely old man."

Jim left the barn half angry, marched to the house, and stormed inside where he grabbed up J.W. and hugged Lis-Beth fiercely.

"Did you talk to him?" LisBeth wanted to know.

Jim nodded. "And a lot of good it did. For a brave man, LisBeth, your brother is a real coward."

But Soaring Eagle was to overcome his fear. He spent the rest of the day while Carrie Brown was teaching school praying. Early in the afternoon, LisBeth and Jim saw him ride out of the farmyard on Bear. He had pulled on his ceremonial shirt and moccasins, and was riding bareback.

Carrie Brown had worn a cornflower blue calico dress to

school that day. She stayed at her desk long after the children had departed, preparing an especially challenging vocabulary quiz for the next day. She was writing on the blackboard, her back turned to the door. In his moccasins, Soaring Eagle was able to climb the stairs, enter the schoolroom, and slide into a seat in the back row unnoticed. He sat quietly, watching her concentrate, becoming more aware of his own racing pulse. When she finally turned around, she started and then smiled an appropriately friendly smile that changed into something else when he stood up and she saw his ceremonial shirt.

He ran his hand across the beading on the chest of the shirt and said, "I have a story to tell you, Carrie—a Lakota story." He cleared his throat and began to talk. "Once, there was a Lakota boy who was frightened and angry. He had lost his way in the world. But as he went along, a little red bird flew down from a tree. She whispered to him not to be afraid, and she led him through many things that frightened him. When she had to fly away, she left part of herself in the little boy's heart. And whenever he was afraid, he would think of his friend.

"The Lakota boy grew up and saw this little bird, and she had changed into a young woman. She was so beautiful that he wanted to take her in his arms and keep her for himself. But he thought, *you are too old. You are too poor. Your life is hard. You cannot ask such a beautiful thing to come down so low and live with you.* So the young man went away. There were other women who tried to woo him, but he could think only of his friend.

"And then one day the Lakota man learned that the young woman was sick. She was far away, and he could not reach her in time to help her get well. By the time he found her, she was well again, and more beautiful than ever before. And the Lakota man still feared. *You are too old.*

You are too poor. Your life is hard. You cannot ask such a beautiful thing to come down so low as to live with you."

Carrie walked to the edge of the desk and whispered, "And how does the story end, Soaring Eagle?"

"Well, the Lakota man did many things to show the woman that he cared for her. Still, whenever they were together, unspoken words hung in the air like fog. One day, the man's friend reminded him that if he did not speak, then he would die a lonely, old man, never having known joy for fear of having pain."

Soaring Eagle walked slowly up the aisle and looked up at Carrie. She had never seen the light in his eyes, the look on his face, and her heart began to thump as he said, "Tell me, Carrie Brown. If an eagle were to ask a red bird to share his nest, would the red bird accept? Would she stay when the winds blew, when there was little food, when the nest was poor, when the cliffs were high. Would she want to share such a life, or would it be too much for the eagle to ask? If she came to the eagle's nest, what kind of children . . ."

The question about children was interrupted by the joyful cry of a tiny redheaded woman flinging herself into the arms of her beloved man of God. But it was answered in time.

Jesse Red Eagle King, tall and athletic, was thoughtful and quiet. He studied law.

Alfred Red Eagle King, wiry and strong, homesteaded in Wyoming.

Walter Red Eagle King, the brilliant one, was working his way through the University of Nebraska when he contracted diphtheria and died.

The well-known Lincoln hosteler Augusta Hathaway saw to it that Walter was buried in Wyuka Cemetery beside his paternal grandmother, Jesse King.

John Red Eagle King went east to his father's alma mater, Beloit, later to become the pastor of a tiny church in Dakota.

Rachel Red Eagle King, the first girl, lived only three days.

LisBeth Red Eagle King accompanied her husband to China as a missionary.

And their parents lived and labored and loved in a tiny village on the Cheyenne River with few people knowing or caring about the battles waged and won and lost for the hearts of a few poverty-stricken Lakota Sioux.

When Carrie Brown King was laid to rest beside her beloved Soaring Eagle, only a few Lakota joined the grown children who traveled home to gather around their mother's grave. Their wavering voices sang a hymn of praise, for that is what Mrs. King had ordered.

"Don't you mourn for me," she had said. "You sing praises. Soaring Eagle said he would wait for me just inside the gate. I'll see Walter and Rachel. Don't you mourn." Carrie had looked up at her children and smiled, her blue eyes sparkling. Then she had looked past them—upward—and died.

The mourners finished their hymn and worked together to fill in the grave. As they finished, the prairie winds came up, tossing the ocean of grass that began at the edge of the tiny cemetery, rolling on over the hills southward. A shadow darted across the weedy ground and the King children shaded their eyes and looked up, watching the eagle soar into the distance.

Jesse murmured, "Ma and Pa would have loved that. They always loved to watch those birds ride the wind."

I have fought a good fight, I have finished my course, I have kept the faith: Henceforth there is laid up for me a crown of righteousness . . .
2 Timothy 4:7–8

ABOUT THE AUTHOR

Stephanie Grace Whitson was born in East St. Louis, Illinois, and received her B.A. in French from Southern Illinois University in Edwardsville, Illinois. A full-time homemaker, Stephanie has been married to her husband, RTW, who shares Rides the Wind's initials, for over twenty years. The Whitsons live on ten-and-a- half secluded acres in rural Nebraska where they homeschool their four children.

Stephanie is an avid quilter with a special interest in antique textiles. She is also a partner in Mulberry Lane, Inc., a business that designs and markets pewter jewelry.

The story of Jesse King and her descendents was inspired by the lives of pioneers laid to rest in an abandoned cemetery adjacent to the Whitson's property.

To receive information about future works by Stephanie, write to her at:

Stephanie Grace Whitson
3800 Old Cheney Road #101-178
Lincoln, NE 68516

Look for these other titles by Stephanie Grace Whitson in the *PrairieWinds Series.*

Walks the Fire
A Novel

This is the extraordinary story of Jesse King, a pioneer woman who is taken in by the Lakota Sioux after her husband and child are killed on the trek across the Nebraska prairie. As she teaches God's Word and adjusts to life with the tribe, she finds an unexpected peace and sense of belonging. She builds lasting friendships and finds love with Christian Sioux brave, Rides the Wind, raising his son Soaring Eagle and their daughter LisBeth. The first in the *Prairie Winds Series, Walks the Fire* is a tender and beautiful love story as well as a thrilling adventure.

0-7852-7981-4 • Hardback • 312 pages

Soaring Eagle
A Novel

The author of *Walks the Fire* continues with the story of LisBeth, Jesse's daughter. After losing her husband at the battle of Little Big Horn, she returns home and finds that she has lost her mother also. Without them, she must find who she really is and where she belongs. And on that journey, she will find her half-brother, Sioux warrior Soaring Eagle. The second book in the *Prairie Winds Series* unites three very different people—a young widow, a disillusioned soldier, and an angry Sioux warrior—to create a moving novel of romance and faith.

0-7852-7617-3 • Hardback • 312 pages